# ARSON!
## THE DAKOTA SERIES

# ARSON!

## THE DAKOTA SERIES: #1

by
**CAP IVERSEN**

Boston ♦ Alyson Publications, Inc.

Typeset and printed in the United States of America.

This is a paperback original from Alyson Publications, Inc.,
40 Plympton St., Boston, Mass. 02118.
Distributed in England by GMP Publishers,
P.O. Box 247, London N17 9QR, England.

This book is printed on acid-free, recycled paper.

First edition, first printing: June 1992

5  4  3  2  1

ISBN 1-55583-197-4

For my mother, Juanita

God did not make all men equal,
Colonel Samuel Colt did.

# PROLOGUE

They came in the middle of the night, about a dozen of them, riding hard, and carrying torches. Shadows fell across their stern faces as thundering hooves pounded into the yard. At first, a solitary rifle tried to stop them, but they kept coming, like killer bees swarming a rotten carcass. Another rifle joined in, but the hand behind the trigger was young and inexperienced. It took only one shot to silence it.

The barn was the first to go. Dry straw and old lumber exploded into an unconquerable inferno. Ropes, flung carelessly around posts then stretched tight, pulled the corrals and fences to the ground. Frantic animals kicked at the stalls. Wild-eyed horses and mules, their ears pinned back against their heads, sniffed the air, their nostrils flaring at the dangerous smell of smoke. Breaking free, they stampeded through the thick smoke, blind and dazed, out of the flaming barn, and disappeared into the night.

The house, a Queen Anne Victorian, elegant and grand against the silver backdrop of the moon, was next. The inhabitants inside fought against the flames. But the heavy velvet draperies and red oak furnishings ignited like moth wings. Choking from the dense black smoke, the inhabitants, like the panicked barn animals, were forced to flee.

Outside, sitting on their horses, the men with the torches waited. The patriarch of the family, dressed only in nightclothes, ran from the burning house, stopping in front of his assailants. There were too many of them, too many to fight successfully, and he dropped his rifle in surrender. One by one, he scanned their cold faces. Some wore masks, but he knew them, knew who they were, recognized each one by turn. None of them were bad men, bandits or outlaws or vigilantes. They were men he had walked the same street with every day, attended church with on Sunday mornings. Despite that, he knew his life was about to end on that blazing mountain. The rigid faces of the men on horses told him so.

The men moved towards him. One of them shouted, "Get a rope!"

A woman screamed, a small child cried and clutched her mother's skirt. From the barn, a young man ran to free his father as he had tried to free the penned animals. Thumbing shells into an empty rifle, he raced towards them. A masked man lifted his gun, aimed, and fired.

"Daniel!" his mother called as he fell to the ground, his rifle settling not far from his grasp.

Six men pulled the patriarch to a tree, a spidery manzanita protruding among the boulders.

"Let my family go," he pleaded. "They have no part of this."

"Sorry, Ben, you and yours had your chance..."

More shots were fired, quelling the cries of the woman and child. A rope was placed around the old man's neck as he was hoisted onto the back of a horse. At a sharp slap to its rear, the horse sprinted out from under him. His hands tied behind his back, the old man struggled and kicked to free himself from the tangled rope. The noose tightened, slowly squeezing the life from him.

With a mighty groan, the Queen Anne collapsed, toppling to the ground, a blazing bonfire lighting up the night sky. The men on horses watched as it burned. Then gradually, subdued, their shoulders drooping, their hard faces slackening, they rode out. None would look back.

At dawn, dying flames flickered in the charred ruins. A mule nuzzled placidly at the barren earth as if last night had never happened. The Colsen family, and everything they had built, were no more than an angry memory in one man's mind.

# I

I drew a hand that was either going to make me rich or get me killed. Pete threw an extra card on the table. Holding my breath, I lifted the left corner, just a little. A one-eyed jack winked at me. Slowly exhaling the stale air in my lungs, I rehearsed the lines over and over again in my mind: Just a coincidence, boys, pure coincidence.

The saloon doors parted with their usual creaking hinges, letting what was left of the setting sun filter in, then shutting it back out, like a curtain momentarily lifting. The room was dusky, cloudy. You could almost see vapors rising off the sawdust floor.

From the corner of my eye I watched as he stepped tautly to the bar. He was a stranger in the true sense of the word, a strange man walking awkwardly through a room full of men who looked, played, and fed alike. His was a different world. From somewhere back east, no doubt. A sharp air of intelligence snapped briskly in the way he walked and moved. Out of place among the grizzled goat-smelling men drinking whiskey, playing cards, coughing and hacking as cigarette smoke scorched their lungs and Red Eye scalded their throats, the stranger sparkled like a brand-new copper penny. A penny I wouldn't mind sticking in my pocket.

He ordered sarsaparilla, then wiped the dirt from the ring of the bottle neck before taking a swig. Strange, all right.

I could only watch him with my right eye, my left was securely centered on the five cards in my hand. He said something to the saloonkeep, the saloonkeep nodded at me.

I threw a wad of bills, all that was left of my money, in the middle of the table. Jess grunted at Ray, then they both added the same amount to the pile. Pete hesitated.

The boy with the sarsaparilla looked at me. Couldn't help myself, I looked at him. But only for a second.

"You're full of shit," Pete said. Guess he needed Jess and Ray's affirmation. He turned to them and said, "He's full of shit." They nodded in agreement.

"If I'm so full of shit, fat man, put your money down, and stop holding up this here card game." It was said without animosity. I did not care if he continued playing. There was already enough money on the table to keep me drunk and entertained for a while.

The boy left the bar and walked towards me. Silver dollars scattered angrily across the table. Pete's contribution.

"Excuse me."

I looked up. He was standing directly over me. Habit, I guess, I shielded my cards from his view.

"Are you Dakota Taylor?"

Real nonchalant-like, I took a drink of whiskey and chewed on the tip of my cigarette. "Who's asking?"

"I'm Benjamin Colsen, Jr." He stuck out his hand.

He talked funny, had an accent or something. Course everyone at the table noticed. In these parts people with accents were treated about as kindly as steers with foot-and-mouth disease. You did not find too many funny-talking folks this far west. Or such dapper dressers. He wore a white silk shirt, with a hundred miniature pearl buttons, under a tailored knee-length coat. His boots shined so bright they must have just come out of the package.

The kid was something new, and Jess and Ray snickered behind their cards. Soon enough, they would be taunting him something awful. Good. Break their concentration.

Seeing as how I ignored his outstretched hand, he let it drop to his side. My inhospitality must have annoyed him. He squared his shoulders, cleared his throat, and got a prideful look on his face.

"I'm looking for a gunfighter."

That drew loud guffaws from the boys around the table. Ray's gold front tooth, a tooth he was mighty proud of, twinkled on and off like a star.

Jess said, "Try the General Store. Hear they're running a sale on gunfighters."

Everyone laughed like hell. Except me. At that moment, I cared nothing about nothing, not even a good joke, and was irritated by the interruption. There was some big money in front of me, money that should have been mine a whole five minutes ago. Now, I'm not a superstitious man but luck has a way of coming and going, changing from good to bad, if you don't give it your full attention and keep your eye on it.

Biting down hard on my cigarette, I stared a hole clean through them cards, seriously attempting to ignore the peppery smell of talc the stranger was wearing on his clothes or in his hair somewhere. Men were not supposed to smell like that. Most men smelled like the outdoors, or like their horses. This one smelled, well, fine. And because of it my cards were starting to blur. Benjamin Colsen, Jr., was going to bring me bad luck. Could count on it.

"You going to play poker or ain't you?" I snapped at Jess.

"Yeah, I'm going to play. Just hold your horses..."

Easing from one foot to the other, the kid showed signs of impatience. "I need someone to track down some men for me. I don't exactly know who they are, I need someone to help me find them."

Prim and proper with his clipped accent and uppity carriage, he reminded me of a schoolmarm. Mrs. Applegate, the schoolmarm. Except she was old and white-haired, bespectacled and cronish. He was young and lithe, with the eyes of a fawn and a neck as sleek as a thoroughbred's. Dark hair, dark eyes; he was easy enough to look at, that's for sure.

The cards were starting to disappear.

"Sorry, Junior, I'm a gunfighter, not a Pinkerton detective."

Fawn-eyes blinked at me, but his snotty disposition didn't change none. "A gunfighter is what I'm looking for."

"I don't think you fully understand how it works. You tell me who you got a beef with, you pay me, say, two hundred dollars." I glanced up real quick to see if this price bothered him any. It didn't. "I hunt him down, shove him a little, until I make him mad enough to draw on me. He ends up dead. That's how it works. I don't do no detective stuff."

Pete looked at me. "Let's see your cards."

Slowly, full of mystery, I laid them on the table. Full house. Two jacks, three beautiful ladies, a colorful bounty. Had to admit, it looked suspicious even to me. But, the Lord is my witness, I did not cheat. This time.

Grunting like a hog, Pete leaned his fat belly over the table to get a closer look. Ray looked at Jess, Jess looked at Ray, doubt just dancing all over their faces. Fawn-eyes, with his irritating accent, said, "He's cheating."

Jess looked at Fawn-eyes, Ray looked at me. Pete shouted, "You sonofa..."

Ray's hand left the table, dropping into his lap. And that was about the dumbest thing he could have done. The old boy had a long-barreled Remington .44 hiding snugly in his waistband. I had eyed it long before we shuffled the first deck of cards. In fact, I knew the make and model and location of every firearm in the saloon. Small details like that is what kept me a living, breathing gunfighter, instead of one of them dead historical ones.

Kicking my chair back with enough force to slam it against the wall, I jumped up, both six-shooters out, their hair triggers quivering, ready to discharge. The men froze. Everyone in the room froze. They knew who I was. Knew my reputation. Except Junior. Fascinated, he watched me with obvious pleasure, as if he had never seen gunplay before. I thought for a second he was even going to help me out. Instead, he passively folded his arms and sized me up, seeing if I was worth his money.

"Geezus, boys, there's nothing that makes me sorrier than sore losers."

None of their guns had cleared their holsters. Ray was twitching to kill me, that's for sure, to slip that Remington out of his coat and take my heart out with it, so I leveled him with mean eyes.

"You boys ain't nothing but harmless lard farmers. Don't make me kill three harmless lard farmers, because when I die the Good Lord is going to say, 'It wasn't a fair fight, Dakota.'"

Slipping a pistol back in its holster, I reached down and gathered up as much money as I could with one hand. Cautiously, my eyes watching their faces, not their hands, which were in clear view, I backed out of the saloon and into the street. Before the doors swung shut, I tipped my hat, and said, "Thank you, kindly." Then I ran like hell.

Hudson had been crowded when I'd arrived that afternoon. It was Friday and the saloons and cathouses were already packed with sore-muscled farmers looking for something or someone sweet to get them through the weekend. I had been forced to tether my buckskin mare at the livery stable way at the end of town. She seemed to be a mile away as I darted down the street, careful not to knock anyone over or get trampled by a wagon or lose my money.

I frog-leaped onto the mare's back and quickly swung around in the street, my gun still fanned out in front of me. No one was there. No one had followed me. Guess they knew better. Raking her side lightly with my spur, we hightailed out of town in a cloud of dust. It would be a long while before I was welcome in Hudson again. It didn't matter. There was nothing or no one I wanted to come back for.

Eight dollars and twenty-seven cents. The sole sum of eight dollars and twenty-seven cents. Shit. A beautiful hand like that and I'd grabbed eight dollars and twenty-seven cents. There must have been fifty, maybe a hundred dollars laying on the table. I had thrown ten dollars into the pot myself. Walked in with ten, won, and walked out with eight. No wonder they hadn't followed me. They were probably laughing their fool heads off.

Stuffing the money in my pocket, I sauntered down the trail. No big hurry, no place to go. If I rambled for a couple of days I would end up in Flagstaff, which was fine with me. I had a friend in Flagstaff, a piano player at the Cactus Saloon. He had sharp green eyes, copper hair, and a soprano voice that could take him to the opera in San Francisco, excepting he had to stay in Flagstaff to take care of his sick mother, the meanest woman I ever met. Rusty was charitable enough though, charitable and affectionate.

I dropped the reins and let the buckskin decide which way to go. It was a game we played, sort of like tossing a coin or throwing a feather to the wind. She knew the easiest trails, the towns with the best restaurants, the saloons with the best-looking men, and the livery stables with the best-tasting oats, better than I did. Her nose was as keen to the whiskey, her ears as in tune with the player piano, as mine. If she wanted solitude, she would take us into the hills and we would have solitude. If she wanted excitement, she would find the red lights.

She must have had enough excitement for one day. She took us deep into the desert, farther and hotter than I like to go. We rambled past ten-foot cacti and baby junipers turning bloodless in the heat. Dry tumbleweed bumped silently against sandstone boulders even though there was no wind, not even a breeze. Tumbleweed just flat had a wandering spirit of its own. The sun was hot, Arizona was ugly. Not much scenery to look at, not much of anything to look at.

Twenty minutes passed before I heard the sound of hooves coming up behind me. They were coming fast. I was not worried, didn't even turn around. The fat boys would not come after me in the searing heat for a lousy eight dollars.

Junior reined in beside me. Breathing hard and sweating pellets, he must have run his horse all the way. It was frothing. He was riding a brown Tennessee walker–looking thing with its mane cropped short and its tail bobbed. I always noticed horses. Horses and men.

"What the hell did you do that to that horse for?"

"What?" He inspected the horse to see if he could find anything wrong with it.

"Made it look stupid. Geezus, no self-respecting horse wants to walk around with a tail like that."

"I bought it this way. My father bought it..." Surprised that he was even arguing with me, he sighed with great exasperation.

Then he stopped the stupid-looking horse and stared at me. "Are you going to help me or not?"

"Depends."

If I had gotten the full hundred dollars off the table I would have said no and continued rambling to Flagstaff. But Rusty's mother hated my guts and did not appreciate me visiting when I didn't have any money in my pocket, which, come to think of it, was the only time I did visit.

"On what?"

"On what you need. Thought I explained that to you."

"I need protection."

"I ain't no baby-sitter." Nudging the buckskin, I trotted ahead. From his gallant steed, he shouted, "You'll be a rich man when it's over. I promise."

I stopped and turned around. "How rich?"

The sun was gone, melted into the desert like butter on hot flapjacks, but its leftovers splashed deep scarlets and purples across the sky, giving me something majestic to look at now that I was not interested.

"We'll camp here. Right here in the thorny old desert with the lizards and rattlesnakes. Ever see how big a gila monster can get? Saw one the size of a small boy one time. Mean, too."

Course I was trying to scare him back home to his mama. But Junior leaped off the walker without fear. "I live in Arizona. Go find something to start a fire."

I stayed on my mount, watching his darkening shadow grapple with his bedroll. "Just one thing you ought to know, Junior, I don't take orders."

"That wasn't an order it was a ... request." He led his horse to a clearing, unbuckled the cinch, and looked back at me still sitting stubbornly in the saddle. "I don't particularly like giant lizards or I would do it myself."

Good enough. I slid off, gathered some twigs and dried acacia seedlings, and got a fire going. Luckily, Junior was prepared. The boy had everything in his saddlebags. I had maybe half a dozen pieces of jerky. They'd been there a couple of months and were getting moldy, but they were still edible. He put coffee grounds in a tin pot and boiled up some coffee. With a buck knife he opened a can of hash and stuck that in the fire. This was great. I was hungry.

Neither of us said much as we ate. I made a few comments about the coffee being good, that sort of thing, but I'm not a big talker. Apparently, neither was Junior. He did not respond, just stared into the fire, eating his hash. Every once in a while his eyes got all red and watery like he was about to cry. I thought it was the smoke from the campfire.

A coyote let loose a howl that would have made a ghost shudder. It sounded as if it were two feet away from us. But it was somewhere far, far away. Junior glanced at me quickly, as if my presence alone, here in the dark, reassured him. I sort of chuckled. Despite his outdoor culinary skills and cavalier attitude, the kid was not used to the wilderness. He probably didn't even know where he was.

"How far are they?"

"Who?"

"These invisible men you want me to track down."

"Not much farther. We'll be there by dark tomorrow."

"Where's there, Junior?"

"My name is Benjamin. My friends call me Bennie. You can call me Benjamin, not Junior. No one calls me Junior."

As soon as I started to like him, he stuck his nose back up in the air, and I decided I didn't like him after all.

"Where's there, Junior?" I repeated.

"The Double C Ranch just outside of Turnpike."

I nodded. I had heard of Turnpike. Cattle town. "What does the Double C stand for?"

"Colsen and Colsen. My father and older brother, Daniel, run it ... ran it. That's where we're going."

"Is this a family feud or something? They send you out to hire a gun?"

"Not exactly. I'm on my own."

Patiently, I tapped the side of the hash can with a spoon. Yeah, Junior remembered to put spoons in his saddlebag. I never did. "Are you going to tell me what's going on, or am I going to have to ask questions all night?"

He hesitated, struggling for words that would make his story less of a reality, a little easier to tell. "A few weeks ago some men, maybe ten or twelve of them, I couldn't really tell, there were too many hoofprints, rode onto our ranch and burned it to the ground. They hung my father and killed my family."

"All of them?"

"My father, my mother, brothers, sister..."

I stared across the desert into a vast emptiness, a flat dark wall, as his voice trailed off. I didn't look at his face. Even the night could not hide anguish like his.

"My sister, Marcie, was nine years old. Sammy was eleven."

Grimacing a little, I stretched a tight muscle in my neck, and hunched closer to the fire even though it was hotter than hell. I always carried a pouch of tobacco around my waist or in my saddlebags. Removing the pouch from my gunbelt, I neatly rolled a cigarette. I offered it to Junior, but his mind was miles away. He didn't see or hear me and I kept the cigarette for myself.

"Do you have any idea who would want to do a thing like that?"

"No."

That answer was not good enough. I glanced up at him, waiting for a better one. He stared at me, the entire campfire outlined in his eyes.

"No," he repeated. "I've been away at school. I study law at Harvard. I only came home during school breaks, which wasn't very often. My father and Daniel ran the ranch. I didn't know anything about it."

"Where were your folks from? Your voice is different."

"England, originally. We came over on a steamer fifteen years ago. I remember very little about it, I was only six or seven. I was considered the intellect in my family. I've been in boarding schools most of my life."

I did some quick calculations. That would make him twenty-one, twenty-two years old. Older than I first figured. Smooth and fine, he looked younger. He had lived a protected life, one of academics and leisure. Probably the toughest thing Junior ever did was make his bed in the morning. Until now. Fate was one hundred percent unreliable.

Once I had done some figuring on my own age. I was somewhere around the thirty-year mark, but I had no way of telling.

Even Ma had not kept a proper date. "Before your daddy went off fur trading," she told me when I got the notion to ask. The question made her uncomfortable, and when she answered it, she answered sternly, like it was my fault she could not keep track of my birth. Or maybe because I was forcing a lie from her.

I did not believe for a second my daddy had ever been a fur trader. My daddy was not an adventurer or a man who would leave his family for a winter. Not because he loved us so much, but out of fear for his own safety, and stinginess for his own comfort. I was nothing like my father. That was a fact we were both proud of. Looking in the mirror, I just estimated thirty. I wasn't gray or anything, but too many days in the sun and wind, and watching too many men die, had put lines on my face where they did not belong. Lines that would not show up on Junior until he was a hundred.

"Your folks were in Turnpike for fifteen years before the trouble started?"

"We moved there from Boston. My father retired five years ago and purchased the land then. His dream was to own land, settle in the West, and run a ranch. He had such admiration for the pioneers who uprooted everything and moved west. He wanted to be a cowboy." Junior sort of smirked at me when he said the word *cowboy*. "Finally he did it. He boarded up the house and sold everything that didn't fit into the wagon. My mother gave up everything, her friends, her church, the children's schooling. Everything. Now he's dead. They're all dead." Suddenly angry with his father, Junior shook his head and reached for the coffee pot. I started to warn him it was hot. He burned his fingers slightly, ignored it, and filled his cup. "Daniel believed in his dream and became what my father wanted him to be. A cowboy. Not me. I always felt safer in the cities."

"What did he do before he became a cowboy? In Boston?"

"Sold tea."

Another quick glance from me.

"Seriously. He had an import business. He imported tea from London and sold it to American companies. He was successful at it. I suppose you could say we were privileged."

"What about ranching? Was he good at that?"

"My father was an astute businessman. From that angle I assume they were doing well. My schooling never suffered. Daniel ran the ranch, the physical side of things."

"The foreman."

"I suppose."

Lifting my hat, I wiped the sweat from my brow. Thick of night and it was still hot and dry. Dry, suffocating heat that sucked the breath from your lungs.

"I can't see a man making enemies selling tea. Anyone in Turnpike carry grudges?"

"None that appeared serious or deadly. Last summer during break, I overheard Daniel and father arguing over a man named James Anderson. I think he owns the ranch bordering ours."

"What were they arguing about?"

"I'm not really sure." There was frustration in his voice as he mentally kicked himself for not knowing more. "It had something to do with fence lines. Anderson wanted to buy some footage where his fences were, and had been for twenty years. Father wanted the fences down. Daniel was neutral. He didn't see any harm in letting Anderson leave them there. It was an ongoing argument, I do remember that much."

"Ranchers fighting over fence lines ain't uncommon. But I can't see anyone killing kids over it."

"Me neither. At one point, Anderson offered to buy the land. Father said, 'Over my dead body.'"

"No shit?" That was something to gnaw on. "Do you own the land now?"

He nodded. "I own it."

"Think this Anderson fella is capable of killing for it?"

"I think anything is possible, everyone is suspect. Especially him."

With the heel of my boot I kicked a stray coal back into the fire. I wanted to be as nice as possible now that I had heard his story. I said real gently, "I'm sorry about your family, Junior. Real sorry. But I still don't know what it is you want me to do."

His face hardened. All the light vanished from his eyes. "I want you to kill them. Find out who they were, who did it, and kill them. It's what you do, isn't it?"

I shuffled uncomfortably. "Yeah, that's what I do, up to a point. I mean, I don't go around slaughtering people indiscriminately, and you're talking about a dozen men. You're studying to be a lawyer, you should know there's laws and courts to take care of this sort of thing, even out here. Maybe you believe in your father's cowboy stories more than you realize."

Evenly, he said, "I am not stupid. I know what I'm doing. I talked to the sheriff, Sheriff Bid Wilcox in Turnpike. He said there was no evidence, and there were no witnesses. He even insinuated that my father may have had something to do with it. He isn't going to do anything. He isn't even going to investigate. My feeling is, he doesn't want to get involved or get people stirred up. Maybe he was even a part of it. Who knows."

Now that got my back up. A lazy, useless sheriff was just about the most annoying thing to me. That and a preacher who sins after telling everyone else not to. The way I figured it, if sheriffs would do their jobs then common folks like Bennie would not have to hire a gunfighter like me.

"I'll pay you two hundred dollars for every one of the bastards you bring down. That is your asking price. I'll pay you more if necessary."

More quick calculations. That was a lot of money. Higher than what I could count in my head. I had never tasted that kind of money before. Course I had never killed that many men in one sitting either, and I had no way of knowing how dangerous these men might be. But I was sure of one thing: they were cruel, unconscionable. Even I drew the line at women and children. Most hired guns did.

Doing the killing was easy, spending the money would be the hard part. Junior was right, I would be a rich man. The possibility of being a rich man was a mighty convincing incentive.

I spit tobacco on the coals. They hissed. Slowly, I nodded assent. "You got yourself a gunfighter."

# 2

Like Junior said, we reached the outskirts of Turnpike before nightfall. We did not ride directly into town. The Double C Ranch lay four miles out. The land was Hades above ground: dry, rocky, and barren. Where night winds had blown the top layers of soil away, deep cracks zigzagged along the desert floor like cobwebs spreading across a broken windowpane. Our horses clip-clopped across as if we were riding on cobbled streets. It had been a long time since rain had brought relief to this part of the country.

Yet sprawling ranches prospered to the north and south of us, and herds of cattle languished in brown fields. As far away as Montana I had heard of the wagoneers that had settled in Turnpike. Depending on who was doing the telling, there were tales of stalwart cattlemen taming the desert or tales of how the desert was taming some loose-headed cattlemen. Through my eyes, it looked like the desert was winning. I would not put a donkey on this land, let alone a cow.

The Union Pacific Railroad had finished linking tracks with the Central Pacific in Sacramento, California. Throughout the plains and deserts, the railroad companies had laid tracks that sprouted out of the main trunk like tiny rambling branches.

Across rivers, across mountains and gullies, across Indian territories, steadily on the move, the trains ventured into regions where a man riding a beast would not travel.

The Iron Snake was what the Navaho called the belching creature wending its way across sacred burial lands. Filled to capacity with white faces carrying treasures, permanent fixtures like chairs and beds, photographs and Grandma's Bible, to the Indian it meant the white faces planned on staying a while. I had ridden up on a couple of burned-out hulls lying on their sides, the photographs and books scattered across the desert, the spoil of Indian attacks. The Indians did not appreciate the Iron Snake.

The cattlemen of Turnpike sure did. Union Pacific laid tracks right down the middle of town. Ranchers no longer had to drive their herds hundreds of miles to market in the blistering heat. They drove them into town and loaded them onto cattle cars.

A year-long stream seeping into underground wells, steadily flowing from the rocky cliffs, provided adequate irrigation, although things got pretty scary during the dead of summer.

Yep, to an outsider Turnpike looked like the worst place on earth to raise cattle, but to hear Junior tell it, Turnpike was a cattleman's delight. Thanks to the railroad and that tiny stream up in the mountain.

We rode up onto that mountain. Way up. No vegetation, no trees, just sand-colored dirt and sand-colored boulders. The only relief came from the sky, as blue and clear as the eyes of a child. Everything else was broken, twisted, parched. What shrubbery was left had bent to the ground, tired and hopeless. Only God knew where that stream was. The earth was not giving away any hints.

"How much farther?"

"We are on Colsen property now. The house is ... was a hundred feet around that boulder. Father called it Big House Boulder. As soon as we rode around it we could see the house. It loomed up on us like a ship floating on a lake, peaceful and calm. The boulder was my indication that I was getting close to home."

I stopped the buckskin on the crest, took off my hat, wiped my face on my sleeve, and looked across a sand-colored valley. My eyesight wasn't too good. One doc told me I should be wearing spectacles. He told me that two hours after I shot a pistol out of Max Weiner's hand. Max Weiner was a crackerjack shot and a raging buffalo who pretty much had the townsfolk of Arcada, New Mexico, scared witless when he was drinking. After I took his trigger finger off, folks were mighty obliged. Word spreads fast through cow towns and farm towns where people have nothing but the bellowing of animals to entertain them. Men walked up to me, patted me on the back, bought me a whiskey in admiration. A couple of hours and a half dozen straight shots later, they were cussing me and demanding I draw. Whiskey courage is what a young brave called it. Farmers, cowpokes, schoolboys, it didn't make a difference. You could not talk a man out of killing you just to see if he was better than you.

Problem was, and I will go to my grave before I admit this out loud, I was aiming for Max Weiner's heart. And Dakota Taylor became a legend because he was too vain to wear spectacles.

Leaning in the saddle, I squinted across the ugliest damn valley I had ever seen in my life and tried to focus in on the gray woolly things grazing below.

"Sheep!"

Bennie ignored me and rode around Big House Boulder to where the house used to stand overlooking the valley. Hot on his tail, I followed him, cussing all the way.

"Your father raised sheep in the middle of cattle country? Where grass is as rare as fish? No wonder they killed him."

Junior kept his nose in the air. Being the son of a dead sheep farmer was a circumstance he was determined to be proud of. "My father traveled thousands of miles in a boat because he believed in the American dream of free choice and free enterprise. It was an ideal he was passionate about. Maybe you are right, maybe it got him killed."

"That's all fine and well but ... sheep? They ruin everything. Eat the grass off at the root and there ain't much grass out there." I paused, petulantly reflected on the situation, and said the only thing left to say. "I hate sheep."

"Too bad."

"Why didn't you tell me?"

"Would you have come?"

"Heck, no."

"Well, there you have your answer. And the sun is going down, it will be dark soon." He trotted away and hollered over his shoulder. "It's too late to leave."

"Sheep ... geezus."

He was no longer paying attention to me. The subject of sheep, pro and con, was an argument he had heard many times and was obviously bored with. He dismounted and stood over five mounds lined in a neat row, each two feet from the next. They were covered with rocks to keep the wild animals from digging. Rugged wooden crosses, twined in the center with strips of leather, were pounded at the head of each mound. There were no inscriptions to identify the graves. By heart, he knew who rested underneath each rock pile. He laid wilted flowers he had picked along the trail from Hudson on each grave, then he knelt down and mumbled a prayer. Out of respect, I removed my hat and bowed my head. But I didn't say no prayer.

When Bennie stood up he magically converted back to the efficient schoolmarm that had hounded me all the way here.

"I was able to reconstruct one of the bunkhouses. It's small but it has a working stove and two cots. We can stay there until I get the big house rebuilt."

It was the first time I noticed a stack of lumber leaning against the charred mountainside. Next to it was a pile of rocks standing taller than a man. Foundation rocks. Bennie was not wasting any time. He had already marked out the building site. It was not much smaller than the house that had previously stood.

Anger was a tangible thing. Something you could taste on your tongue, feel in your gut, marry and live with the rest of your life. It would not surprise me if Bennie, with his delicate student hands, rebuilt the entire ranch on rage alone. For the first time, I actually empathized with the kid.

"I'll fix us some supper." At the door of the bunkhouse, he turned around. "Are you going to get off your horse and come in?"

I had to seriously think about that. It had been a long day's ride. Hungry, I could use a good supper. Hot and sticky, I could use a good washing up. And Junior was right, it was too late to leave. I would only fumble blindly back down the mountain. I would stay. Just until morning.

Before dismounting, I took one last look at the trouble milling in the valley below. I shook my head, wondering what I had gotten myself into this time.

The bunkhouse was small, more like a miner's cabin. There was a wood-burning stove in one corner and a table in the middle of the room. A fancy lantern with stained glass and tassels sat on the table, probably the only relic left from the big house. Although there was some daylight left, Bennie lit the wick. The lamp was ridiculously pretty for the rough interior of the cabin.

Two canvas cots sat side by side against the far wall about a foot apart. I noted that: about a foot apart. Above them was a small paned window obscured by cobwebs and dust. It was the only window in the cabin. You could not see out of it.

Bennie was a hell of a cook. The only place I had gotten better lamb chops was at the Cactus Saloon in Flagstaff. Miz Mary Turner cheerfully cooked me up a storm of them whenever I was in town on Saturday night. She would probably bat me in the head with a frying pan if I said so, therefore I was not going to say so, but Bennie dang near did a better job than her. He dropped a tin plate in front of me then sat across the table, the light from the fancy lantern splattering across his cheeks like rhinestones.

"What are you going to do?" he asked, sopping up bean juice with a biscuit.

I shrugged. "Don't know."

He looked at me, sharply. Very bad-humored boy. "Don't you have a plan?"

"Sure. I plan to find out what happened. How is that?"

"How are you going to do that?"

This time I was serious. "Don't know."

"Look, if you don't know what you're doing here..."

Angrily, I shoved my plate aside. "No, you look, Junior. I got a lot of thinking to do, a lot of planning. I ain't going to ride into Turnpike and shoot up the town. And I ain't going to report to you every time I think a thought or make a move. Now I got my business to do. You just go ahead with your own business and let me do mine. I ain't going to need your help."

"Fine." Stiffly, he got up from the table without finishing his dinner. He did not appear to be real upset or anything, just exhausted. Sitting on the edge of a cot, he pulled off a boot.

"I'm tired," he said, sounding like a little kid.

Immediately, I was sorry for yelling at him.

He stripped off his shirt. His chest was surprisingly brown and muscular for a bookworm's. The tan was new, probably acquired from gathering his pathetic hill of rocks.

To let him know I was sorry, I said, "The best thing to do is to ride into Turnpike tomorrow and sniff around, see if I can find this Anderson fella."

Unbuttoning his jeans, he slipped them over his butt and down around his ankles. "That's fine. Make sure you..."

He stopped mid-sentence, figuring I would just jump on him again, and slipped under the blanket. He was lean, cool, and brown, and I watched him for a few seconds longer. He was asleep before I finished my chops.

I don't get up early in the morning. All that crap about country folks jumping out of bed when the rooster crows wasn't written about me. Most of the time I don't get up before noon. I had heard Bennie rustling around by the stove, smelled coffee, but I nose-dived back to sleep.

Blazing through the window like a scorpion sting, it was the damn sun that finally woke me. I kicked the blankets into a tangled mess trying to escape it. It sought me out and stung at me, turning my mattress damp and sweaty. Grudgingly, I got up.

The coffee pot was full, a plate of mutton stew and eggs sat warming on the stove. They had been there for a while. Sweet kid. Disregarding the coffee, I picked up the plate and hobbled bare-foot to the open door.

There he was, shirtless, carrying stones from the pile, laying the foundation. I crammed a rubber egg in my mouth with my fingers, watching him intently, trying to figure him out in my head. I didn't especially like the kid, not really. He hadn't done anything to earn my like or my dislike. But I simply could not keep my eyes off him. It had been that way since I first saw him in the saloon. Not that he wasn't pretty, but I have seen and touched pretty before. Rusty was pretty, and I would never stand in a doorway partially dressed and be completely pleasured watching him haul rocks back and forth.

There was something about Junior that fascinated the brains right out of me. I didn't know what it was. It wasn't the money. Two hundred dollars for every bastard I brought down was enough to hold any man's interest, I guess. But what bastards? No witnesses, no evidence. Shooting ghosts was not going to earn me a cent.

If I had an ounce of them brains left, I would have saddled up the buckskin and rode out of there. And I almost did just that. Then Bennie looked up from the lumber pile, hesitated, and gave me a half-civil wave. I went into the bunkhouse to put my boots on.

You would have thought I was riding in with the James Gang the way folks stopped and stared. A woman grabbed her kid from the walk and held onto his hand. Afraid, I guess, that I was going to bend down and kick him or something. I tipped my hat. "Mornin', ma'am."

Businessmen left their shops, stood on the street with their arms folded across their chests, and watched as I rode by. Dozens of eyes peered out from behind sun-streaked windows. Like mirages shimmering in desert heat waves, they were faceless, mere reflections hiding behind drawn shades when I looked their way.

This type of unfriendliness was unusual for a town as active as Turnpike. A town with a train bringing people in and out with everyday regularity was usually eager to embrace potential customers. A town with a train usually meant strangers walked easily among them, unnoticed and unprovoked. Already they knew I wasn't any old stranger. I was Bennie Colsen's stranger.

Turnpike looked exactly the way I figured it would look. Another cow town wanting to be a city. Brown weathered buildings lined each side of the street, mostly small mercantiles. There was a livery stable, blacksmith, barber shop, saloon. All the necessities. The buildings just kept stretching across the desert. One long main street.

The only building anyone had bothered to paint was the church. It was a small country church with gables and a bell tower that disappeared into the sky. It stood alone, off the main road, within walking distance of town, shining as white as angel wings. Guess God must have been worth the extra effort.

Railroad tracks came smack down the middle of the street. To keep the wheels from getting caught in the grooves the wagons and stagecoaches kept off to the side. At the very edge of town, covering ten acres, was a combination depot and cattle-processing company. The loading docks spilled onto the main street. Just pull up, load the cattle, and be gone. It simplified things, that's for sure.

But the only real distinctive thing about Turnpike was the smell. It smelled like five hundred head of cattle were cooped up in small pens in ninety-degree heat. And there were.

I stopped at the saloon. A rickety sign overhanging the door, sort of lopsided and faded, just said: *Saloon*. It was a dusty place, dark and empty, except for two old fellas talking in a far corner. They were drinking heavily. Town drunks, I assumed. I didn't pay much attention to them, they paid lots of attention to me. I ordered beer, it was too early for whiskey.

The bartender, a squared-jawed Irishman by the name of Charlie Eagleton, was about as friendly as the rest of the towns-folk. Like the boys in the far corner he was eyeing my guns. Either people in Turnpike did not wear guns or mine were real frightening. Good. I wanted to instill a little fear into them, like Dracula coming down from the mountain.

"Know where I can find James Anderson?"

"You got money, mister?"

I flipped a coin towards him. He slammed the beer down. Foam sloshed over the side of the mug onto his already sticky countertop. Then he turned his back to me and pretended to busy himself at the cash box. Staring at the back of his head, my neck reddening at his rudeness, I reluctantly concluded it was too early to kill the bartender.

Instead, I placidly took a swig of the beer. Lukewarm. I almost spit it out. It was obvious I was not going to find any talkative people around. I figured I would just rinse my mouth out with the beer and go on over to the sheriff's office.

Discreetly, real friendly-like, a strong hand rested heavily on my thigh, and started moving slowly up. Normally I would have swung around and shot somebody – didn't like a hand getting that close to my guns. Now, I could not say I recognized the hand, but I'd recognize the scent of this man a mile across a sandstorm.

In a sexy, gravelly voice, he said, "Dakota Taylor."

A slow, easy smile swept across my face. "Ryder McCloud."

He was tall, slender, with brown wavy hair, a mustache, and bluish gray eyes. Handsome. Looked a hell of a lot like me. When we spent time together in Santa Fe folks were always mistaking us for brothers. Excepting he held one card higher than mine: he had dimples. They flashed at me.

"What are you doing in Turnpike?" he grinned.

"What are you doing in Turnpike?" I grinned.

We were both hired guns. We both knew that. And we both knew we were up to something. I could outshoot him. We both knew that, too.

"Got me a respectable job with one of the ranchers around here," he said.

Yeah, bullshit. I swished lukewarm beer around in my mouth to keep from choking. "Me, too."

"No kidding."

"Dead serious."

"So what are you carrying them for? All bright and shiny?"

"You know me, Ryder, I was born with these here guns attached to my sides. I even sleep with them."

"I know. Made sleeping with you kind of dangerous."

I looked down at his waist. Two Colts were strapped on tight. "Don't remember you sleeping with yours."

"Nah. These are for coyotes. Got to protect the boss's newborns from coyotes."

"What boss?"

"Told you." He picked up a toothpick off the bar and stuck it between his teeth. "Got me a job with a cattleman, protecting fence lines, baby cows from rustlers, his daughter from randy, young farmboys." He laughed at himself.

I laughed, too. He was cute when he laughed. Something he did a lot of, not like Benjamin Whatshisname.

"Who are you working for, Ryder?"

"J.T. Anderson. James T."

Somehow I wasn't surprised. He rolled the toothpick around on his tongue, purposely looking real, real good.

"Rumor is, the Colsen kid went and hired a gun."

Geezus, I had only been here for one night.

"Who's that?"

He grinned big and wide. "I thought about taking the job myself, he's one fine-looking boy, colder than ice cream, but fine. Unfortunately," he shrugged, "the money wasn't there."

"You know anything about them killings?"

"Sure. Old Man Colsen lost his head, killed his family, and hung himself."

I really laughed. Loud. The two drunks in the corner turned around to look at me, then shook their heads. Laughter must startle these people.

"Before or after he burned his ranch?"

"I can see you don't believe me. Don't matter, I only got here a few days ago myself. I'm just repeating what folks are saying."

"That's what they're saying? Even if it were true, why would he do it?"

"Don't know if you noticed this, Dakota, but people around here aren't real friendly. Especially when it came to a family of redcoat sheep farmers. They gave them a hard time, pushed them out of town, out of the church, put a lot of pressure on the old man. Besides, they were flat broke. The bank was foreclosing on them."

"Broke?"

Ryder nodded slowly. "I don't know what the kid promised to pay you. He ain't got half a cent to his name. Only thing he has is that pile of rocks he's living on. Unless, of course, he's paying you with something other than gold. You've always been a sucker for a pretty face."

Not that big a sucker.

"Why does Anderson want that land?"

"Hell if I know. And it ain't just Anderson. It's everyone. Every cattleman and businessman in this town is tripping over each other to get that mountain."

"Why? I've seen it. It ain't nothing but rock."

Ryder shrugged, growing bored with the conversation. If memory served me, he was capable of playing long and hard, but it was difficult holding his attention when it came to serious matters. "Like I said, I only got here a few days ago. I'm just repeating gossip. But it appears some boys are willing to kill for it. Otherwise, we wouldn't be here, would we?" His hand was back on my thigh, squeezing gently. "It's a lazy hot day. They got some rooms upstairs with lots of shadows and curtains to cool things down."

That was mighty tempting. Making long, leisurely love to Ryder McCloud on a hot, sultry day was an event I would normally ride fast and furious to attend. It was the heat that had driven us indoors in Santa Fe for two wild, drunken weeks. I had a warm spot tucked inside me belonging to Ryder. Every time I looked into his eyes, I saw my eyes. When he talked, I heard my voice. Being with Ryder was like being with myself without the lonely.

But I got this instinct, sort of like a sixth sense or something, so sharp it has kept me alive way past my due time. It was that instinct that warned me a man was about to draw seconds before he did. An instinct that told me to turn west when I was heading east just before a blizzard crossed my path. An instinct I trusted and acted on, no questioning. It was that instinct telling me now that Ryder was in town to kill Benjamin Colsen, Jr., and I was in town to protect Benjamin Colsen, Jr., and whatever fumbling I might do in life, I never ever mix business with pleasure. Anyway, I haven't yet.

"You're turning me down," he said, slightly puzzled that I would. Ryder had some good instincts, too.

Nodding slowly, I freed myself from his grasp, and gently rubbed his shoulder before walking away. I had a hunch I'd be seeing Ryder McCloud again real soon.

# 3

Sheriff Wilcox's office was five buildings down from the saloon. Like the saloon it had a simple sign hammered to it that said: *Sheriff.* Imaginative people in Turnpike. The shades were partially drawn, the door bolted. Cupping my hands over my eyes, shielding them from the glare, I peeked through the murky window. No one was home.

Next door to the sheriff's office was the General Mercantile. A handwritten sign stating *We Have Everything* was taped to the window. Above it, another sign read: *No Sheep Farmers Allowed.* Under no condition would I consider myself a sheep farmer. Not for love or gold. I went in.

The store was empty. I rang a brass bell sitting by the cash register, then hung on the counter, patiently waiting. Folks around here sure took their time. So far, they appeared slow and suspicious. I had the uncomfortable feeling I was being watched by a hundred pairs of eyes hiding in the walls and ceilings and rafters. I almost peered over the counter to see if someone was hiding behind it.

"What ya be needing?"

The proprietor's name was Dusty Jacobs. An old gent, he had a long gray beard and ears that poked straight out from the side of his head, making him look sort of comical. He seemed polite enough, though.

"I'll take some of them." I nodded toward a jar of penny candy brightly wrapped in foil. I had come in for nothing and settled for the first thing I saw.

A kid, in a large cap and baggy drawers, stood next to me. First he stared at my Colts, looked up at me, then back to the Colts. Admiration pushed his eyes open big and wide. He watched intently as Jacobs bagged my candy, hanging on to every word that came out of my mouth.

"Just come in on the train?"

I smiled slightly. Jacobs was waiting for me to lie. Now, I sort of figured I was going to have to lie my way all the way down the street and back again, but this one would be too obvious. My boots were scuffed and dirty, the back of my jeans stained. Saddle-worn and grimy, any fool could tell that.

"No sir, rode in."

He pushed the bag towards me. "That'll be three cents. Only locos ride across the desert now that we got the train."

"I hear that," I chuckled.

"Go on, Jesse," the shopkeep suddenly scolded the floppy kid. "Get on home."

The kid backed up a bit but he stayed put. He was used to being scolded by the shopkeep.

"What brings you to Turnpike? Looking for work? That's what brings most cowpokes in."

Now was the time to lie. He had given me an opening. "Sure am. I heard James Anderson was hiring. Know where I can find him?"

Placing his elbows on the counter, Jacobs hunched up his shoulders, and nodded towards the window. "Might try the depot. He's usually got business there."

"Thank you kindly."

I started to ask about the killings, he had been friendly enough, until I remembered the sign in the window. The Colsens would not find sympathy here.

The kid followed me out the door, dogging my footsteps. I stopped, spun around, menacing-like, then threw him a piece of candy. Catching it, he giggled, and popped a yellow gum ball in his mouth.

"Mister?" He squinched up his face as if he were about to tell me something important.

"Jesse!" He wasn't the only one who had followed me out the door. Standing on the walk outside his shop was Jacobs. Next to him stood a burly man wearing a meatcutter's apron stained with blood, looking as scary as all hell. "Best be getting on home. Now!"

It was more than a demand, it was a threat. Hesitating only slightly, the kid flashed me a sorry look, then disappeared around the corner like a scalded cat. I studied the two gentlemen coldly. They remained sober, almost frozen in place, like two wooden statues with no expressions, no blood pumping through their veins. One thing was clear, the threat had been made for my benefit.

At the Rhinehart Cattle Company and Depot I climbed a fence and looked out over acres of dusty pasture land. All the corrals were crammed full of sleek, fat Herefords ready for the market. A wealthy man's bounty. By evening they would all be gone, loaded into cattle cars and shipped halfway across America.

I jumped off the fence and went into a long, flat building. It was a warehouse, had a tin roof. It was cool inside. One portion of the building was used as a slaughterhouse. Sides of beef hung from the ceiling on hooks. There were twenty men working inside, gutting and skinning. Not the most pleasant job but it kept their families fed.

In a room off to the side was a cooler. Blocks of ice, some weighing in at two hundred pounds, were stacked to the ceiling to keep the meat from spoiling. It was so hot outside the ice was melting fast. I was already standing in an inch of water.

I stayed there a while watching the men work. Six pulleys, small, but made out of heavy-duty steel, lined the ceiling. The men strapped a harness around a full beef, then pulled on the rope, hoisting it through the pulley to the ceiling, where they settled the beef on hooks. With all the pulleys operating, the work looked effortless.

"Can you tell me where I can find the boss?" I hollered to one of the workers.

Without stopping his task a Mexican fella nodded towards the back.

Partitioned off from the rest of the building was a small room serving as an office. A desk sat in it. On the wall hung a calendar, a photograph of a thin-lipped woman holding a baby, a tea-stained Wanted poster – looked like Buffalo Bill Cody – and a train schedule. A chunk of flint, about the size of my fist, sat on the desk, a paperweight or something. I picked the flint up and rolled it around in my hand as I stood reading the schedule. The train would be in that evening.

"Can I help you?"

Casually, I turned around.

"I'm looking for the manager."

He stuck out his hand. "That's me. Frank Rhinehart."

Putting the flint down, I shook his hand.

He was a little man, not more than five-four with two-inch heels on. He was thin, balding, with a sparse mustache, weasely eyes, and pox all over his cheeks. No, sir, I did not like the looks of this fellow at all.

"What can I do for you?"

"Well, sir, I got me a herd that needs to be transported to Flagstaff."

A keen and excitable businessman, he scurried behind his desk, sat down, and rummaged through his papers. The guy liked his job.

"When were you planning to move them?"

"End of the month sometime."

"I see, I see." Clucking like a hen, he studied his appointment book. "That would be perfect. We have empty cars heading for Flagstaff on August 25. How would that work out?"

"All right."

He tapped his pencil on his bottom lip, stifling the urge to chew on it. He had a whole drawer of chewed-up pencils. "How many head are you moving?"

"Couple of hundred."

"And what is the exact destination?" He scribbled notes like a crazy man.

"The Flagstaff Wool and Dye Company."

Sputtering a little, he stopped scribbling, and studied me skeptically. "I'm afraid I didn't catch your name."

"Taylor. Dakota Taylor."

Eyes went blank, his face turned a shade whiter. But he was not afraid of me, he did not show any fear, and I did not like that.

Even though he knew the answers to his questions he continued to ask them, his voice pricking with sarcasm. "What would be the name of the ranch this herd is coming from?"

"Double C."

"Exactly what breed of animal would we be transporting?"

"Sheep."

Tired of the game, he threw his pencil on the desk, and puffed up his little chest. "The Rhinehart Cattle Company and Depot does not transport...," he wrinkled his brow as if he were about to say something dirty, "...sheep."

"How come?"

"Because that is our policy."

"Seems like a pretty damn dumb policy to me."

Getting up from the desk, he shrugged. "Terribly sorry. If I can be of further assistance..."

"Nope." I grabbed his hand and shook it real friendly-like, just to annoy him. "Thanks for your help." When I reached the door, I stopped and turned around. "Yeah, maybe you can. Do you know where I can find James T. Anderson?"

"I think you had better leave."

"Right."

Outside I sat on the walk. To shield my eyes against the sun and my face from curious passersby, I pulled the brim of my hat down. I unwrapped a piece of candy, slowly chewed it, taking my time. Five minutes later the back door of the warehouse slid open. Rhinehart jumped on his horse, gave it a swift kick, and galloped out of town. I chuckled to myself. James T. Anderson would know I was looking for him before the sun went down. Ryder and Rhinehart would make sure of that.

Now that I had gotten the hornet's nest good and stirred up, I walked back to the sheriff's office. The shades were up, the door slightly ajar. Tapping lightly, I did not wait for an invite, and pushed the door open.

Bennie was right. Wilcox was fat and lazy. Round as a cornfed turkey. He sat with his feet up on the desk, cleaning a shotgun.

"What can I do for you?" he asked without looking up.

Noisily, being careful to annoy him, I scooted a chair close to the desk and sat down. "I want to know about the killing of the Colsen family."

Alarmed, he finally looked up from the shotgun, his eyes swinging around the room until they rested heavily on my guns. His feet hit the floor and he leaned forward, narrowing tiny pig-eyes at me, eyes way too small for his moon face.

"Who are you?" Speaking took some effort on his part, he was a heavy breather.

"Name's Dakota Taylor, from the Pinkerton National Detective Agency." I flashed a deputy's badge I had taken off a wounded Texas Ranger in El Paso at him. "I was hired by the surviving members of the Colsen family to investigate the circumstances leading up to the murders. I would appreciate any help you can give me, Sheriff."

The sonofabitch believed me. Nervously, his pig-hands tapped the desktop, yet, at the same time, he seemed genuinely flattered that a big-shot detective like me was courting his knowledge. He cleared his throat and became real professional all of the sudden.

"We did a thorough investigation of our own, of course."

"Of course."

"The only conclusions we could come to, after studying what little evidence was left behind, was that it was a horrible, tragic murder and suicide instigated by Ben Colsen himself."

"Yeah, that's horrible and tragic. But what's the reasoning behind that? In Boston, Ben Colsen had a right impressive reputation. He was a highly respected citizen."

"If you had known him before he died, you would have seen he wasn't the same man. Not the same man at all. This is hard country. Hell, I don't have to tell you that." He grinned at me, buddy to buddy. "It takes a certain breed to stay alive out here. Ben Colsen and his family were products of the city. Country like this ... the sun, the hard ground out there, can break a man's back, and make you crazy if'n you ain't strong enough."

"Crazy enough to kill his own wife and kids?"

"Boy howdy, you should have seen and heard him last time he came into town. Cursing and a-hollering right in front of the womenfolk. I thought I was going to have to lock him in one of them jail cells just to calm him down."

I looked at the empty jail cell, looked at the sheriff, looked at the nicely polished shotgun lying in his lap, and wondered how much of this was true.

Noticing my concerned expression, he leaned forward and squinted at me. "I told all of this to that boy of his when he came in a couple of weeks ago. Course he didn't want to believe any of it, and I can't say I blame him. I'm sure he'd like to remember his papa the way he was, but Ben Colsen ... Truth be, without speaking ill of the dead, that entire family was...," the sheriff tapped the side of his head with a pudgy finger, trying to stifle a laugh, trying not to show too much disrespect, "...crazier than one of them German clocks."

Except for what the sheriff was telling me, and the gossip of hostile townsfolk, there wasn't any reason not to give Bennie and his family the benefit of doubt. "According to my investigation, my witnesses believe there were twelve, maybe more men involved. They told me there were fresh horse prints all over that ranch after the killings."

"What witnesses?"

"My many witnesses."

"He doesn't have any witnesses," Frank Rhinehart growled from the door. That was fast. Anderson must live nearby.

"Howdy, Frank," I said.

"This is Dakota Taylor, Bid. He's been employed by the Colsen kid."

"I know. He's with the Pinkerton..."

"He's a hired gun, you dumb..." Frank stopped short of cussing the sheriff. "He's been snooping around all morning asking questions."

Wilcox waited for me to contradict Rhinehart's accusation. "Sorry to disappoint you, Bid."

"Excuse me." Heaving himself out of the chair, Wilcox walked over to a bureau standing next to a gun rack housing a fine collection of rifles polished prettier than my two pampered

Colts. His stomach was so big, his shirttail rose up in the back and his pants drooped halfway to his knees, exposing the top of his rump. Without thinking, he caught the right side belt loop and pulled them up. I'd recommend suspenders for a problem like that.

He leafed through a pile of papers sitting on top the bureau. His professional manner dissolved as quickly and noticeably as it had appeared.

"Are you aware, Taylor, that you are wanted for questioning in the murder of a marshal in Tombstone?"

Yeah, I was aware of that. Time to go.

"Arrest him," Frank demanded.

"You can try," I chuckled with an air of arrogance. I had never seen the inside of a jail cell from the inside, and I wasn't about to let these two bumblers change that. "You're talking about arresting Dakota Taylor, fastest gun in the West and East. The man who shot a milk pitcher out of his own mama's hands when he was eight years old just for practice." I strolled towards the door. "I wouldn't mess with him if I were you."

"Arrest him," Frank repeated. "What the hell is wrong with you?"

In order to keep control of the town and the law, the citizens of Turnpike had hired a spineless sheriff. Wilcox was no more capable of locking me in one of his empty cells than he was capable of wrestling a bear down and arresting it. Still, for Rhinehart's sake, he gave it a good try.

Timidly, without much conviction, he said, "You're under arrest for the..."

We were interrupted by a ruckus in the street. I was out the door first. The two men plowed through at the same time, momentarily jamming together in the doorway. People were milling in a tight circle around a buckboard in front of the General Mercantile. Two men were shouting at each other. One was the store owner, Dusty Jacobs. The other had an accent and was shouting quietly. No shit. Bennie had the ability to shout quietly. It had something to do with his infinite pride. Rhinehart dissolved into the back of the crowd where he could see, but not be seen. Me and the sheriff walked into the circle. The sheriff, bless his lazy heart, did nothing. Out of curiosity, I watched as Bennie tried to hold his ground.

"Your credit is no good," Jacobs said.

"My credit was good last week."

"That was before..." Jacobs attempted to wave him off.

"Before what?" Bennie prodded. "Before you knew who I was?"

The buckboard was loaded down with lumber. While Jacobs confronted Bennie, face-to-face on the walk, the meatcutter held onto the mules' harness to keep him from driving away.

"You haven't paid since then."

Bennie looked astounded. Loved that look. "In a week? Since when do you collect on debts in a week?"

Someone shouted from the crowd, "Since we don't want no smelly sheep farmers around here!"

"That's right!" someone else chimed in.

Bennie ignored them. "I will pay for this load of lumber and the previous load of lumber at the first of the month like everyone else."

"Go back to England, redcoat!"

"We don't want your kind around here!" This came from a grandmotherly type, which would have shocked me excepting Rusty's mother came to mind.

Still ignoring them but feeling the pressure, Bennie moved towards the buckboard. He was surrounded, outnumbered.

"You're gonna end up like the rest of your family!"

Geezus, what hateful people.

The store owner grabbed Bennie's elbow. Bennie pulled away.

"Give us the gawdamn water!"

What gawdamn water?

He tried to get into the wagon. The meatcutter, standing two feet taller than Bennie, grabbed him around the waist and pulled him down. In a calm rage, Bennie pushed him against a post. He whacked his head hard on the post, shook the dizziness away, then exploded towards Bennie. Bennie tried to sidestep him, but the giant threw a blow and hit him squarely on the chin. Bennie went down.

Seeing him sprawled on his back in the street, his silk shirt all dusty and dirty, just irked the living hell out of me for some reason. Before I knew what my body was doing, I propelled through the crowd and landed on the meatcutter's shoulders. He swatted me off like a bug.

I lifted my face out of the dirt, spit out a few pebbles seconds before the giant grabbed me by the collar and threw me against the buckboard. I lunged at him, he slapped me aside. His size, weight, and meanness meant nothing to me. I was in a no-nonsense fury. Agilely, I leaped to my feet and started swinging. A blow landed on his thick neck. It hurt my hand. Didn't hurt him at all. I kept swinging. Blow after blow after blow bounced off him as if he were a sack of flour.

Then, like a vise grip, his massive hand clamped around my throat, and he squeezed tight. Blood drained from my head, threatening to blow out of my ears. I coughed, and this funny gurgle came out of my throat. I felt him crushing my windpipe. With sad feebleness, I clawed and scratched at his hand.

Mercifully, the butcher was not a killer and he released me seconds before I lost consciousness. I slid down the side of the buckboard onto the ground, coughing and spitting blood. He snorted a little, checked to make sure I was good and broken, and turned to walk away.

Don't know what made me this stupid, but before he could leave, I kicked him hard behind the kneecap. Bellowing in agony, he swung around. As if I were a limp chicken, he picked me up and started pounding on my face. I got in a few licks, not that it did any damage, but it momentarily kept him off my face.

"Awright, awright, Bobby Joe, that's enough." Wilcox finally drifted out of the circle and put a stop to all the lawbreaking going on under his nose. "You had your fun. Go on, go back to work." He waved his arms, shooing the crowd away. "All of you. Break it up now."

I guess they did what they were told. Lying there on the ground, I watched their feet shuffle away. My nose was bleeding. My ears were bleeding. My eyes were bleeding. With a dirty forefinger I wiggled my two front teeth. They were okay.

"Can you stand?"

That was Bennie. He grabbed my left arm and tried to lift me. Then another hand wrapped around my right arm and gave it a good tug. I squinted through a veil of blood into Ryder's goofy grinning face. Deliriously, I tried to grin, too, but it hurt.

"Crazy bastard," Ryder laughed.

Together they lifted me and somehow got me into the buckboard. With his hat, Ryder gave the mules a smack, and Bennie and I bolted out of town, painfully bumping all the way. I thought my ribs were broke. I hunched over, hugging myself as if that would keep them from falling into a million pieces inside me.

"Are you all right?" Bennie tried to drive the team and nurse me at the same time.

Still hurting, I did not answer him. I could not answer him, my mouth would not move.

"Are you all right?" he repeated, more insistently.

"No, I'm not all right," I sort of shouted. "I just got the shit kicked out of me by a ten-ton bull, thanks to you. Course I'm not all right."

He got snotty, his concern turned into peevish coolness. "You're supposed to protect me, that's your job. If you don't want this job then..."

"I'm the one with the broken nose. Ain't that good enough?"

Again he studied me with a mild hint of disgust. Then he sort of half-assed smiled. "It's not broken. At least, I don't think it is. Anyway, thank you, that was humiliating."

That was my reward. A meek thank-you. And somehow – a real mystery to me – it was good enough.

We continued to bump through the desert, bump harder up the mountain, me just sitting there with my mouth hanging open. Had to admit, I was good with guns, not so good with fists.

# 4

Bennie put a lamb chop on my eye to bring the swelling down. I did not see how that was going to do a bit of good but Bennie said it was the coolest thing in the cabin. Rinsing torn rags in water, he gently wiped away dry blood and dirt. He had a soft touch. Almost worth getting beat up over.

But not quite. I suppressed some anger as Bennie calmly patted down a lump on my forehead. It had been too early for trouble, too early for a confrontation. One of the finest methods of Indian attack was to smoke your enemy out, bring them into the light of day. For me, it was important to get a good look at my adversary, and offer him a fair fight, face-to-face. The fairest fight he would ever get from a gunslinger. Brawling in the street was no way to settle anything. Especially when you got the worst of it.

Bennie should not have been in town. Judging from the hostility of the crowd, what Colsen blood had been spilled did not satisfy them none. He could have gotten himself killed. He could have gotten me killed or forced me to kill prematurely. Timing was the most important element to a gunfighter.

"Did you follow me into Turnpike?"

"No," he answered, indignantly.

"Then what were you doing there?"

"I needed to pick up lumber. I'd like to finish the house before the rains start."

"Why didn't you tell me you were going? I could have ridden in with you, kept an eye on you."

Inspecting my face for more injuries, Bennie decided he had done the best he could, and shrugged. A black eye would be riding with me for a couple of weeks. "You told me to tend to my business and let you tend to yours."

"That I did say. But part of my business is keeping you alive."

"You did a fine job of that," he smirked.

Sometimes I felt like popping him a good one. "Don't do it again. I think it's best if you keep a low profile and avoid Turnpike altogether. You either stay on this mountain, or you let me know where you're at and when you are going to be there. I can't be watching your back and mine at the same time, Junior."

"Whatever you say." He said it, but he didn't mean it.

We stayed quiet for a while, just the sound of him rinsing the rag and squeezing out pale pink water. The subject was a touchy one, and I already made up my mind I was not going to mention the gossip about his father being crazy, but I did not like being lied to. My sixth sense was warning me, big and bold, that Bennie was not telling the whole truth.

"People in town are saying your folks were broke."

"They say a lot of things."

"Then why didn't you prevent an argument today and pay for the lumber? Knowing how they feel about you and all."

"Because I don't have any money."

I stared at him for what seemed like an eternity. Slowly, in a low voice, I said, "What do you mean, you don't have any money, Junior?"

As expected, he bit his lower lip, got defensive. "There's money. Don't worry about it. And you will get paid when and if you ever do your job."

I slammed the table hard with my fist, flinching at the sharp pain zigzagging through my rib cage. Rickety and old, the table wobbled and almost collapsed. "Put it there then. I want to see it. You said a dozen men. I want two hundred dollars per man, whatever the hell that adds up to, right here, right now, or I'm riding out of here come morning."

It was sort of demoralizing, but I did not scare him either. Him and Frank Rhinehart. Think I was going to have to be a little rougher on both of them.

"It's in a trust fund in Boston," he said, simply.

"A trust fund?"

"Well, yes, you don't really expect it to be under my bed. It's my inheritance. There's paperwork to be done, debts to be paid, before they can free it. Things like that don't happen overnight."

"How long?"

"It could take weeks, maybe longer."

I calmed down some. It wasn't Bennie I was mad at, not really. It was the swollen lip, the bruised ribs, and too many questions that had too many quick and unsatisfying answers.

Mysteries were not solved easily. I liked things plain and simple. When things got complicated, I got moving. Not because I was a coward or an imbecile, but because most things just aren't worth fussing about.

Honesty was what I needed from Junior to make my job easier. As long as there was money in the bank, waiting to be counted and shelled out, it did not matter to me if his old man was a lunatic or a sheep farmer or the most hated man in the Americas. I was hired to do a job. I wanted to keep that job simple as possible.

"Why is the bank foreclosing on this property if there's money?"

"I don't know anything about that." Vaguely, he gazed out the dirty window. "That guy, the one who helped you in Turnpike, he's a hired gun for Anderson."

"How did you know that?"

"Is he a friend of yours?"

"An old friend."

Shaking his head and muttering to himself so I couldn't make out what he was saying, Bennie threw the rags in the rinse water, then headed for the door. "I have to unload the wagon."

It was still ninety degrees outside. Mid-afternoon and hotter than hell. I did not want to unload lumber in the heat, but sitting around talking wasn't doing any good, so I put my hat on, righted the crooked table, and followed Bennie out the door.

For every two-by-four he unloaded, I unloaded two. I don't know why. Guess I just needed to work up a sweat and work off some tension. We toiled side by side, as active as two bumblebees, as silent as two deaf mutes. I watched him out of the corner of my eye, he watched me out of the corner of his eye. And every time his eyes rested on me for more than a few seconds I unloaded three times the amount of two-by-fours. Don't know why. Until the day I die I will not know why it was important to impress Bennie Colsen on that mountain.

My feelings for Junior were hard to call. I felt them running back and forth like a wild mustang caught in a snare. They made no sense, had no strategy, they were just on the run. Anger would quickly be replaced by a tenderness I did not know I was capable of feeling. Greed was replaced by concern. Protective one minute, I'd want to knock his head off myself the next. Back and forth. Up and down. Maybe it was purely physical.

Overheated, he stopped working and sat down to rest. Reaching for the bucket of water, he poured some over his head, then he shivered and shook the water off like a little pup. Dewdrops quickly formed on his chest and shoulders, glistening in the sun like diamonds. He leaned over to hand me the water bucket. I shook my head no, picked up six times the two-by-fours. I think it was purely physical.

"I really don't care if I die." It was said in a whisper, an afterthought I accidently overheard.

"That's a morbid thought, Junior."

"I mean, I didn't hire you because I'm afraid of dying and I want someone to watch my back, as you put it. Those people in Turnpike don't frighten me. James Anderson doesn't frighten me. Neither does Ryder McCloud."

"How do you know about Ryder McCloud?"

"I told you, I am not stupid. I know what I need to know. It simply proves that Anderson is guilty. Why else would he hire a gun?"

I stood in the back of the wagon and dropped lumber over the side. "Makes sense. Think he wants you dead so he can claim the mountain?"

"I'm sure of it. But I'm not afraid of him. And I'm not afraid of you either."

Grinning, I took my hat off and wiped my forehead with my forearm. One was just as damp as the other. "Junior, why do you think he wants this mountain bad enough to kill for it?"

Sincerely at a loss, Bennie shrugged. "I don't know. To attach it to his ranch, I suppose. To get the sheep out of his way. To have more grazing land for his cattle. There's many reasons."

"Do you think it might have anything to do with water? Someone in town hollered something about water."

"There is a drought. I might have more water than most people do. I don't know, Dakota. Your guess is as good as mine."

"I suppose Anderson is the one to ask. If I ever get a chance to talk to him."

"I didn't hire you to talk to him," he said, dryly.

"What do you know about Frank Rhinehart?"

"Rhinehart?"

"Yeah, that little slimy guy that runs the depot."

"Not much. He came here once to discuss something with Father. He was the only human being from Turnpike that ever came up the mountain to visit. That made it memorable." Junior smiled, slightly. "Neither of them seemed pleased to be talking to each other."

I jumped off the buckboard, warming to the information. "How long ago was that?"

"Three months ago."

"Do you have any idea what they were discussing?"

Junior shook his head. Any useful information evaporated with that one gesture. "I'm sorry, no "

"Was it a hostile meeting? Did he say anything threatening?"

"No ... not necessarily."

Disappointed, I placed my hands on my hips, kicked a stone across the clearing, and stared into the valley. I wanted to nail Rhinehart to this cross and have the job done. Nice and neat. Wash my hands. Go on home.

"I'm sorry."

"It's okay." Resigning myself to the fact that Junior knew about as much as I did, I gloomily pulled the last of the lumber off the buckboard.

"With another hired gun in town, things have gotten rather perilous, don't you think? Anderson means to kill me, too."

"No doubt."

"Sometimes I think it would be a welcome release."

"From what?"

"From this..." He stopped, then quickly added, "My actions are based solely on principle."

I glanced up from the wagon. A tiny droplet of water jumped from his hair and ran down his nose, resting on his bottom lip. I could almost taste it.

"Revenge." I said.

"Yes."

Surveying the burned-out yard, he pictured scenes only he had witnessed. "I'm the one who found them. Luckily I was scheduled to return home the day after it happened. Otherwise their bodies would have been exposed for months. They didn't have any friends in Turnpike. No one would have called on them.

"Marcie was lying over there, behind the house with mother, as if they had escaped out the back door. They had been shot three or four times. Sammy was still in the house. I found Daniel outside the barn. He was trying to let the animals out, I imagine. Daniel loved animals. Father was over there, hanging from the tree."

I followed his gaze. There was no tree.

"I chopped it down. It was the only tree left on the entire mountain. It never bloomed or leafed, it was a like a twisted skeleton standing there, colorless like everything else. Mother loved it. She held out hope that it would turn green. But I had to cut it down." Intense, almost mad, he held my gaze. "Wouldn't you?"

"Chop down the tree?"

He smiled, oddly. "No. Want revenge."

"Yeah."

With exaggerated blitheness, he shrugged his shoulders. "There you have it. So do I."

Suddenly, he leaped to his feet and jerked his head towards Big House Boulder as if he had seen a ghost. I was beginning to think Bennie was riding backwards in the saddle. Maybe Wilcox was right. Maybe the Colsen family was crazy.

"Someone's coming."

Then I heard it, too. Shale crunched under shod hooves. Two riders, one was heavy in the saddle, the other light. Quickly, I reached for my Winchester standing against the buckboard.

"Go get your gun."

"I don't have a gun."

"You don't have a gun?"

"I don't know how to shoot."

"Geezus..." I pushed him aside. "Go in the bunkhouse, or take cover behind those rocks."

Course he didn't listen to me.

My footing slipped most of the way as I scrambled up the east side of Big House Boulder and crouched behind a jagged wall of granite at the top. From there I could see who was coming before they got too close. The muscles in my neck tightened, my shoulders knotted, as I laid the rifle on a boulder and scoped in the riders.

I relaxed, lowered the rifle, and slid back down the boulder.

"It's okay," I said to Bennie.

Seconds later, Ryder ambled around the corner leading my buckskin. He stopped in front of the building site.

"Howdy, boys."

"Howdy, Ryder."

"Does this here nag belong to you? I found her in town. I figured whoever owned her had to get out of there pretty fast. You're the only person I know who usually has to leave town without enough warning to take your horse with you."

"Yeah, she's mine. Appreciate you bringing her all the way up the mountain."

Ryder was no longer looking at me, or listening to me. He was staring at Bennie with what could only be described as bold, unmitigated lust. What could only be described as bold, unmitigated jealousy started creeping up my spine before I had a chance to wrestle it on the ground and step on it.

"What ya building?"

Consistent snot that he was, Bennie shot him a dark, dirty look and turned away. We watched as he disappeared into the bunkhouse, slamming the old door shut behind him, a cloud of dust rising from the unswept steps. Purely satisfied with Bennie's reaction, I grinned at Ryder.

"Cold as ice cream," he chuckled.

"Tell me about it." I took my mare's reins and started to lead her away. "Like I said, thanks for bringing her. I would invite you in but Junior would probably stick a knife in you."

"Actually, I didn't come here just to deliver your horse. I have a message from James T. He wants to arrange a meeting."

"About what?" I nearly jumped two feet in the air. Silent as a cat, Bennie had come up behind me. He carried an ancient musket that would have blown off his face if he'd pulled the trigger. Guess it was his way of trying to scare Ryder off. I did not want to discourage him, but Ryder would not be easily scared of a dusty old musket. You could stick a Gatling gun in Ryder's ear and it wouldn't worry him none.

"Where the hell did you get that?" I said, afraid he might hurt himself with it.

"About what?" he repeated, ignoring me like I was some pesky insect.

"The message is for Dakota here."

"I don't care. What does Anderson want to talk to him about?"

"The boss doesn't tell me his business, I'm just delivering his message. Can you be there around ten?"

Ten was too early. I wouldn't be fully awake if I had to do some serious shooting. "Make it about noon."

"You're not going." There it was, another command.

Junior was issuing orders and interfering with my business again. Kicking hard clumps of sand with my boot, I felt my face redden, my temper running. "Course I'm going. I've been looking for an opportunity to talk to Anderson."

"Not in his territory. You won't stand a chance. He has dozens of men working for him."

"Ryder will protect me." I grinned up at him.

"You bet."

"Then I want to go," Bennie said. "I want to know what he has to say."

"Alone," said Ryder.

"You're going to stay right here. I mean it, Junior. I'll hog-tie you if I have to."

Bennie wasn't satisfied, not even close. Folding his arms, he stared at me as if he could hypnotize me with those damn eyes. I stared back, holding his gaze, trying to look serious and frightening at the same time. I could be just as stubborn as him, maybe more so.

Ryder shifted in the saddle. Leather creaked as he leaned over and looked down on us. "Sort of like being married, ain't it?"

# 5

At that moment, I would have given two hundred dollars times one dozen men for one cool, clear morning; for one glimpse of the emerald pastures of Montana, for the damp and musky forests of California, for the sweaty rains of Texas, for the blue-and-purple seas of the East Coast. Six o'clock in the morning and this country was still hot and ugly. A reptile, the size of a bobcat and the color of driftwood, skittered past my horse. Spooked her for a second. Spooked me, too.

Yeah, I was out of bed. Snuck out, careful not to wake Bennie. He had been badgering me most of the night over this Anderson business, and I didn't want him badgering me early in the morning. There was nothing worse than crawling out of bed and being challenged before you have a chance to wipe the sleep from your eyes.

Nor did I want him following me, which I pretty much figured was his intention. I leaned over his cot, listened for his steady breathing, made sure he was sleeping, before barefooting it to the door. As an added precaution, in case he was tricking me and just pretending to sleep, I threw his riding gear over the cliff. Bennie may have been the one with all the book learning, but I was smarter than him, no doubt about it. My kind of smarts came with the territory.

I rode around for hours, snooping here and there, examining the mountain and the flatlands surrounding it. Maybe the earth would give me some clues, crack open its secrets, and whisper to me who killed the Colsens. For the longest time I didn't discover anything. Then I rode up on some dead steers, their carcasses tanning in the heat. The vultures had already gotten to them, there wasn't much left but bone and hide.

Covering my nose, I dismounted and inspected the bodies. No violence had come to them, neither man's nor beast's. I ran my hand over a graying brand, two A's linked together like a chain. Maybe they had died of old age. Then I squinted at the sun. It rested on the earth like a big orange ball resting on its belly. Most likely they had died of heatstroke.

Before long I was riding on Anderson's land; dry as Rusty's mother's toast. I rode for miles through flat, sandy fields. Clumps of Herefords chewed at the soil, they had nothing else to chew on. I squinted at them, checking for signs of illness, an illness that may have fallen the older steers. From a distance they seemed bored but healthy.

Just before I reached the gate I trotted through a herd about two dozen strong. Upon closer inspection they did not look so good. They looked like they should be dropped; it would have been the merciful thing to do. Their rib cages resembled dugout canoes. The hide was clustered, peeling on their rumps like they had mange.

An arched gateway marked the entry point. DOUBLE A RANCH, in carved lettering, ran along the arch. Anderson must have a son he was proud of, too. The brand on the dead steers belonged to him. I passed under the arch. No one was around. I didn't think I was too early. Although I didn't own a pocket watch, I watched the sun, and it was in the right position.

The house stood directly in front of me like a giant sandcastle. Designed after a pueblo, a white man's pueblo, it was made out of sand and clay. The color was baby-shit yellow. Fancy for these parts. It had two terraces. A smaller building rested atop the larger bottom. I don't know how they got it that funny color.

Chickens squawked and fluttered in the air, making a whole bunch of unnecessary noise when I rode through them. A shaggy old dog, looked like it had mange, too, came bounding off the porch, barking and nipping at the horse's hooves.

Finally the door of the house swung open and Ryder stepped out on the porch. He whistled for the dog. The dog was deaf, didn't pay attention to him.

"Afternoon," I said.

Ryder just nodded with that sexy grin on his face. "The boss is waiting for you inside."

He pushed the door open for me, stepping back to let me enter. Suddenly there was a burst of activity at the barn. Seven men led their horses out, saddled and ready to ride. They were armed with rifles and handguns. Panic shot through me like a poisoned dart. Briefly, I thought about Bennie alone on the mountain. Was this a trick? Had I been purposely pulled off the mountain?

But, by the way the cowhands' saddlebags bulged, and the way they tied their bedrolls down, I realized they were prepared for a roundup. One that would keep them busy for several days.

Ryder poked my ribs, pushing me inside. "You're a curious man," he chided, with a hint of affection that was present whenever he spoke to me.

"James T. has some sick animals out there."

"You noticed those? Can't keep anything from you, Dakota."

We walked into a large room, kind of empty, with a few chairs scattered around. Indian blankets, some the size of Texas, lay on the floor and hung from the walls. More Indian artifacts, including a couple of scalps, were displayed in a glass case lining one entire wall. Ryder called the room a foyer.

"A what?" I laughed.

Before he could repeat it, two heavy wooden doors pushed open. A large husky man with silver hair and sideburns practically charged into the room.

"Come in, come in, Mr. Taylor." Anderson grabbed my hand, squeezed hard, and shook it like we were old drinking buddies or something.

He sure was friendly. The way he had come through them doors I thought I was going to have to draw on him right then and there.

Standing back, he kind of looked me up and down, sizing me up, which was okay because I kind of looked him up and down.

He was an older man, had a rugged face as sun-worn and calloused as his hands. Hard work had been a constant companion. James T. Anderson had probably never sat out a day in his life. He was top-heavy with wide strong shoulders. Soft around the waist, his belly hung over his belt, but he wasn't round fat like Wilcox. His legs were thin, and he had a slight limp from carrying too much top bulk around.

"We were about to sit down to supper," he said. "Of course you'll join us."

Heck, no, I didn't want to sit down and eat with this man and his family. I was beginning to think no one had warned him that I was the enemy. That I was not an invited guest who had come to dine with him, but a gunslinger sniffing out my prey.

Before I could protest, he nudged me into the dining room. It was the largest dining room I have ever seen in my life. The table was bigger than Bennie's cabin. It was laid out with linen napkins, fine china, and expensive silver utensils. There was ham and roast beef, pies and biscuits, and all sorts of vegetables in the center of the table, enough food to feed me for a year or two.

I have to admit, I was stunned into silent submission. Luckily, I had shaved and washed my face that morning, outside in a wash pail to keep from waking Bennie, but I still was not dressed for this type of table setting. Rusty's mother would have yanked my ear off if I had sat at her table in dirty jeans.

Then, for some reason, Jesus came to mind. And I pictured that big old buffet table he was sitting at minutes before they nailed him to a cross.

A young man and an older woman, dressed formally and both looking handsome, stood behind their chairs, waiting for instructions to sit down.

"This is my son, Zeth, and my wife, Grace." Anderson took his wife's hand and stroked it affectionately. "They are the pride of the Double A."

Removing my hat, I nodded. "Afternoon."

Zeth was his father's son, all right. It was the same curly light hair, broad shoulders, and thin hips. It would not be long before he was limping like his old man. Flickering with youthful expressions, his circular face had a lunar look. He didn't look anything like his mother, who had strong features, a hooked nose, and a prominent chin.

Anderson pulled his chair back and plopped his bulk down. That was a sign for everyone else to do the same. So I took a deep breath, wiped my dirty hands on my dirty jeans, and did what they did.

"Ham, Mr. Taylor?" Mrs. Anderson held up a plate of meat, a pretty plate of blue rose china.

"Thank you, ma'am."

Zeth took a chair next to Ryder, tactfully leaning into him when no one was watching. But I saw. It was in my nature to notice affection between men. When our eyes met, he reddened and quickly looked away. Something was stirring in that boy's chest, that's for sure. I was willing to bet the money I hadn't earned yet that Ryder was having some fun with the boss's son.

A flurry of noise from the kitchen caught everyone's attention and temporarily halted the serving dishes. A woman loudly scolded someone in broken English. Then the door of the kitchen was flung open and two men, wearing riding chaps and weighted down with lariats, stomped into the dining room. Immediately, they froze.

"Sorry, Boss..." one of them mumbled. "Didn't realize..."

"Come on in, boys," Anderson said, heartily. "Here, sit down, have something to eat."

Twisting their hats in their hands, they looked about as uncomfortable as I felt. They wore six-shooters, strapped on low. Those were not hunting wild dog guns. Those guns were trouble guns. And, as far as I could tell, I was the trouble.

"No, sir, we were just on our way out."

Anderson looked at me. "This is my foreman, Maury Keats, and his right-hand man, Pat..."

"Jordan, sir."

"Hard to remember that, son." He nodded an apology. "This here is Dakota Taylor."

They glanced at each other, then at me. Suspicion registered on their faces. Maury was a stringy fellow, an old cowhand, with ice blue eyes and leather skin. Jagged lines crisscrossed his weathered face like scars. Pat was younger, stouter, with a square jaw and a full head of hair. He watched me more carefully than Maury did. Once Maury recovered from the shock of me dining with the boss man, he regarded me with an airy detachment most weather-beaten men possessed.

"We just wanted to let you know we're ready to move the herd into the canyon," Maury said.

Anderson nodded with some trepidation. "No more than twenty-five head at a time, Maury. No more than that. And stay with them."

Junior had pointed out the boundary lines one evening. From the top of the mountain you could see flatlands as far as your eyes allowed you to see. Once in a while a small butte, hidden behind a haze of salmon-colored heat waves, dotted the horizon. None of the flatlands belonged to Junior, only the mountain and its peaks and crevices and valleys. The canyon belonged to Junior.

Whether or not they knew I knew this, I could not tell. Anderson had his eyes on me, gauging my reaction. I said nothing, just reached across the table for the sweet potato pie as if their conversation was none of my business. Which it wasn't. Letting Anderson's cattle graze in the canyon was of no importance to me. If Junior wanted to fuss about it, that was his problem. He did not hire me to keep sick cattle from grazing. If he had, I would have met Anderson's men at the canyon entrance with a loaded rifle.

"Go ahead and take them out."

"Yes, sir," said Maury.

"And for gawdsake," he suddenly shouted, "don't let them founder."

"No, sir." They nodded and practically backed out of the dining room.

"Dakota rode through a herd of sick Herefords on the way in," Ryder said.

"Did you?" Anderson's voice boomed across the room like God's. Everyone visibly stiffened, except Ryder. He winked at me, delighting in my discomfort.

"What do you think is wrong with them, Mr. Taylor?"

My mouth was full of potatoes. I took a quick drink of water and swallowed hard. "Looks like mange to me." I wasn't no cow doctor, I didn't know what was wrong with them.

He stopped eating, and pointed his fork at me as if it were my fault. "Dehydration," he said, emphasizing the D. "In a week or two they'll swell up, fall over, and maybe even explode from the heat."

"James..." Mrs. Anderson scolded.

"That's a real shame," I said. Meant it, too.

"So far I've lost fifty head that way in the past month. And I'm not the only one. Every rancher in Turnpike has lost cattle, some as far north as Pender. Joel Webb, he has a spread to the south of us, lost two hundred head."

Now wasn't the time to go into my theory about how insane it was to raise cattle in the middle of the desert so I just said, "It's been a dry summer."

An Indian woman, short, with a pleasant plump face, came from the kitchen carrying a platter of fruit to the table. She carried it atop her head as if it were a bucket of water. She began to pick up empty plates. She was Hopi. One of the gentler tribes.

"Let me help you with those," said Mrs. Anderson.

It annoyed the hell out of me to see Indian women waiting on white men. But as more settlers moved farther west, and governmental treaties became as worthless as an outlaw's promise, it was getting to be a common sight.

"Well, gentlemen," James T. boomed again. "Let's go into the study for brandy."

No one else was finished eating. But the boss had spoken, and Zeth and Ryder pushed aside their unfinished lunch and followed him into the den. So did I.

"Cigar?"

"Yes, sir."

I slid a slim cigar from between his fingers. A man could easily get used to this kind of pampering. A slight twinge of guilt flitted through me as I thought about Bennie sitting on his mountain with nothing but cornmeal and mutton, a meal that was already getting tiresome. I felt like a Yankee traitor.

"Have a chair, Dakota," Anderson commanded. He put a match to his cigar and sucked heavily. "Don't mind if I call you Dakota, do you?" he asked between puffs.

"No, sir."

Leaning over, he lit my cigar. I chose a straight-backed, red velvet chair next to the fireplace. The fireplace was made from small sandstones that had been carried from the mountain and bleached in the sun. It was a great gaping black hole that had not been lit in months. No doubt, since winter. Above it hung a hand-painted portrait of Anderson and his family. The painting was recent, although Zeth looked like a gangly schoolboy. Sitting next to him was a young woman with wheat-colored hair and sapphire eyes. A sister.

Bennie would have loved this room and its frilly ornaments. His lamp would have looked good on the mantel. Even though the outside of the house was rugged adobe, the inside was cool, cluttered, and comfortable, like an old farmhouse.

"Where are you from?" Zeth handed me a fishbowl brandy glass, his fingers lingering on mine longer than necessary. This was the first time he had spoken. He took a chair next to me, we were knee to knee. Ryder stood at the door, watching, smiling.

"California."

"California?" His smile showed true appreciation. "I'd love to visit California. Everyone that's been there says it's the prettiest country in the Americas."

"Yeah, it is."

"What part of the state are you from?"

"San Francisco."

Another appreciative grin. "Hear tell that's a wild city. Folks say it's more lawless than Tombstone."

"That's why I live there. Tombstone is a nunnery in comparison."

James T. grunted a brief approving laugh, but stayed silent. Zeth had taken over the conversation, making small talk. It was his role to pry, to get information that his father could either use or discard. Puffing on his cigar, Anderson tilted his head forward, deep in thought, as if he were going to nod off. I wasn't fooled. I had met men like Anderson before. He was sharp, intuitive, counting every hair on my head.

"What are you doing in Arizona?" Zeth continued.

"I have friends here." That was true. I had come to see Rusty, although I hadn't done that yet.

"Do you have family in these parts?" Anderson came back to life.

"They're in San Francisco. My ma and pa. I don't have any brothers or sisters."

"Families are important, son."

"Yes, sir."

"The most important part of your life."

"Yes, sir." I hadn't seen mine in five years. Furthermore, I had no desire to.

"What's your father do for a living?"

"He's a preacher."

Ryder chuckled. I glanced at him. He arched an eyebrow, grinning wide, as if he were convinced I was pulling everybody's leg. I wasn't. It never occurred to me to lie to these people, which was strange. Inventing stories was a fine habit of mine.

"That's an honest profession. About as honest as it gets..." James T. broke out in loud laughter at his own joke. Then, abruptly, he stopped. "You seem to be a good man, a smart man."

"Thank you."

"The Double A Ranch could always use a good man, if you're looking for a job."

"I already have a job, sir."

Nodding thoughtfully, and without malice, he said, "With Ben Colsen's boy?"

"You heard about that."

"I heard."

Gingerly, he stood and slowly stretched the stiffness from his back and legs before he could move. He walked to a mahogany desk under a window, opened a drawer, and removed a pouch. It looked like one of them money pouches you get from the bank. Carrying the pouch over, he dropped it on the table beside me. It jingled for a second as its contents settled into place.

"That's two thousand gold pieces. There's plenty more where that came from."

Real money. I could smell it. Bennie's assets or inheritances or trust funds were nothing but promises. I could not eat or drink or gamble promises. I needed cold, hard cash, like what was sitting on the table smiling at me.

# 6

There was a quiet in the room that was interrupted only when James T. reclined back in his chair and groaned slightly as a dull ache pricked his spine. Zeth got up and refilled the brandy glasses, keeping his back to me. Ryder caught his eye and, for a second, I thought I saw real warmth exchanged. The money pouch stayed on the table. Everyone averted their eyes, too uncomfortable to look at it.

"Our wells are drying up," Anderson said, so quietly I was not sure I understood him. "Come the end of summer there won't be a teaspoon of water left. By then, it won't make a difference to any of us, anyhow. Our cattle will be long gone."

"I was at the Rhinehart Cattle Company and Depot yesterday. The corrals were full of healthy-looking steers."

"Most of the ranchers are selling out early, trying to make a profit before they lose too many head. Until relief comes we have two choices, and only two choices: sell out, or let them die of thirst. In this country relief can be years away."

"Is that why you're moving your cattle into Colsen's canyon?"

"In and out. Twenty-five head at a time, just enough to keep them alive. I'm not greedy." He paused, then mumbled, "I figure the boy has enough worries to notice my cattle."

"You're right about that."

"Ol' Ben Colsen," he chuckled with a surprising hint of admiration, "he would have noticed. That tinhorn had the nose and eyes of an Apache."

That he had brought up the subject of Ben Colsen carelessly, and with humor, I found curious. Would a man speak of someone he had murdered that casually? And with that much sympathy?

Now that he had, I felt free to broach the subject on my own. "I was talking to Sheriff Wilcox..."

The mere mention of his name brought a contemptuous snort. "Wilcox," he muttered, "that bastard."

"He said Ol' Ben Colsen was a lunatic. That he killed his own family."

"I know what they're saying, son. Ben Colsen was saner than you and me. He wouldn't touch a hair on them young 'uns' heads."

Zeth handed his father the brandy, sat on the arm of his chair, and squeezed the old man's shoulder. "It's the water shortage. It has folks saying and doing things they wouldn't normally do."

I almost said, like killing children and hiring gunfighters? But, it served me more to keep quiet and let them do the talking. I found it odd that it was in this house Ben Colsen and his family would be spoken of gently. Odder, still, that it was in this house the dead would earn a smidgen of respect.

"Is there water in the canyon?"

Zeth nodded, slowly. "It seems the only water left on earth is in the canyon, but it's drying fast. The sheep know how to find it, almost instinctively, and the cows follow them."

Anderson chuckled again. "Them critters aren't as dumb as they look." Then he suddenly turned serious. "What do you think, Dakota? Do you think stealing water for thirsty animals is wrong?"

"There's no such thing as right or wrong in the West. A man's gotta do what he's gotta do." Thoughtfully, I chewed on my cigar, willing to put myself in James Anderson's situation. Standing in another man's boots was an easy road to understanding. Would I let my cattle die? I didn't think so. How far would I go to keep them from dying? I didn't know. "What are you going to do when the canyon runs dry? You'll have dead cows, and Bennie will have dead sheep."

"That will never happen."

I grinned and shook my head. The stubborn optimism of a cattleman always made me smile. "This is dry country. Drought is a gamble cattlemen face every summer."

"That's true enough for most places. But not in Turnpike, Arizona."

"This is desert. Drought affects everybody everywhere."

Anderson tapped his burned-out cigar on his knee and eyed me with quiet intensity. "Have you ever heard of the Eternal Spring?"

"Can't say that I have."

"It's an Indian legend. Would you like to hear it?"

"Sure." I felt like a kid about to be told a bedtime story.

"When a Hopi tribe was released from bondage from the Navaho, they were led across the desert by their gods into a new land." He paused, checked to see how I was enjoying the tale so far. "You should be familiar with this story, Dakota, your father being a preacher."

"Moses and the Promised Land."

"That's it." He nodded, pleased. "When the tribe arrived at the promised land there came a great drought. It lasted for a hundred years. The grass died, trees, birds, animals, every living thing shriveled and died. But the Hopi survived, and with them, the Arizona lands. Their gods, hearing the cries and prayers of his people, struck a boulder, and from that boulder came the eternal stream of water, the eternal stream of life. Without it, life dies." Anderson relit his cigar. I watched the smoke drift out of his mouth and curl lazily up to the ceiling. "Legend says that boulder is up in them mountains."

Of course.

"Most folks would say water flowing from a rock is geologically impossible, it's just a myth. What do you say, Dakota?"

I shrugged. "I have no problems with myths. I've heard wilder ones than that and they made me wonder. There's more to Indian legends than we'll ever have the privilege to know."

"The Eternal Spring is located on that mountain. I promise you that."

James T. was fanatically serious. There was no point debating him. He had a belief. One that helped him get out of bed every morning.

Respectfully, I said, "I haven't seen it."

"No one has ever seen it," Zeth said. "Part of the legend is that it's invisible to the human eye."

"Now that's a legend that's going too far." I smiled at Zeth. Grateful for the smile, he blushed, his ears turning crimson. I turned back to his father. "If no one has ever seen it, how do you know it exists? And what makes you think it's on Colsen's mountain?"

"Oh, it's there, son. I know it, can feel it in my bones. There's enough water on that mountain to turn this entire valley into an oasis. Where else would it be coming from? If we can find it, channel it, we could..."

"But the mountain don't belong to you. Neither does its water."

"You're right. It belongs to Benjamin Colsen, Jr." He drew my attention back to the money pouch. "And that belongs to you. You can take what I've given you, get on your horse, and ride out of here tonight. Or you can bring me back the deed to that mountain and triple what you have."

"How am I supposed to do that? He ain't going to sell." I stared at that little gray bag with its pretty yellow contents all snug inside, wanting it something awful. Mine. All I had to do was get on my horse and ride. No blood had to be shed, no killing had to be done. The easiest money I had made in my life.

"I don't care how you do it. I don't want to know how you do it. Just do it."

"Didn't you hire Ryder for that?"

"He trusts you," Ryder said.

I almost laughed. Bennie trusted me about as much as you could trust a wounded cougar. "He don't trust me, don't trust me at all. At this point, he don't trust no one, no how. You ain't going to get that deed from him. Not peacefully."

Anderson's calm, patronly eyes turned ruthless, and his voice grew harsh. "Now I don't want to hurt him, I promise you that. It's the last thing I want. But I stand to lose everything I own. I came to this land forty years ago, me and my wife, on one of the first wagons heading west. Frank Rhinehart and Joel Webb were in the train, too. We broke an axle up by Pender way, and we decided to stake out a claim and settle right here. There was no locomotive then, no town, no water wells, nothing but forty years of hard labor. And I ain't too proud to say the three of us, me, Webb, and Rhinehart, built Turnpike from the ground up, making it what it is today. My life is right here. My children's future is right here. It's like you said: a man's got to do what he's got to do."

"Yeah ... well." Scared of the thoughts I was thinking, I took a deep breath and steadied myself. Was Bennie safe with me around? Was he safe from me and what I might do for them gold pieces?

"Maybe we can work together," Ryder volunteered. "I can take care of the part that you can't do. If it comes to that."

I knew what that meant. I never knew a man as passionate and warm when it came to loving who could become so cold when it came to killing. Not even me. Ryder did not look or think twice. He could kill someone, turn around, order a whiskey, drink the whiskey with the fella still bleeding behind him. Not me. I usually had to hide in the livery stable, sulking, convincing myself that I had done the right thing. It would take some mighty big convincing when it came to Bennie.

"Whatever is done," Anderson boomed, "I don't want to hear about it."

Geezus, you would have thought we were talking about drowning a litter of pups.

The door of the study burst open. A woman, tall and strong, her jaw set rigid, slammed into the room with enough wrath to make it explode. It was the young woman in the portrait. The soft tranquility the artist had added to her eyes and lips was gone; her attractive features barely contained her rage. She folded her arms and stared at us, one by one, like we were a pantryful of rodents.

"Ruth Ann..." Anderson started to say.

"What are you doing, Papa? Bringing in another hired gun?"

Determined to be a good host, Anderson cleared his throat. "This is my daughter, Ruth Ann. Ruth Ann, this is..."

"I know who he is. Everyone in Turnpike is whispering about him. Whispering and gossiping like they do about everyone. Whispering, 'Dakota Taylor, cold-blooded murderer.'"

"Bennie Colsen hired him, Ruth Ann," Zeth said, weakly, "Papa didn't."

Nice try. But this woman could not see or hear, she was consumed by fury.

"Why don't you leave what is left of those people alone? Hasn't Bennie had enough?" Although she was staring at me, she was addressing her father.

"This is none of your business, girl. You go on back and..."

"What do you mean, it's none of my business?" She whirled around to face him, her voice growing more desperate, more strident, but she wasn't shouting. "How can you sit there and tell me it's none of my business?"

"This is men talk, Ruth Ann. You go take care of your son like you're supposed to do. Now."

They were squaring off, father and daughter. Anderson and Anderson. They looked alike, talked alike, carried around their importance with a regalness reserved for royalty. But his eyes were warm, betraying a sorrow his harsh words attempted to disguise. Hers were cold, vengeful. Only proper breeding kept her from destroying everyone in the room without mercy. She was a wounded lioness. That made her more dangerous than the old man.

"Men? You call yourselves men? You should be ashamed of what you did. Of all the killing and bloodshed. You should be ashamed, Papa."

Old Man Anderson stayed silent. Somewhere, not so deep in his conscience, he was ashamed. A shamed man doing what he had to do. Ruth Ann stayed firm. Her eyes red, tears threatened to spill down her cheeks. Tears of anger. Tears of frustration. I've had my share of those.

Tenderly, Zeth took her arm and started to lead her out of the room. "Come on, Sis, let's..."

Jerking away, she pushed him back. Her voice was calm. "You're nothing but cowards, all of you, with your guns and ropes. You, Ryder McCloud, are a coward." He flashed his dimples at her. Then she looked straight at me. "And you, Dakota Taylor, are a coward."

Her shoulders stiff as a flagpole, her head held as high as a strong-willed filly, she stomped out of the room. Not because she had been ordered to, but because she was about to cry, and she'd be damned if she'd let any one of us see her cry.

Ruth Ann's outburst embarrassed the men in the room enough to cut short the puffing on cigars and the sniffing of brandy, as we plotted to steal Bennie's mountain.

We had been good and told off, taken a good tongue lashing. I scratched the back of my neck, wishing for a good strong smoke, not one of these namby cigar things. I had forgotten my tobacco in my saddlebags.

Anderson wasn't in the mood to host anymore. He stood up, patted my knee. "Think about what I said, son." Painfully, he limped out of the room.

The gold went into my pocket. There had never been any doubt in my mind that I was going to take it. Putting on my hat, I nodded at Zeth and Ryder. Zeth looked like he had the need to apologize or something, but I said, "Thanks for the supper," and stepped out into the foyer.

A little boy, not more than a year old, was playing there, chasing a ball. I liked kids. I stopped to watch this one play. He had on miniature boots and a miniature hat. It would not be long before he was packing big guns.

The ball rolled towards me. I stopped it with my boot, then bent down and picked it up. Expectantly, he stared up at me with a wide toothless grin, waiting for me to throw it. He had dark hair, dark skin, and the eyes of a fawn. Similar to the brown eyes that had been snapping at me just yesterday. A baby Bennie Colsen.

Mama Bear stepped into the foyer, ruining our fun.

"Danny, come here. Come to Mama."

The little cowboy ran clumsily to her like young legs do. Protectively, she clutched him to her breast, eyeing me with the same contempt she had in the study.

Puzzled, I squinted at her, looked at the baby, then back at her. And, at that moment, she knew that I knew. The revelation did not seem to bother her any.

"Leave," she said so coldly I felt myself shiver.

There was nothing to say, nothing to explain, no purpose in defending myself even though, strangely enough, I felt I should. I turned and walked out the door. Ruth Ann Anderson would be a formidable enemy.

Outside, I found my buckskin at the entrance of the barn, gobbling down a bucket of grain. We had both been well fed. I had come here to confront a killer. Issue him an ultimatum. Shake him up, scare him, warn him: Dakota Taylor is gunning for you. What I found was an old man, bent over from hard work, trying to hold his family and his home together. A likable man. Was James T. Anderson Ben Colsen's murderer? I sniffed the air, stared vacantly across the desert, waiting for that sixth sense to provide me with an answer.

"What's it going to be?" Ryder stepped out of the shadows just as I swung into the saddle. "You took the gold."

Wordlessly, I leaned over, lifted his chin, and kissed him full on the mouth. He grabbed me by the back of the neck, dang near pulling me off the horse, and held me there for a long time. I felt that old familiar stirring deep in the pit of my stomach. If I would have accidentally fallen off that horse, we would have stayed on the ground for a couple of hours.

The buckskin danced around his feet a little, and he reluctantly released me. To spend the night with Ryder would have been a pleasant ending to a strange day. The gold growing warm in my pocket indicated that I no longer had any commitments to Junior. But I had me a good hunch Zeth was waiting in the barn.

"Missed ya, Dakota."

That was one thing we always agreed upon. However far the distance between us, no matter what the other was doing at any given moment, I always missed Ryder McCloud, and he always missed me. I looked towards a perfectly sliced half-moon lighting my way.

"If you're ever in California..." Lightly, I kicked the mare and trotted through the arch, heading west.

Swear on my grandpappy's grave, I was heading for California. Maybe stake a claim. Buy me one of them dude saloons on the waterfront in San Francisco. Talk Rusty into coming west and singing for me permanently. Two thousand gold pieces could do a lot of settling down for a man if he's ready to settle down. Course it could also front a heck of a poker game. Gold and San Francisco: a troublesome combination if there ever was one.

Then the buckskin stopped at the bottom of the mountain. Swear on my grandpappy's grave, it was the mare's idea not mine. If I rode back up the mountain, I would have to face Ryder sooner or later – that was inevitable. Glued to the saddle while the mare refused to budge, I sat there for hours, looking west, thinking of how cool northern California was this time of the year.

I don't know how long I sat there, don't remember much of what I was thinking while I sat there. I do know I was thinking about the fog drifting like wispy ghosts under the street lamps along Market Street ... Then I started thinking maybe it would not take that long to finish building the big house. I mean, at least I could leave him with a house to live in ... But, then, I started thinking about the hootin' and hollerin' going on at the Barbary Coast Saloon on a Friday night. I could almost smell the brandy on the breath of the reveling gold miners, the mildew on the red velvet draperies ... Then I thought about this little girl, her life snuffed out prematurely, no fault of her own ... Course I thought about the men, thought about the crisp nights, the tranquil water lapping against the boats docked in the bay. And the sailors, lonely and tired, drunk and free-spirited ... Then I thought about Bennie, haunted and hunted ... Thought about Ryder McCloud ... Thought about Bennie and Ryder McCloud ... Bennie's musket and Ryder's two slick Colts.

My brain hurt, my eyes burned red, and my legs were numb with saddle ache. The sun came up, the black walls lifted around me.

"Come on, horse." I nudged the buckskin in the flank and we began the long, tedious climb up the mountain.

It would have been like throwing a lamb to the wolves.

T he ropes were tightened securely to the right and left beams. I fastened the lead guy line to the mule's harness and goaded her on. Like a sphinx rising from the ashes, towering above our heads, the eastern wall of the big house lifted from the sand, and came to rest snugly on its foundation.

"Hold it there," Bennie shouted.

"Whoa, whoa."

Working fast, he hammered the framework into place to keep it from teetering and crashing. After tethering the mule, I joined him, working beside him. Then we raised the three remaining walls. Pride escalated with each hammer blow, with each bolt anchored into place.

The sun lashed at our backs like a mean old slave driver frowning down at us. We worked with it, keeping our shirts loose, letting it bathe us in sweat and slow-cook us. It was hard work, mighty hard work. The work bruised my muscles, dislocated my bones, and I fell into bed exhausted and content, too tired to lie there and think bad thoughts.

By early afternoon of the next day we were finished. The skeleton of the big house was complete. One more week of work, and Bennie would be living in it, working in it, studying and playing in it. For him it was a return to normalcy and a civilized way of life. I was comfortable enough in the bunkhouse.

Hands on hips, Bennie stood back and admired our work. I had to admit, it looked pretty sturdy. I had never built a house before; I was a gunfighter not a carpenter. But as I stood by his side, watching him smile in appreciation, I seriously considered changing professions.

He was in an unusual mood, cheerful and almost trusting. Something had changed since my last ride up the mountain. Two weeks had passed, and he hadn't said a word about my meeting with Anderson, did not ask a single question. When I had dragged around Big House Boulder, way past my bedtime, Bennie had been sitting on the porch. Somber and gloomy, he was the only chilly, dark fog Arizona would see that time of the year. He was whittling pegs with my bowie knife to anchor the frame when I stopped the horse in front of the bunkhouse. He didn't say anything, didn't acknowledge my arrival, but the fog lifted a little. Immediately I noticed he was a lousy whittler.

Sliding off the horse, I sat next to him, took the pegs and my knife, and started shaving off the rough edges. As if noticing me for the first time, he examined me closely. My ears and neck warmed under his gaze. When I was halfway finished, he said, "I didn't think you were coming back."

I wasn't going to tell him that I almost didn't.

Something changed inside me right then and there. Five minutes earlier, if I had dropped dead, it would have been one pitiful graveside burial. The preacher would have preached a short sermon. He would not have said Dakota Taylor was a good man or that he had done anything to make the world a nicer place, unless removing obnoxious rogues for a price was a virtue. I was not a good man, nor was I honest or caring. I was nice to my horse. That was it.

All of the sudden, with Bennie leaning against my arm, watching me whittle, I wanted to be. I wanted to be good and honest and important. The thought got me so excited I started whittling faster, and when I finished I cast the peg into a pile of badly whittled pegs and said, "Well, let's get the house built."

Climbing the mountain that morning had made me a changed man. But I wasn't the only one who was different. Bennie had done some thinking, too. There was a bounce in his step, a light in his eyes that wasn't there two weeks ago. His voice was softer and more respectful when he talked to me. Maybe it was because the house was close to completion. Accomplishment usually lifted a burden or two off a man's shoulder.

Or maybe someone reminded him that he could kill more flies with honey. In my case, that was degrading but true. When he turned that rare smile on me and said, "It's almost finished," I would have lassoed the moon for him.

"Now we have to seal it up and put the roof on, as soon as we can get more lumber." Squatting on his haunches, he picked up a stick and marked figures in the dirt, multiplying how much more lumber we would need. "I doubt that Jacobs will let me purchase any more, especially not on credit. You might have to steal the rest of it."

"Better than getting my nose broken for it."

His laugh was sudden and musical, echoing across the canyon. Bennie Colsen laughed. It was the first time I had heard Bennie Colsen laugh, and I had a good feeling it was the first time it had happened since the killings. It gave me an odd pleasure that I had been the one to instigate it. That alone was worth its price in gold.

I removed a smaller version of the money pouch from my holster. The real thing was tucked away safely in my saddlebags. Gathering a handful of gold pieces I slowly rained them to the ground in front of him.

"There you go. That should take care of your debt at the General Mercantile. Don't worry about getting the rest of the lumber. I'll get it. One way or another."

"What is this?"

"Money. What's it look like?"

Carefully, he picked it up, like it was dirty long johns or something. "Where did you get it?" he asked, accusingly. He knew I had come into this partnership dead broke.

"Anderson gave it to me."

"Why did Anderson give you money?"

"To talk you into selling this place to him."

"I'm not selling the ranch. Not to Anderson or anyone else."

I shrugged. "Can't say I didn't try."

"Are you on his payroll now? Are you working for him? Tell me the truth, Dakota." The thought disturbed him.

"See, I'm sort of in this funny position. Anderson pays me all this gold, but I'm not working for him. I'm working for you, but you haven't paid me enough to buy a warm beer at the saloon."

I think I embarrassed him. His cheeks flushed, turning a shade of pink. Forgot about his dang pride. He didn't say anything, just stared past me at the house and spread his hands out like he didn't know what to say.

Crouching next to him, I pulled his attention back to me. "I want to do what's right, Junior. For the first time, I want to do what's right."

"What is the right thing?"

"I don't know. I'm trying to figure that out."

"Do you think I'm wrong?"

"No. I understand what you're doing, believe me, I do. I know you're hurtin' and you're mad and you want to get even with the people who did this. But what if innocent people get hurt in the process? What if people who never had anything to do with killing your family are ruined?"

"I don't know what you're talking about."

"I'm talking about the water. No one has any water. Cattle are dying, things are drying up, and once they do, they aren't going to come back. People like Anderson who have worked all their lives to tame this country are going to lose everything. Do you understand what I'm saying?"

"Sure. But what does that have to do with me? And why should I care what happens to James Anderson? He murdered my family."

"I guess you shouldn't. There's an almighty drought affecting folks all around you. Haven't you noticed you're the only one who has water left?"

"Of course."

"A lot of people are desperate for your water, maybe desperate enough to kill for it. I believe that's why your family was killed."

"Anderson killed them for the water?"

"Anderson, Frank Rhinehart, Joel Webb, or anyone else. Take your pick, Junior."

"What am I supposed to do? Carry it down the mountain? I don't know where the source is coming from. If I did I'd divert to the valley. Father would have done the same thing, if they had given him a chance."

Surprised and excited with his answer, I pushed him on, maybe a little too hard. "Would you? If we found the source would you let them channel the water?"

He paused, hesitating, confused now. It was the word *them* that threatened him. Them. Them who slaughtered his family. Instantly, he grew cold again.

"I would have at one time. Now it doesn't matter to me if their children die of thirst. They can burn in hell for all I care."

Momentarily defeated, I fell back on my butt, landing in the hot sand. He was right. He did not owe anybody anything.

"Speaking of children, do you know anything about Anderson's daughter, Ruth Ann?"

"I know she exists."

"She has a little boy. He's got giant brown eyes. Kind of like your eyes."

"Well, he's not mine."

"Did your brother look anything like you?"

"Daniel was in love with her if that's what you're getting at."

"Old Man Anderson know about it?"

"They both knew. He didn't like it, my father didn't like it. It was just another reason for them to batter each other. I don't know how Daniel handled the situation, or what he did about it – he never confided in me. He left at night and returned early morning. I assumed he was sneaking onto the Double A Ranch to visit with her. Father tried to stop him, but Daniel wouldn't listen. I didn't know about the baby. I don't know if my father knew about the baby. Like I said, Daniel and I didn't talk much."

"Why not? I always figured if I had a brother I'd have someone to talk to, a built-in best friend. Isn't that what brothers are for?"

Bennie picked up a handful of sand and let it drift slowly through his fingers. "I'm going to tell you a secret, Dakota. A

Colsen family secret. I've never told anyone." He smiled, faintly. "I don't know why I'm telling you. Most people would find it shameful. My family did. So if you want to ride out of here after you hear it, I don't care. It doesn't make a difference if you stay or if you go."

My right eyebrow lifted a little. I didn't believe that for a second. "I can't imagine you telling me anything that's going to get me riled. I've done more than my fair share of unmentionables. There ain't much that shocks me, Junior."

"I never got on with my family. Maybe my little sister, she was too young to be disillusioned by her big brother. My mother wanted to be close but she was worried about father. She didn't want any more dissension in the family, and was afraid to oppose him, so she kept quiet and agreed to most everything. There wasn't much communication between us. I came home and everyone stayed very quiet. They only spoke with me when it was necessary."

"Why?" All this time I had pictured a close-knit family sitting down to tea and crumpets.

"When I was quite young, maybe ten, I revealed something personal, very private about myself to Daniel. He promised he would never tell a soul."

"What was it?"

Dark eyes pierced mine, searching right down to the core, seeing if I was worthy enough to tell, if I could be entrusted. Or, perhaps, to see if I was going to cause him some trouble. Whatever dark secret Junior had to tell was enough to alienate his family. I alienated mine, but I was a hired killer, a man with a small dose of morals. I was promiscuous and greedy, a drunkard, a cheat, and a liar. Yet I was still a likable enough fella. A skunk with a stripe as wide as mine could stand my smell and enjoy my company. Was it possible that Bennie Colsen, with them choirboy eyes, shy voice, and gentle ways – when he wasn't peeved, could stink worse than me? It sure didn't seem likely.

"I told him that when I got older, I wasn't going to marry a woman." Loosely, he pitched a rock across the yard. "I was going to marry a man."

I didn't flicker an eyelid, didn't wrinkle my brow. I almost laughed. Almost threw my hat in the air and shouted hallelujah.

But Bennie, looking all sad and pained, continued spewing forth his confession, somber as all hell.

"Later, Daniel and I squabbled over some childish thing, I don't even remember what it was. To punish me he ran and told Father what I had said. A part of me had meant it, but at that age, how could I possibly guess the impact it would make on my relationship with my family? From then on, I was in and out of boarding schools and seldom allowed home. Once I was shipped back to England. Of course, it was in the guise of higher education." He grew quiet, assessing memories, watching ghosts act out past roles. "My father, when he spoke of it at all, called it a Whitmanish sort of thing."

"What's that?"

"The poet, Walt Whitman."

I shrugged, a dull, blank look on my face.

Bennie smiled patiently at my ignorance. "*Leaves of Grass,* a book of poetry..."

Suddenly he leaped to his feet and ran to the makeshift lean-to I'd hurriedly built to house our riding gear. Scattering the contents of his saddlebag, he found what he wanted. He returned to me with a thin paper-covered book. It was all dog-eared and yellow, like it had been read a hundred times or so.

He held the book in his hands as if it were a baby bird that had fallen from the nest. Flipping the pages carefully, he stopped at one particular well-read passage. "This is from 'Calamus,' one of my favorite poems. 'For the one I love most lay sleeping by me under the same cover in the cool night. In the stillness of the autumn moonbeams his face was inclined toward me, And his arm lay lightly around my breast, and that night I was happy.'"

After he read it, he took a deep breath and stared at me as if that were supposed to ring a bell or something. It was pretty, all right, and I found the conversation fascinating, and I enjoyed being read to almost as much as I enjoyed being made love to. But Junior had lost me a long time ago. In my rogue mind, I did not see the shame of what he had confided, therefore, I could not understand the significance of the poet. One thing I did understand was that this poet was important to Junior.

"My father wouldn't allow the book in the house. I keep this copy nearby at all times, mostly in my saddlebags. It's quite special, and relatively difficult to find. He wrote most of it during the Civil War, when camaraderie among men wasn't uncommon. You may read it, if you like." He added with mild diplomacy, "Do you know how to read?"

"Course I know how to read," I answered a little too defensively. "I can do some writing, too."

Truthfully, my reading and writing was sorely limited. And if this Whitman fella's writing was anything like that Shakespeare fella, I could pretty much forget understanding a single printed word.

"It's been rumored among certain quarters that Mr. Whitman has undesirable affections similar to mine. Of course, it's just a rumor and I shouldn't repeat it carelessly and speak ill of him. He'll no doubt marry some day." Bennie shrugged, frowned, laughed it off, all at the same time. Poor kid was confused as all hell. "Of course that doesn't mean anything. We all marry eventually."

"We?"

"Uranians. Sodomites. Homosexuals. There's a German scientist, Krafft-Ebing, I believe his name is, who has done some studies in Europe. When I was in England last year he published a paper on the subject. It was all very academic, mind you, certainly not meant to be scandalous."

Uranians? Sodomites? Homosexual? Bennie's vocabulary was a might difficult to comprehend. Still, I could hardly wait to tell Ryder. All this time we thought we were just being randy cowboys. He would have a good laugh, be proud to call himself a uranian or a sodomite, the same way he was proud to carry his guns and the title gunslinger. Ryder was a renegade, no question. If he were Apache, he would be riding and fighting alongside Cochise.

"Maybe that's why I feel so cheated, so completely abandoned. Or maybe it's guilt. If I had been a normal son I would have been here. I would have died with them."

I hated that kind of talk. But Bennie didn't need no lecture from me. He was so baffled about all this uranian stuff that anything I said probably wouldn't make sense, anyhow. Instead I attempted to joke him back into his good mood.

"Why didn't your old man just make you stay on the ranch? Teach you how to hunt and kill and scalp? Make a man out of you?"

"Like you?" He was smirking, that's for sure, but it was a playful smirk.

"Yeah, like me."

I smiled. And with pure affection, he smiled at me. Couldn't help myself, I moved in close. I reached up and touched the tip of his temple where his hair was damp from the heat. My hand felt as coarse as sandpaper scratching along his cheek. His skin was hot, moist, burning under my fingertips. He didn't say anything, didn't move or stop me. He just held my eyes, with a slight smile playing on his face. I brushed his lips with mine, barely, briefly, not knowing which of us I was teasing, me or him. Dropping his hand to my shoulder, he squeezed gently, acknowledging a mutual want. His arms slipped around my neck, wrapping hard around me, almost knocking me over. He hugged me like I was his best friend. Maybe I was.

A rifle cracked in the distance.

Startled, Bennie jumped to his feet. "What is it?"

"Shhh..." I put a finger to my lips, listening to the hollow sound reverberating through the valley.

In rapid succession, three more gunshots rang out. Lambs called in the valley, their cries becoming more frantic with each gunshot.

"The sheep," Bennie groaned.

"The shots are coming from the north."

Running wide open, I jumped on the buckskin. Bennie followed close behind.

"Stay here," I said.

"I want to go with you."

"Stay here." Lo and behold, if he didn't do what he was told this time.

I fled, my ears to the wind, trying vainly to track the sound of a gun.

# 8

The mare stumbled down the seldom-used paths of the northern side of the mountain. Rocky and steep, unstable in most places, her steel shoes slipped in the loose shale. We rode down at an odd angle. Her back legs bent at the hock, she hopped like a jackrabbit. I tilted all the way back in the saddle, pulling the reins tight to keep her from tumbling.

A couple of times, we both almost went down. I thought about turning back and finding easier access into the canyon. But I heard another shot, closer this time, and pushed her on.

Twenty minutes later I was at the bottom of the canyon. In contrast to the stark shout of the gunfire, there was an easy quiet there. Moving slowly, I inspected the ever-shifting silt for tracks, the white thorn for recently broken branches, the ground and surrounding rocks for empty shells. I began to think I had come to the wrong place.

Something moved. I removed my rifle from the boot and cautiously approached a hedge of brush. An old ewe staggered out from behind a dead acacia bush. She dropped to one knee, forced herself up, and dropped again, a victim of the gunman. I couldn't leave her to suffer. I lifted my rifle and quickly put her down.

Most of the sheep had already scattered, going into the cliffs for protection. Farther beyond where I had left the old ewe, a half dozen more lay on the ground like discarded heaps of cotton. This time, the gunman had been merciful – their throats had been cut. A dozen more, dazed and disoriented, stumbled in circles. Burgundy stains soaked their wool. Some, with the right amount of doctoring, could be saved, but the others would only die a slow death.

I couldn't say that I liked sheep, couldn't say that at all. But I figured them to be harmless animals, harmless and tranquil, and it sort of got my back up seeing them aimlessly slaughtered. One by one, I put the wounded out of their misery.

It occurred to me that I was standing smack dab in the middle of the canyon. Whoever had shot the sheep might still be up in the cliffs eyeballing me right now. The sound of my rifle would only alert them to my presence.

Bennie had told me that during the winter months the runoff from the surrounding cliffs formed a natural creek bed that stayed wet throughout the summer. I was standing in it. It was dry. Mosquitoes swarmed a two-inch puddle that had turned to slush. That was the only earth water I had seen the whole time I was in Turnpike. Two inches of puddle sludge.

It was here that Anderson brought his cattle, apparently to no avail. Sheep droppings were fresh, but the cow manure was dry, already turning to straw. Off to the side was the skull and hide of a Hereford. The eternal water Anderson had been relying on, had been thieving bit by bit, was gone. His cattle had found no relief here.

Leaving the creek bed, I followed the canyon around wall to wall, looking for an entrance or an exit. There wasn't any. It was solid rock wall all the way around. Steep and treacherous; only a phantom, nimble and swift, could kill a couple of dozen sheep, and scurry back up the cliffs before I arrived. Ryder was such a phantom. He was also an expert marksman. Involuntarily, my shoulder blades squeezed together as I imagined him scoping me in with his high-powered carbine. His eyes were on me, watching me, no doubt grinning at my stupidity. I could feel him. But where was the jackal? And how did he get in?

I searched the ground for tracks, attempting to distinguish horse hooves from hundreds of fleeing sheep prints. The sheep had panicked, crisscrossing back and forth, destroying any clues that may have been left behind.

The north wall of the canyon swept around in a splendid curve, connecting with the western wall. Bennie's side. Thick with loose rocks, immovable boulders, and dead prickly brush, it was even higher and steeper than the western wall.

Balls of wool clung to the white thorn. Short, hollow tunnels burrowed through the brush. It was a partial trail, an animal trail. Sheep, mountain goat, and white-tailed deer could travel freely on the closed path. A horse or a cow would find it tough going.

It wasn't fair to the buckskin, but she had gotten me in and out of situations rougher than this, and I pretty much figured there wasn't anything she couldn't do. Steadily, I climbed, following sheep droppings, trying to stay on their path. The higher we climbed the more of a vertical slant we fought against. Halfway up the mountain the horse refused to go farther. She reared back on me, coming to a complete stop. Just because I was crazy and wanted to break my neck didn't mean she was. Dismounting, I took my rifle and climbed the rest of the way on foot.

Hot and merciless, the sun beat down on my head, penetrating through my thick felt hat. I lifted my collar to protect my neck. Clothes could not shelter a man against mountain heat. Yet, to discard them meant instant death.

White thorn and manzanita tore at my shirt and jeans. A hawk circled overhead, swooped gracefully, and glided in close to see what I was doing on its mountain. Still, there was no sign of sheep, no sign of man, just the hawk, before it glided away with a farewell screech.

After an hour, I stumbled into a clearing a hundred yards wide. Massive boulders ascended out of nowhere, blocking my path. They looked ancient, prehistoric. The solitude of the mountain, the absolute isolation, only intensified my feeling of being completely alone. It was the kind of feeling you noticed when squatting in the middle of the desert or on a mountaintop. Small, frail, unimportant, like a speck of dust on a prospector's boot.

Off to my right, a ridge, about a foot wide, circled the boulders, then disappeared behind the cliff. The drop was drastic, a long flight downward. The ridge appeared to be carved from smooth light granite. Granite was tricky. Tough and unbreakable in most places, it could be as unsteady as sand where you least expected it. The sheep couldn't have been dumb enough to go around that. Could they?

I thought long and hard. I had two choices: crawl over the boulders as if I were a gawdamn spider, or do a light stepping dance around that ridge. Neither choice appealed to me much.

Removing the bandana from my neck, I tied it around my forehead to keep the sweat out of my eyes. If I was going to walk a precarious ledge, a foot wide and a thousand feet above ground, it would be wise to see what I was doing. I cursed a little and wished I was lying under cool sheets between Rusty's arms at the Cactus Saloon. Then I took my first step. My back pressed against the rock wall as if I were part of it, I clung to the smooth boulders and sidestepped carefully. The rock was fiery hot. It blistered my palms within seconds.

Midway across I stopped and forced myself to look down. From where I stood, perched like a wise but wingless eagle, I could view the entire valley. On my left were the sorry gray flats of the Double A Ranch. To my right, the steep, rocky mountain of the Double C Ranch. I did not realize the conflicting ranches were that close. If I had been wearing spectacles I probably could have seen the shit yellow of Anderson's house.

Then, I noticed, at the bottom of the canyon, a trail leading from the fields of the Double A straight onto the canyon floor. On foot or horseback, the trail was invisible, camouflaged behind boulders. From up here, you could almost follow the pattern of footsteps. Good guess them footprints belonged to Anderson's men. Maybe Maury. Maybe Pat. Good bet Ryder. Any one, two, or a whole posse could have ridden in, shot the sheep, and been back out again in minutes.

Hanging a thousand feet in the air when the gateway I was looking for was below me left me feeling pretty foolish. I checked the sun. I still had plenty of time to climb down and catch the culprits.

I turned back. My foot slipped in the loose gravel. Catching my breath, I steadied myself. Calmly, I wiped sweat from my eyes. A low grumbling rumble vibrated under my boots. With little warning, the level gave way, crumbling underneath me, an avalanche of rock and dust.

Suddenly I dropped, as if dropping off the earth, and slid down with it. Quickly flipping over, I rode the wave more wildly than I had ridden a bull that dragged me halfway across the plains. My chest and belly grinded against the sharp shards of rock flowing down the cliff like a sand-colored waterfall. Frantically, I grabbed at anything, trying to break the fall. A juniper bush, fried golden brown from the sun, jutted from the wall of the cliff. It tore at me as I slid over it. With about ten feet to go before I catapulted over the edge, I grabbed the bush, snagging it with both fists. It whipped me in the face, then sprung down as if my weight were too much of a burden for the dying shrub. But its roots were embedded deep in the rock wall and it held.

Sliding to a halt, I shielded my head as a hailstorm of rocks followed me down. I held tight against the force of the impact. My legs dangled over the edge. The jagged rock sliced into every limb of my body. My hands were sweaty, slippery. I couldn't hold on much longer.

I mumbled a fast prayer that the shrub would hold, gritted my teeth, and slowly began to claw back up. Broken fingernails dug into the side of the cliff, my muscles felt as if they were being ripped slowly from the bone as I pulled. Blindly, my right foot sought out the smallest crevice on which to rest, then my left. Inch by inch, I scaled the wall until the top ledge came into view. When I reached for it, my hand slipped. Shale blasted me in the face and I scooted back down a foot. Grunting, with one final burst of strength, I heaved myself up and back onto the platform. I sat there, panting heavily, blinking dirt from my eyes, taking deep steadying breaths. That was close.

Humble as all hell, I rested my head against the boulder and tried to relax. The silence was broken only by a stray pebble skipping down the cliff. It would take a month's worth of might to climb back down the mountain and get my horse. I knew a fellow, a hard-talking gambler, who whistled a high-pitched whistle through his teeth, and his horse would gallop across the Great Plains to save him from whatever folly he had gotten himself into. Mine wouldn't. Mine was too sensible.

Thirsty, sore, aching like a grandpa, I sat there for a few more minutes and picked sharp slivers of shale out of the palms of my hands.

Then I heard it. At first it sounded like musical notes, little bitty angels singing. I cocked my head, straining to hear. Scrambling to my knees, I pushed aside piles of broken rock and shale.

Geezus ... there it was. Thinner than a reed; a puny, crystal stream of water. The Eternal Spring.

It was not my desire to die on that mountain or any other mountain. But the needle-thin stream of water was everything James T. said it was. Mythical. Magic. And I was drawn to it like most fools are drawn to myths and magic.

A man could wander in these cliffs for weeks without ever finding his way out. Eventually, he would die of exposure, hunger, thirst. Or, one blunder and he would drop out of the sky like a bird with broken wings. The mountains were not friendly, and a man had no business challenging them.

But the utter importance of the spring, its capacity to save Bennie's life, to revive Anderson's failing cattle, outweighed the dangers of exploring any further. Plain old curiosity, and my hankering to be a hero, may have had something to do with it. Ma always said that heroes and the curious die young. I was perpetually tempted to see if she was correct.

Hero looking for applause and gold, or fool looking for magic, I was determined to follow the stream to its source. I studied the steadily sharpening incline as intricately as one of them scientist people study the stars and sky, willing myself to do it without fear. The walls were slick and flat with few places to anchor my feet. There was no juniper bush to break my fall.

Climbing on my hands and knees, I took the wall like a monkey skittering up a banana tree. I moved quickly but cautiously, not looking down. I stopped only long enough to catch my breath, to wipe away dust and sweat stinging my eyes, to dig the heel of my boot firmly into the side of the cliff. But I did not stop long enough to think about what I was doing.

My blue denim shirt was in tatters. I ripped the tail into strips, placing them under loose rocks to make sure I had a trail to follow back out. Staying as close to the stream as possible, I kept my ear to the stone wall, listening, sniffing at the water. It whispered to me, pushing me on.

At the top of the cliff, I climbed out on a flatland only a hundred feet wide. The flat was dotted with assorted boulders, some smooth and round, others sharp and jagged. All had been beaten, shaped, and designed by the harsh, rugged elements, eroded into intricate designs. Sparse, bent brush bowed to the sun. The ground was hard orange clay. Dust storms had blown the topsoil away.

There was no sign of water. No hint whatsoever. There was no place else to go, I was at the highest peak. From here, I could shout at God. To go higher I would need a ladder to heaven. To go lower, I simply had to climb back down. The source had to be here somewhere.

I wandered around, poking here and there, kicking the sod with my boot, pushing aside stones, checking for moisture. There were no clues. On my hands and knees, I scanned the ground inch by inch, feeling for dampness. A slight warm breeze brushed against me, cooling me, cooling the land, but still there was no sign of water. The top of the mountain was as dry and barren as the bottom.

Two boulders, taller than me, were lodged together. Stone arms twisted around stone arms like two lovers forever immortalized in a granite embrace. At the bottom of the boulders was a portal the size of a bear cub. I squeezed through the hole and emerged on the other side. The music got louder. Covered discreetly by a flat gray rock, purposely hidden, was another hole. It was an opening in the ground, an entrance to an underground cave. I pried the rock loose, pushed it aside, and peered into the cave ten feet down. The music became a symphony. Water rushed like an ocean inside the mountain.

Barely a foot wide, the opening was too small for a large man. Luckily, I was slender, not too broad, and had a lot of experience getting in and out of tight places with ease. It was snug, but I squeezed through the hole. The drop wasn't severe. I landed on my knees, splashing in two feet of water.

This wasn't possible. Legend or not, water should not be running through a mountain in the middle of the desert. But I was not one to question myths or magic.

Inside was radiant orange. Ribbons of yellow and red bounced off the walls. Light reflected off the water, giving the walls a fluid quality, as if there were flames dancing in the cave. There should not have been any light or colors. It should have been dark. Except for the small opening there wasn't anywhere for the sun to enter. Yet the light existed, gold and splendid in its brilliance. Mystic and godlike, the cave was like a temple. A shiver shimmied up my spine.

Careful not to desecrate this holy place, I waded gently through the water, vaguely wondering if I were the only human being to set foot there. No one could travel freely up and down the cliffs. Those who succeeded would find nothing. The flat rock covering the opening was Nature's way of protecting her secret. Or a delicate coincidence, like the weather-carved portal between the entwined boulders.

In ten minutes, I had the answer to my question. I was not the first. Men of magic had been there before me. Deeper into the cave ancient Hopi drawings, dyed in various earth tones and depicting primitive ritualistic sacraments, were carved into the rock walls. They were difficult to read, like nothing I had seen before. On the embankment, cutting and grinding stones lay nearby, a long time abandoned. A circle of rocks, strategically placed, still held ash and charcoal in the middle. Eagle feathers, tied together with leather and beads, lay next to the forsaken campfire as if they were a bouquet of desert flowers. Pieces of flint were piled next to the feathers. All the treasures an Indian had to offer. No money, no silver or gold pieces, just humble pickings off the earth. It was the mark of a shaman. A medicine man.

I slid by, leaving it untouched. I knew enough about native culture to know that it was an altar, gifts left for the water god.

The farther I went the brighter the odd light became, melting away shadows, lighting up the walls as if they were lined with torches. And the higher the water became. Already it was to my waist and deepening fast. It was deepening too fast. I stayed close to the narrow shore, holding on to keep from slipping on the slick rocks underfoot. As the water swiftly deepened, I took my boots and hat off, cast them ashore, and prepared to swim.

Eventually I let go and swam the rest of the way. There were no currents, no ripples. Just a placid, clean body of water. It felt cool on my wounds, almost healing. With long even strokes, I swam farther into the cave, rounding bends. No one was there to keep me company but the water god. Playing a little, I dived deep, then surfaced to shake the water from my hair. I floated on my back and spouted water from my mouth. After weeks of dry hot land, I savored the cool liquid and almost forgot why I had made the journey.

Then I stopped in the water, bobbing at the surface, staring straight ahead.

Someone had been there before me, all right, and it wasn't no medicine man. Directly in front of me, standing taller than a building, was a rock wall. Sandstone boulders, some of them four feet in diameter and weighing four hundred pounds, were piled high on top of each other. It was not a natural phenomenon. The wall was manmade. Someone had built a dam, stopping the water flow.

The water channeled through small openings throughout the cave and trickled down the north side of the mountain, relieving some of the overflow in the underground cavern.

Barefooted, I gingerly climbed the wall, then slid over to the other side, landing in a foot of mud and slime. Small trickles of water escaped from between crevices, providing a minimal amount of moisture. It was hard to tell, but from the way it looked the water had been dammed for a couple of months, maybe longer. It was only a matter of weeks before the flow would stop completely. When it did, the water tables in the valley would dry up, along with the town of Turnpike.

# 9

My clothes were dry before I reached the bottom of the mountain. I found my horse waiting loyally where she dumped me, chewing on dead brambles as if they were sweet oats. Bored, content, she didn't look as if she were hurting much. I sure did. I looked like I had been chewed up and spit out. But my spirits were high, and I felt revitalized, thanks to the water.

Elated by my discovery, I wanted to jump on the horse, race to Bennie, and tell him what I had found; I wanted to parade through Turnpike with the news like some kind of peacemaker: "It's okay, folks, I've taken care of everything." Except for a few nagging questions. Who built the dam? Did Bennie already know about it? And did it have anything to do with the killings? The last question seemed almost too obvious.

Vultures dipping low and lighting on the carcass of a dead sheep dampened my spirits a little, reminding me of why I had come into the canyon. Envisioning an aerial map in my mind's eye, I scouted the canyon walls until I found the trail that led onto Anderson's property. Well worn, the trail had been used often. For two families that spent most their time feuding with one another, they sure blazed a path straight into their respective backyards.

I took the trail, not riding long before I spotted a lone figure up ahead. He was off his horse mending fences. The sheep killer was long gone, but I was still mad enough to punish anyone remotely connected to the Double A. Madder still that Anderson and his boys had easy passage into the Colsen camp, and, quite likely, used it the night of the killings. The fence mender was on Anderson property. That was good enough reason to teach him a lesson.

Furiously, I galloped across the burning sand, barreling down on him. Zeth Anderson saw me coming, lifted his hat, ran his fingers through his curly hair. I reined the buckskin in so close she butted him with her chest, pushing him against the barbed wire.

"Hey..." he protested.

I whipped out a pistol and pointed it straight at him. The horse kept him penned against the fence. Automatically, his hands went in the air.

"What's the problem, Dakota?" His voice was a mixture of anger and fear. "This is Anderson fence line. I'm not building on his property."

Sliding off my horse, I plucked his six-shooter out of the holster. "Did you hear any gunshots around here?"

The chamber was fully loaded.

"A couple of hours ago, about a dozen of them. I thought it was Colsen target practicing."

I went to his horse and removed his rifle. It, too, was loaded. I pumped the cartridges out on the ground. Neither gun had been fired any time soon. It looked like they had never been fired, period. A kid's shiny new birthday presents.

"Got dead ewes lying all over the place."

Tentatively, he lowered his hands. "Sorry to hear that."

"Did you see anybody ride through here?"

"No, I just got here a few minutes ago. I've been patching fences up by the east fork."

Handing back his pistol, I looked towards the east fork and estimated how much time it would take him to move from there to here. I did not figure Zeth for a sheep killer. He was a kid, almost angelic-looking, in many ways more guileless than Bennie. But I've been wrong before. Once or twice.

"Do you know anything about that trail back there?"

"The one leading into the canyon?"

"Guess you do."

"My sister used it often."

"To visit Daniel Colsen?"

He paused for a moment. Quietly he debated whether or not he should confirm their relationship by feeding me more information. "They met in the canyon every night. She still brings the baby out sometimes. For her own reason."

"Anybody else know about it besides you and her?

"Sure. Everyone knew about it."

"Is that the way your old man brought his cattle in?"

Again he hesitated, not sure he was supposed to reveal that either. The kid didn't trust me, but he reckoned it was best to keep telling the truth unless he wanted the barrel of a gun shoved up his nose.

"Yeah." He knew what I was getting at. His face reddened, he shuffled his feet.

"So anyone could have gone in. Pat ... Maury..." I wasn't going to say it, but I sure was thinking it: Ryder.

"Suppose they could have," Zeth answered, forcibly. "Our men aren't sheep killers."

"Or people killers?"

"No," he said, firmly, looking me directly in the eyes.

Suddenly overcome with fatigue, I sighed audibly. There were too many dead ends. Anderson was my ace in the hole, and according to all the evidence, my prime suspect. But I wasn't so sure.

Zeth noticed and smiled sympathetically. "Looks like you've been mauled by a lion."

"By a mountain."

I thought of telling him about the Eternal Spring but decided against it. Zeth was harmless, but like most young men bullied and commanded by their fathers, he was immature. Naive in an attractive way, he could not be trusted with important business. Without meaning any harm, Zeth would run home, hand the news to his father, then wait patiently for his praise. I didn't want James T. to know yet.

Ruth Ann was the one I needed to talk with about the dam. She had come in and out of the canyon freely. Perhaps she had seen something, heard something. Maybe Daniel had given her some information. First I had to win her trust.

"What is it you're looking for, Dakota?"

Realizing I had drifted off in thought, I glanced back at him. "I'm looking for the man who killed Bennie Colsen's family."

"It wasn't one man, it was more. Are you going to track them all?"

"If I have to. To start with, I'd be satisfied with the head of the man who led them in."

"My father?"

"More than satisfied with him."

"He didn't do it. Pa was home eating dinner when it happened, drinking brandy in the study. I was with him. It sickened him when he heard the news."

"I thought the Andersons and Colsens were unconditional enemies. You would have thought, at the very least, he'd be pleased. He makes no secret over wanting that mountain, or what he's willing to do to get it. Including hiring guns."

"Bennie Colsen hired the guns," he said tiredly, "not my father."

"Guess he had good reason to."

Bending back down, Zeth resumed his work. He yanked a strand of stubborn barbed wire, rusty and twisted. "It's reaching the point where folks, including my pa, are willing to do whatever they have to do to save their cattle." The barbed wire gave on the second yank. "But he didn't kill anybody. One of them Colsens was the father of my sister's baby. His grandchild. But I guess you already had that figured."

"A bastard child."

"Don't make no difference. He still has Anderson blood."

"Yeah, and an English sheep farmer's..."

Zeth stood up quickly, threatening with the wire snips. My muscles twitched, fingers automatically loosened. It took me a few seconds to realize he wasn't using the snips as a weapon, but to emphasize his words.

"My sister was in love with that sonofabitch. God knows we didn't like it, and Pa did everything to stop her. But he didn't have any part in the killings. What he said to you were the words of a desperate man standing to lose everything. No one can be blamed if anything happens to Bennie if he don't share that water. Ben Colsen was a mean old cuss who wouldn't listen to reason. It had nothing to do with them being English or sheep farmers. You can't hold a man's nationality or profession against him."

Calmly, I shrugged and looked down at the snips waving under my nose. "Don't have anything against English sheep farmers myself."

Guess he must have realized how reckless it was shaking a tool at a legendary gunfighter. He kind of chuckled, squatted down, and started yanking at another piece of wire. "Bet you don't."

He looked up from his work, watching me the way he did in the study that night. The way I was always watching Bennie. Maybe he was not as naive as I thought. Bet he was kind of lonely. I was. I had been in Turnpike for two weeks and I was lonely enough to make a fool of myself. Course Zeth had Ryder to keep him company, and Ryder could be pretty good company. Better than Bennie.

I crouched next to him, real, real close. "You say your old man had nothing to do with it. Let's say I believe you. If you know who did, give me some names."

Again he smiled, almost shyly, avoiding my eyes by studying the calluses on his hands. Being this close disturbed him. He was having trouble breathing, focusing. Abruptly, he looked back at me, honesty turning his face sunset red.

"I don't know, Dakota. I swear, I just don't know. Sometimes I think if I did, I'd kill them all myself. I would do it for Ruth Ann, for Danny, for making us live under this shadow. Ever since it happened people have been fighting among themselves, blaming each other and pointing fingers. You can see the mistrust on their faces when you ride through town. Turnpike hasn't been the same. For anyone."

Danged if I didn't believe him. Although Anderson made it clear he was a danger to Bennie, I did not believe he had anything to do with the killings. He was pompous, proud, used to getting his way like most self-made men. But he wasn't a baby killer. One-on-one, face-to-face, he was capable of fighting Ben Colsen to the death. And he was sure enough capable of hiring gunslingers to scare Bennie into selling. It took a special kind of evil to gun down small children, the kind of evil James T. did not possess. The man who killed the Colsens was a man you would not feel comfortable sitting in the same room with for a long period of time. Anderson was not such a man. Frank Rhinehart was.

"What about Frank Rhinehart?"

"At the depot?"

"Yeah."

Zeth snickered lightly. "Him and Pa have known each other forever. I never did take a liking to him."

"Your pa said they came over in the wagon train together."

"They did. He's old name in Turnpike."

"Do you think he's capable of leading men up that mountain?"

Another light chuckle. "Frank's afraid of his own shadow. He talks mighty big, men who hold a lot of possessions and power do, but he's a coward when it comes right down to it. I don't think he carries a gun. Never saw him with one."

Zeth's hand was on my knee. He had placed it there casually, as if he were just resting his arm. He fingered a small hole in my jeans. The tip of his finger felt cool on my hot skin. "Ryder talks about you like he's talking about the moon and stars."

"Does he."

"He told me about the time you spent together in Santa Fe, the crazy things you did. Like when you both got drunk and broke into the sheriff's office and released all the prisoners. He said it was the worst jailbreak in Santa Fe history."

I smiled slightly at the memory. "It was just a bunch of drunken Indians. We were celebrating All Saints' Day. The sheriff put the Indians in jail for being drunk and disorderly but not the white folk. We were sitting in the saloon drinking whiskey, getting ourselves all riled up about it. Then the sheriff came along and jailed a friend of ours."

"Black Eagle."

"Yeah. Hell, we had all been drinking, making a lot of noise, but Black Eagle was the only one he penned. He just didn't like Injuns. Me and Ryder figured we should go and let him out. A couple of dozen others came with him."

"He said you were like brothers."

More than brothers. Ryder and I were twins. Lovers. Twin lovers. Immediately I felt a lonely for him that usually kept me warm whenever I replayed our time together. Which was often.

"He says you can shoot faster than a snake can flick its tongue."

"Course he was talking about my guns."

Zeth grinned. "I guess so." Wordlessly, he reached up and unbuttoned what was left of my shirt. His cheeks were apple red, his eyebrows bleached as white as his hair. I could hear him breathing, see his barrel chest rise and fall. Ryder had obviously told him some bedroom adventures along with drunk adventures. Bedroom adventures that were getting him excited.

There was a definite lonely for Ryder. A lonely for Bennie. A lonely that could be patched up right nicely by this fair-haired fellow. Without saying a word, Zeth leaned over and went straight for the hollow of my neck, burying his head deep. He was smooth, even smoother than Bennie. His face was almost hairless, baby fuzz on his cheeks, chin, and upper lip. He would be one frustrated boy if he ever tried to look more mature and grow a mustache. He ran his lips down the long muscle from my neck to my chest, kneading slightly with his tongue, before moving farther down. I winced a little.

"Sorry," he mumbled, then tenderly kissed the deeper cuts on my stomach.

Mute the entire time, I kept my hands to myself and let him take the initiative simply to see if he had the guts to do it. He did. Finally reaching the point where I could no longer control myself, I pushed him into the hot sand. I sure enough taught him a lesson.

One foot looped around the saddle horn, I rolled a cigarette and let the buckskin meander. The moon was massive. Biggest damn moon I had ever seen in my life. It looked like I could reach over and pet it.

Yeah, I felt pretty good. Zeth was a good kid. I laughed at myself and shook my head. Kid? He wasn't that much younger than me. I had this problem of thinking I was older and wiser than everyone. Still, he was good, eager, and strong. Ryder had taught him a few things. A few things that I had taught Ryder.

Now that I had Zeth, I could go without having Bennie a while longer. It took a strong and complex web to hold Bennie. I had weaved that web once, pulling him close, but a sheep killer had ripped it apart. No doubt, it would be a long time before he'd trust me enough to let me hold him again.

I suddenly grew solemn at the thought that I might have to kill Zeth. Killing men I had made love to was not one of my favorite pastimes. The money never seemed worth it. But, if Zeth had anything to do with shooting down a scared little girl...

The cigarette hit the dirt before I had a chance to light it. Quickly I straightened in the saddle and kicked the horse into a frenzied run. Even from that distance I could see the amber glow pulsating in the dark of the night, hear the crackling of dry, dead brush, smell the smoke drifting across the desert like a low fog.

Bennie's mountain was on fire.

# 10

The heat was intense, the fire circling. Ten-foot flames licked at the frame of the big house, gobbling it up like an insatiable dragon. The top of the mountain glowed as if it were the tip of a volcano. Like lava, the fire flowed slowly down the mountain. The ground had been doused with an inflammable liquid, maybe turpentine. The air smelled sweet, pungent.

"Bennie!" I shouted into the roaring wall of fire, half expecting him to walk through the flames at the sound of my voice. I stretched in the saddle and stared into the fire until I was forced to turn my face away from the heat.

The bunkhouse had already tumbled. It was nothing more than a pile of burning kindling. Urging my mount over red-hot stones, I circled the bunkhouse, calling his name. The mare threw her head back, snorted, and fought the bit. To keep her from panicking, I reined her carefully, patted her neck, and talked her through.

I shielded my eyes against the fierce glare and searched the darkness, the ruins, for movement. A slight hope that Bennie would not stay in the bunkhouse drove me closer. He was mad enough to face his attackers, hurt enough not to care if he died. With or without a gun, he would have fought them.

Without a gun ... geezus.

Bitterness erupted in my mouth, a hollow fear fluttered in the pit of my stomach. More desperate, I swallowed hard and called again. Then I sat quietly, listening for a reply that did not come. In the dark, I searched the ground for a body, afraid I might find one. The flames lighted my way, playing tricks on my eyes. They distorted every boulder, every shadow, until I could no longer tell what was real and what was shadows or smoke.

My chaps clung to my legs. Oblivious to the smell of melting leather, of singed horsehair, of my skin feeling as if it were blistering, I moved in closer. I could have stayed there staring into the flaming rubble of the bunkhouse, damning myself, until I ignited with it. But the buckskin wrestled free and took us out of the ring of fire.

Around Big House Boulder I dismounted, safely leaving the fire behind. There was nothing I could do but let it burn out. Come daybreak, I would find him. Dead or alive. All I could do was wait. Bitterly.

I didn't sleep. My back to the boulder, I sat upright most of the night, watching, listening, waiting. There was no life on Bennie's mountain. No call of a hoot owl or cry of the coyote. No night creatures rustled in the underbrush in a hurry to get their business done before morning. Nothing. Just the sound of the fire cracking and popping joyously. An unwanted guest keeping me company, it scorched again what had been scorched only a month ago.

Bennie Colsen would not die a coward. In many ways he was more courageous than Ryder or I. We, too, would have thirsted for blood, meted out revenge in a sadistic fashion, but neither of us would have stuck around after the first fire. Neither of us would have bothered to rebuild. We would simply have moved on. More than I was willing to confess, I appreciated Bennie's courage and stubborn refusal to surrender. But it was that courage, that stubbornness, that might have been the death of him.

Lumber crashed on top of lumber, and another violent explosion of flames and smoke soared into the sky. Temporarily it illuminated the night like a quick flash of lightning.

I was mad. Quiet mad. Dangerous mad like the fire. The kind of mad words could not reason with. It was hard to say when I had been this genuine mad before. In the past, I had killed men without holding a grudge, without anger. The shameful truth was I killed men for no good cause except it was my job. Somehow, before I pulled the trigger, I convinced myself they deserved to die. They had all been rogues, scoundrels. At the very least, drunken fools who messed with the wrong gunslinger. But I had never been personally mad at any of them.

Tonight I was mad. Personally affronted. Bennie's cause had become my cause. Even if Bennie Colsen were dead, if Bennie Colsen never paid me a Union penny to complete this job, I would complete it. I promised myself that.

Then I promised myself if Bennie were alive I would never leave him unarmed again. I would teach him to shoot, to defend himself. I made lots of promises sitting there, watching and waiting and thinking.

The way I figured it, I had been offered two diversions: protecting the sheep and Zeth Anderson. Someone cunning, perhaps someone like Ryder McCloud, old buddy, knew what kind of candy I would stop and pick up along the trail. I never met a man I would not climb down off my horse for, never met a man that could not divert my attention. When it came to men, I was foolheaded. So was Ryder. We were twins. He knew I would stop for Zeth Anderson.

I was also apt to rush into battle without considering strategy. So was Ryder. We were twins. He knew I would come barreling down off that mountain to protect the sheep.

Ryder McCloud was getting me dangerously riled. Since we thought so much alike, since we were twins, he probably knew that. And he would be prepared.

Behind me the fire demurely sank to the ground, a beast belching and burping after devouring its meal, then succumbing to sleep. The popping of dry timber silenced itself like spent firecrackers at an Independence Day celebration. The massive moon, the one that had been teasing me hours earlier, faded against a baby blue sky. Then the sun came out, shining its harsh, startling light on the damage.

Not real eager to do so, I shook the numbness from my legs and walked back to the big house. I made one last promise: if I found Bennie Colsen dead, James T. Anderson was going to ante up, and the stakes were going to be fatal.

Ashes and a few obstinate flames were all that was left of our structure. I kicked at the flames with my boot, squelching them, for no other reason than to work off tension. Hot coals raised their fiery little heads. I stomped on them, too. They turned gray and died. I stood sullenly, hands on hips, looking at nothing.

"Where were you?"

His voice was soft, almost humble, not accusing. I turned on my heels. Bennie looked about as defeated as I did mad. There were signs of a struggle. Charcoal blackened his hands and face, his clothes were torn and peppered with soot. He smelled heavily of smoke. It was difficult to tell if he had fought with a man or fought the fire.

I wanted to hug him, throw my arms around him, and lift him off the ground. Laugh. Thank God. Something.

Instead I wiped my mouth on my sleeve, stuck my thumbs through my belt loops, and said, "Did you see who they were?"

He sifted through warm ashes, tossing aside broken pieces of smoking pine. "I didn't see anything. It was late when they came, I was sleeping. All I saw was the fire. Everywhere."

"They?"

He shrugged. "I don't know. Maybe it was only one."

"Did you hear horses? Could you tell how many...?"

"I don't know." Glancing up from the ashes, he briefly caught my eyes before looking away. "I thought something had happened to you, Dakota."

No. I was fine. Just fooling around in the sand with Zeth Anderson, the enemy. If I had been here I could have stopped it. If it had been one man or twenty men I would have been able to stop them. I knew that. Worse, Bennie knew that. I had to admit, I was hurting with blame.

Bennie bent over and pulled a brass fixture from the ashes, the base of the fancy lamp. It did not make it this time. Still red hot; he quickly dropped it. "They aren't going to quit, are they?"

"They have too much to lose to quit. It's the water they're after, not you. I told you that."

Sharply, he looked at me. "Sometimes I wonder which side you're on."

I didn't bother answering. I just rubbed the tired from my eyes and waited to see what he needed next.

Dusting his hands off on his jeans, he said, "I have to take the sheep to Flagstaff. Anderson is coming after them now, and he won't stop. The herd is the only thing of value left. It's late, they should have been sheared months ago, but if I can get a good price for the wool I can save the..."

He stopped mid-sentence. He had been talking aloud, mumbling to himself, forgetting I was listening attentively. He wandered away from me, not going anywhere, just wandering as if he were in a trance. Frustrated, I followed behind him, grabbed his arm, and pulled him around.

"Save what? Finish what you were saying."

"The sheep."

He was lying. Plain-as-could-be lying. I may have twisted his arm a little. He grimaced and tried to pull free but gave up when he realized my grip was too strong.

"No more secrets, Junior. I'm getting mighty tired of secrets."

A thin veil of smoke harbored on the horizon. The heavier clouds of smoke sank to the bottom of the canyon, a gray swirling nest hugging the canyon floor. "You were right. There isn't any money."

Maybe he figured, at this point, I wouldn't care. Maybe, at this point, I didn't. Revenge was on my mind, not money. "Go on."

"The Bank of Flagstaff is foreclosing on the land. If I don't come up with the money by the end of the month, they'll claim it and auction it off."

"What about your inheritance? Won't they hold off until you get your..."

"There isn't any inheritance." He attempted a smile, about the weakest smile I'd ever seen. "My father wasn't a cowboy, Dakota, he didn't know how to run a ranch. He certainly wasn't making money off it. Before he died I received a letter from him stating he could no longer afford my tuition. This would have been the last year of my schooling at Harvard. He was forced to take out a loan to keep the ranch operating."

"How much?"

"Thousands. He planned to pay it back when he sold the wool. But, without warning, the bank demanded full payment on the loan. He couldn't pay it. I certainly can't pay it."

"Is that common? For a bank to call in a debt early?"

"Not without financial grounds. They knew father would pay it back when he sold the wool. He had done it the previous year." Bennie stared into the ashes. "Losing the ranch was the first time he would have failed. At everything else he had been largely successful. He stayed awake nights, pacing the floor, worried. If I can get the sheep to Flagstaff in time I might be able to save it. Either that or let Anderson's men slaughter them one by one."

I nodded agreement. Taking care of Bennie was going to be rough enough. Trying to keep five hundred sheep alive, impossible. "The sooner they're out of here, the better."

"Do you know anything about herding sheep?" he asked, hopefully.

A low moan rumbled in my chest. "They're your sheep. Don't you?"

"I've never done it before. Daniel took care of that sort of thing. You have herded cattle, it can't be so much different, can it?"

"Yeah, there's a difference." I was really chomping at the bit on this one. As far as I was concerned there was a big difference. A man could get laughed at herding sheep.

Junior purposely overlooked my distress. "You will help me take them to Flagstaff, won't you?"

I sighed, a real painful sigh. My resolve, along with my dignity, wilted and fell like red rose petals from a vase onto a white tablecloth. One by one. Petal by petal. Gaudily apparent. Would there be anything Junior would ask that I would not do?

"Yeah, Junior, I'll help you."

Geezus ... Dakota Taylor. Legendary gunfighter. Shepherd. I was in a sorry state, that's for sure.

Ten minutes later, I had the buckskin saddled and one foot in the stirrup.

"Where are you going?"

"Turnpike."

"Why?" Bennie watched me with wide, worried eyes. Worried I would not come back. Worried the riders would and my gun would be of no use to him. Again.

"There's a few things I need to do before we leave."

"What about the sheep?"

"We'll move them out in the morning. In the meantime I want you to stay out of sight. There's a trail leading into the canyon. You can walk it. Go there and stay with the sheep until I get back." Remembering a promise I'd made, I pulled my Winchester from the boot, cocked it, and handed it to him. "Don't fool with that. It's loaded and there's a bullet sitting in the barrel. If anybody threatens you, if they just look ugly at you, all you have to do is point and pull the trigger. You do know what a trigger is, don't you?"

He shot me a quick, irritable look. "Yes, I know what a trigger is."

"Good boy. I'll give you some shooting lessons when I get back."

Briskly, I jerked the horse around and headed for Big House Boulder. I thought I heard him call, "Be careful, Dakota," and looked back over my shoulder. Bennie stood in the ashes, watching my back, holding the rifle away from him with two fingers.

# II

Seven men froze when I pushed the doors to the saloon apart. Maybe they could sense it, see it on my face. Quiet mad. The kind of mad that usually meant someone was going to end up dead before the day was over. And it wasn't going to be me.

I squinted through a dingy haze of smoke. Legs slightly spread, my arms dangling alongside my holsters, I met their eyes one by one. None would challenge me, none would dare, not with this gleam in my eye. Not with the two Colt .44s, oiled slicker than a city boy's hair, leaning slightly out of the holsters to give me that extra edge.

The two town drunks, sitting at the same table where I had left them weeks ago, looked away, no longer with defiant scowls on their faces. The bartender, Charlie, picked up a shot glass and slowly wiped it clean with a stained towel. He watched me closely, not respectfully or fearfully, just closely.

A young man, a cavalry soldier or something, stood at the bar. He turned his back to me, then purposely placed his right hand on the counter away from his holster where I could see it plainly. No sir, he did not want any trouble. He had come in to rest a spell and have a couple of cool ones before riding on. That's all.

It was the four men at the poker table who interested me. One I didn't recognize, but he was a cowhand. It was written on his face and hands. His clothes practically hollered out his profession. Cattle dust settles into your pores until it can't even be sweated out. The cowhand was only interested in the card game, unaware that the circle he sat in was rife with danger.

The other two were Maury Keats and Pat Jordan. Their eyes were locked on me. In them, I read anger and poorly concealed fear. If they drew on me they would be dead within seconds. No words exchanged, no second chances, no doubt about it. Maury Keats knew that. Wise and seasoned, he knew he was not equipped to challenge a gunfighter. Yet, he was still loyal enough to die for the boss man ... if need be. Pat Jordan had a flicker of confidence, just a flicker, like a man who just might, maybe, possibly, beat the odds. A million-to-one long shot, but maybe, just maybe ... if need be.

The fourth poker player, the jackal, was the one I watched, intently. Ryder threw down his cards, picked up his chips.

"Buy you a drink?" His eyes were smiling, dimples winking. The nicest thing about Ryder was that he was always genuinely pleased to see me. Course that didn't mean much. Ryder would be smiling the morning he grudgingly put a bullet in me. I was going to make dang sure this morning wasn't that morning.

Deliberately, I walked to the bar, staying behind him, watching his hands. My spurs jingled across the hardwood floor like Christmas bells ringing across a stark, snowy mountain. Ryder trusted me a little more than I trusted him. He allowed me to walk behind him, his back wide open. That was fitting. I was far more trustworthy.

No one in the saloon breathed. I heard a pulse beating, thumping rhythmically like a tom-tom, and no other sound. Who the pulse belonged to, I did not know. Maybe it was mine.

Charlie set two whiskey glasses on the counter, then placed a full bottle next to them.

"Don't want any trouble," he mumbled. We looked past him as if he did not exist. For me, he didn't. Nothing existed but Ryder and his two handguns.

The soldier hurriedly picked up his beer and moved across the room, out of the line of fire. Ryder watched him leave, a slight flash of interest twitched at his mouth. Ryder liked soldiers. Soldiers, cowboys, and Indians. No doubt he had been sizing him up before I came along and interrupted. But, as usual, he did not mind the interruption and turned his full attention back to me. Given a choice he would take me. Given a better choice, he would take us both. Today I was too mad to let him have either choice.

I leaned against the counter and searched his eyes, trying to read them. Impossible. They were as ice cold, as cloaked as my eyes. "Is this all you do in your spare time? Sit in saloons, drink whiskey, play cards? Getting into trouble?"

Ryder chuckled. "Ain't much else to do. I don't have a house to build or a pretty-eyed fella to keep me company. Besides I thought you might be coming down off the mountain. I hoped you would."

"Knew I would. You looking for me, Ryder?"

We sniffed the air like two tomcats not knowing when the other would pounce. We had danced this dance before, but not with each other. With others. Smile, cajole them, win them, toy with them, kill them. A gunfighter's dance. We were dancing with each other now.

His eyes narrowed, some of the play left his voice. "No. But it's always good to see you. I figured you'd get bored playing nursemaid and going to bed early. Sooner or later you'd come in and wet your lips. You can't blame me for looking forward to it."

Sweet talk. It took a lot of willpower to ignore it and stay mad. Purposely I thought about the house falling, the burns on Bennie's hands, keeping myself fighting mad.

I chugged the whiskey back. "Had me a hell of a night last night."

"Good or bad?"

"Somebody paid Bennie a visit while I was counting dead sheep."

"Do him any harm?"

"Just a warning."

"If the boy had brains he'd pay attention to the warning."

"I wouldn't work for no coward."

Ryder tapped the countertop with his shot glass. He started to pick up the bottle, paused as he considered what I said, picked it up, filled his glass. Refilling mine he said, calmly, "I thought you were working for James T."

"Don't know what gave you that idea. I'm working for Bennie Colsen. I made that clear right from the start."

This time I sipped the drink slowly. Ryder had a bad habit of getting a man too drunk to walk before he knew what was happening. That's how we ended up in a hotel in Santa Fe. Me too drunk to walk, him just sober enough to keep me on my feet. If I wasn't careful I could easily be guided upstairs.

"You took Anderson's money."

I kind of laughed. "I'll take anybody's money. Especially when they put a ribbon around it and hand it to me."

Abruptly, he looked up from the shot glass. "How much have you gotten from him, Dakota?"

"Who?"

"Bennie Colsen."

"None of your business."

"You ain't getting a gawdamn cent..."

"Maybe not now, but I will..."

Half grinning and half disgusted, Ryder shook his head and stared into his whiskey as if he had seen something there. "Lord almighty, I never thought I'd live to see the day you started thinking with the seat of your pants instead of your head."

"Afraid I don't know what you're talking about."

"You know what I'm talking about. You went and got yourself hitched to that Colsen kid. You fancy him a lot more than..."

"Bullshit."

Brotherly concern replaced disgust and his voice grew soft. "Listen to me, buddy, this ain't the time or place for it. There's a whole den of lions knocking on that boy's door, and you're standing useless against them. The day you start caring about somebody is the day you should hang up them guns, buy yourself a plot of land, plant some potatoes."

I snorted. Me? Plant potatoes? No, sir.

"Caring too much will get you killed."

"Doubt it." I didn't want to look at him any more. My face reddened. Heat prickled my cheeks. His words had come too close, too personal. I stared at the back of the bar, reading the labels on the bottles. Jack Daniels ... Red Eye ... Cripplin' Pete.

"Don't force me to come after you," he said in a low voice, barely audible.

I glanced at him fast and hard, wondering if I had heard correctly. No one comes after Dakota Taylor. No one. I was the hunter, not the hunted. The stalker, not the prey. Avoiding the dragon in my eyes, he looked away, lifted his glass, and drained it.

"You ain't thinking straight," he said, flatly. "You're outnumbered."

"I've been that way before."

"You were paid and you were paid good by James T. I don't want to see you lying face down in the dirt with a bullet in you just because you're pining over some pouty-lipped kid."

"Yeah? Well, what am I supposed to do?" I whispered, viciously. I did not want anyone in the room to overhear me. The conversation was embarrassing enough with just Ryder listening. I did not need Maury and Pat and every cowhand, drunk, and soldier west of the Mississippi thinking I was some lovesick pup.

"Walk away. If it ain't in you to work alongside Anderson for the money, then get out of the way."

"And let him fight Anderson's men by himself? Just step aside and let you gun down an innocent kid that don't know nothing about defending himself? Geezus, Ryder, he doesn't even know how to load a gun."

"Since when are you supposed to give a shit?"

"Okay. Okay." He was riling me so bad, I either had to concede or knock his teeth out. "I don't give a shit. But, consider this fair warning: when you come after him you're going to find me standing between the two of you."

Calmly, Ryder removed a wooden match from his pocket, bent over, and struck it on the heel of his boot. He took a rolled cigarette from his hatband and lit it. Then he held the match inches from my face. Hypnotized by the miniature flame, we watched as he let it burn to his fingertips.

"You have to be careful, Dakota. If you drop one of these things someone might get burned. Someone like that boy of yours." He let the match fall to the floor before crushing it out.

"James T. is getting desperate. He lost twenty more head yesterday. That's about twenty a day. Tell Colsen to deal."

"Did that."

"Tell him again. Be more persuasive this time or I'll have to do the persuading." Lightly, he laid his hand against mine. I gripped my whiskey glass so hard I almost crushed it between my fingers. Almost apologetically, Ryder added, "It's my job."

"You're real good at your job. Real good. But not as good as I am."

I walked to the door, stopped, but did not turn around when he called to me. "Dakota ... if he tries to move the sheep he'll find trouble. We'll be waiting for him at the bottom of the mountain."

"Thanks for the warning." I pushed through the doors. They snapped shut behind me.

"Guess I'll be seeing you at the bottom of the mountain," Ryder hollered.

Not if I could help it.

The town had been deserted when I rode in. Even with a train, Turnpike was the quietest, creepiest town I had ever had the misfortune to visit. Either people recognized the buckskin, or they had some mighty swift gossips going from door to door announcing my arrival. Thirty minutes after I got there, the entire population of Turnpike stood in the street, whispering among themselves.

"Someone burned out the Colsen boy last night."

"Good."

"Didn't kill him."

"Too bad."

"The hired gun is in town looking for revenge."

"Oh, no."

Whispering.

I stood on the walk outside the saloon, ashamed to admit that I was a little unnerved by their sudden presence. Coolly, I lit a cigarette, inhaled deeply, and squinted down the street. Maybe I felt for the first time what it was like to be an outsider. Maybe I felt what it like to be a Colsen.

Awkwardly, I pressed through them. They moved out of my way, slowly. Sometimes they forced me to stop, but only for a fleeting second, never long enough for me get a good look at them. Red faces. Thin lips stretched tight. Profanities remained unspoken. They wanted to spit at me, curse me, challenge me, so great was their hatred, but fear held them back. Good thing. The Colts were still leaning sloppily out of their holsters.

Without looking behind me, I knew Maury and Pat had followed me out of the saloon. They leaned against the hitching post discussing what they should do about me. Ryder stood behind them, warning them not to do anything. I was on a death walk, if need be, and an old cowhand like Maury, or a young stud like Pat, was no match for me. Ryder was my match. But Ryder loved me. Worse, he respected me. He watched me for a few more seconds, then, bored and tired of the heat, he went back into the saloon to court the soldier.

As I walked past the sheriff's office I stopped briefly and peeked through the window. Old Bid was keeping himself occupied by throwing darts at a Wanted poster.

Then I walked past the General Mercantile. Jacobs blocked my path, but scooted over when I got close enough to smell. The meatcutter, Bobby Joe, stood in the doorway of his shop. I grinned and tipped my hat at him. He dropped his arms to his sides and moved, as if he were about to approach me. Then, like smart people do, he thought twice, refolded his arms across his chest, and stayed where he was. Good thing. This time I would have just shot the sonofabitch.

I stopped and asked a fair-haired, gentle-looking woman holding a fat baby where I could find the telegraph office. Surely she wouldn't do something disgusting with a baby in her arms.

At first she wasn't going to answer me. But her good manners got the best of her and she said, curt and proper-like, "Across from the depot."

"Thank you, ma'am."

Nervously she touched her throat, closing her lace collar as I brushed by her.

The telegraph office was a four-by-five hole-in-the-wall directly across the street from the Rhinehart Cattle Company and depot. It looked as if someone had hammered together a coffin, picked up a saw, and cut a rough window out of the center. Other than the window, the building was a flat gray box of wood. How anyone could work in there without drying up like a tumbleweed was a mystery. A Comanche's smokehouse seemed more hospitable.

Lazily, I let my gaze drift to the depot. There was no sign of Rhinehart. The stalls and corrals were empty, unexpectedly quiet. Ghost corrals. There was still activity in the warehouse. I could hear the pulleys clanging against metal chains, hear the grunts of the men working inside.

The train came in, ground its wheels to a halt, and rested there. Eager to keep moving down the track, it impatiently belched steam and deposited a few passengers. The first to get off was a stout gent and his equally stout wife. He dressed like a politician. A gold watch dangled from his paisley vest. He snatched up the watch, checked the time, then turned to help another younger woman off the platform.

She was stunningly beautiful, would even make a man like me look twice. Petite, well dressed, she had long, auburn hair tied loosely in the back. There was something familiar about her. I squinted through the engine steam to get a better look. A ponderous ostrich plume hat obscured her face, and she turned her back to me to lift her skirt off the dusty walk.

Separate from the politician and his wife, she nodded at his gallantry and stepped towards the depot, tapping her parasol ahead of her as if it were a cane. What would a lady like that be doing in a slaughterhouse?

The brakeman released the brake, and the conductor called, "All aboard!" one last time. No one from Turnpike got on board. Most of Turnpike's passengers were the four-legged kind crammed ankle deep in manure in a half dozen boxcars. But not today. The cattle cars remained empty. The loss of the stream was taking its toll.

The train started a slow clatter down the track, taking its noise and activity with it. Shrouded in its dust, I stood on the tracks and watched the caboose disappear into the flatlands of the desert before stepping up to the telegraph office.

Removing a piece of paper from my pocket, I stuck my head in the cutout window box. "I'd like to send a telegraph," I half shouted into the cubicle.

"I can hear you."

A thin man with milk white skin and tiny gold wisps of hair stepped out of a shadowy corner. He was youngish. He had a nametag written in his own handwriting pinned to his striped shirt. It said: *Lester*. Lester was a fussy fellow, and already irritated with me.

With an elaborate sweep of his arm, he snapped his bifocals into place, and started to snatch the paper out of my hand. His hand stopped in mid-air when he got a good look at me. He must have liked what he saw, his voice turned soft all of the sudden and he delicately took the paper, effeminate as all hell.

"Let me see..." he murmured.

This must be one of them uranians Junior was talking about. I had encountered a few of these boys in San Francisco. There were a couple of nightspots I frequented, practically lived in, where men powdered their faces, wore silk clothes, and spoke with low soft voices. And there were women there who smoked cigars, cropped their hair short, and could outride, outshoot, and outdrink any man. Including me, excepting I ain't about to admit it. Those places were dark and secretive. You had to know somebody who knew somebody who would open the door for you. They were also a hell of a lot of fun. I constantly warned Rusty if he wasn't careful he would be walking and talking like them boys. Course Rusty did not care. Course, neither did I.

In the untamed West, without the anonymity or the vast privacy of the city, a boy like that had to be even more careful. Lester apparently kept a couple of masks behind the counter which he could slip on and off with ease. The one he slipped on now was for my entertainment.

After reading my message, he leaned out of the cubicle and said, conspiratorially, "You're Dakota Taylor."

I flicked his nametag. "You're Lester."

"Everyone in Turnpike is talking about you. They're scared to death."

"No kidding."

"Shaking in their boots. I was talking to Jacobs at the mercantile. He said he sold every rifle, shotgun, and handgun in stock. Even the ladies bought up all the derringers. They're afraid you might be sneaking into their bedroom windows at night."

"Can't see myself doing that."

Lester moved closer, touched the cuff of my frayed jean jacket. "I wouldn't mind if you snuck into my window."

"You don't have one of them little derringers hidden under the counter?"

"Lordy, no," he laughed. He had a lilting laugh that made you smile. "You can come and see me anytime. Day or night. I'm not going to shoot you."

"I just might do that." And I meant it, too.

The door of the warehouse slid open, metal sliding against metal, and Frank stepped out with the petite woman. He guided her towards a covered buckboard at the side of the depot. I crouched down a little so he wouldn't see me.

"Who's she?"

Lester leaned out of the porthole. "Oh, that's Mrs. Rhinehart," he whispered.

"His wife?" That bothered me. She was far too exquisite for such a man.

"Don't be silly. No one would marry him. That's why he's so ornery. She's his brother's wife, or some such thing."

"That makes more sense."

Not because it was necessary, but because he wanted to get closer, Lester practically lifted out of the hole to whisper. I could feel his lips flutter against my ear. "She's Indian."

"No shit?" I studied her closely. I suppose she could have been Indian. Maybe half-breed. Most Indian women were too practical to walk tiptoe like that.

"Everyone says so," said Lester, then added with another merry laugh, "except Frank and Frank's brother."

Rhinehart helped her into the wagon, then momentarily caught my eye. It couldn't be helped, me and Lester were staring pretty rude. Frowning like a prune, he started to approach the telegraph office, probably decided he didn't want to scuffle in front of the lady, and climbed into the buckboard. Sharply, he snapped the reins over the horse's back, and they trotted into Turnpike. Frank looked over his shoulder to throw me one last sinister look.

I rested my elbow on the window ledge and brought Lester's attention back to the note. "It's important that my friend get that message right away."

"Of course," he smiled. "I wouldn't want your friend to be disappointed. There is nothing worse than a disappointed man."

"And I probably should mention that it's confidential."

Annoyed at the implication that he was anything but professional, Lester shrank back into his cubbyhole. "All of our telegraphs are strictly confidential."

I did not want to, I could have stayed and played with Lester all day, but I nodded, said thanks, and sauntered back down the street. His invitation for a late-night rendezvous was tucked conveniently in the back of my mind for future use.

In the saddle, out of sight, I kept my eye on Lester and the telegraph office. No need to point out I did not trust anyone in this town. Not even a fellow uranian. Lester poked his head out the door, hung a sign in the window, and scuttled across the street to the cattle company.

Maybe I was handsome, but Lester had to live in Turnpike, side by side with the powerful Rhineharts and Andersons. I would have been disappointed if he had not taken my note to Frank and his boys. In fact, I was counting on it.

Quietly, on foot, I snuck around the corner. With a quick flick of the wrist, I snapped the lock and slipped inside. Then, deftly, I tapped out the message I really wanted to send.

# 12

The sun blazed across the dusty, dry pastures of the Double A Ranch. It scalded my eyes, making me mean all over again. Dried carcasses of dead cattle, same color as the sand, dotted the horizon like small clumps of rock. Buzzards circled overhead, patiently waiting for the others to fall. One smelled death here, sensed the despair of its inhabitants. To keep out the smell and the dust, I covered my nose with my bandana. I felt as if I were a wandering nomad crossing a barren wasteland.

Maybe I could have settled everything right then and there by calling a meeting in the town square and telling the good folks of Turnpike about the Eternal Spring. Together, as a community, we could have climbed the mountain, laid pick and shovel to the dam, toppled the sandstone, and freed the sacred water to refill the wells, real peaceful and pretty-like.

But I had a few things to settle first. Prematurely announcing the mystery of the spring might drive the killer underground. I had a good hunch that whoever dammed the spring killed the Colsens, unless Ben Colsen dammed the spring. That would provide a mighty appetizing motive for murder.

The only way I was going solve anything was to leave the water dammed a while longer and let the wells in the valley continue to empty. It would force the killer to rear his head and come after the water, come after Bennie the way they had come after his family.

I rode under the arch and to the porch. Resting in the saddle for a few minutes, I waited for someone to notice my arrival. No one was around, not even the dog. I knew where Ryder and the hands were. I needed them to stay there a while longer.

There was movement in the barn. I tethered the buckskin and walked to the door. Zeth stood in a stall combing down a brooding mare. He was naked to the waist, his shoulders were turning red, freckling fast. I really enjoyed them freckles yesterday. Intent on combing the mare, he neither heard nor saw me.

Without warning, I pushed through the door, ran up from behind, and shoved him facedown in the straw. Quicker than anticipated, he leaped to his feet.

"What the hell?"

Blind and mute, I did not respond, only pushed him again. Not willing to fight me outright, he inched away. Like it or not, he was going to fight. I wanted that much. I pushed him again, harder, and he fell against the stall. The boards cracked and he tumbled through, landing at the feet of a fat roan. The roan whinnied and pawed the soil.

"What's the matter with you, Dakota?" Zeth bellowed, coming out of the stall, face red, fists doubled.

Told you. Quiet mad. No words. With a steady swing, I slugged him. His head snapped back, but he stayed on his feet. I threw a tight jab to the stomach.

He doubled over, clutched his stomach, and gasped for air. His eyes watered. I thought for a second he was going to cry like a baby. Instead he lifted his head and charged like a brainless bull. He caught me around the waist and pulled me to the ground. Pounds heavier, he maneuvered his bulk until he was sitting on my chest, pinning me down, and walloped me a good one in the eye. Heaving hard, I shoved him off, rolling him in the straw.

Back on my feet, I booted him in the chest, not hard, I did not want to cause serious damage. He grabbed my boot and tripped me back down. I landed on top of him. Placing the palm of his hand firmly under my chin, he pushed upwards, stretching my neck towards heaven. One finger rested alongside my mouth. I bit down hard. He yelped like a pup, loosened his grip, but did not get off.

Together we rolled and grunted in the hay, neither of us getting in any good punches. We rolled under the feet of the mare. Annoyed, she stamped her back foot towards us, barely missing Zeth's head.

I shook him loose and jumped to my feet. Zeth was up. Before I could stop him, he grabbed a pitchfork lying against the stall. He jabbed at me. I held back.

"Dammit, Dakota!" he cursed, taking slight pokes at me. "Come on, come on."

Not fair. I circled him, moved in close, let him take pokes, then leaped back seconds before the fork hit skin. I was quicker than him, lighter on my feet.

"You set me up yesterday," I said.

"I only done what Ryder told me." He was sweating, getting tired.

Cruel as a cat, I continued to circle, taunting him. "He told you to make love to me while he burned Bennie out?"

"I didn't know what he had in mind. He only told me to keep you occupied."

Swiftly, I swept my right leg around and kicked the pitchfork out of his hands. Then I punched him full force in the face. Blood gushed from his nose. Stunned by the dramatic flow of blood, he swayed slightly, then dropped to his knees. Protectively, he lifted his hand to his nose. I felt sorry for him and reached down to give him a hand. But he dived at me, grabbed me around the knees, and we smashed against the wall. Tack and lanterns clattered to the floor.

A shotgun exploded, blowing a hole in the roof above our heads. Just the force of the vibration paralyzed us both where we lay. Ruth Ann stood in the barn door, a vaporous shadow against the western sun, her shotgun smoking.

"Stop it," she commanded.

Thoroughly intimidated, we did what we were told. She lowered the shotgun and stepped into the light. She wore a gingham dress with a wide apron tied around her waist as if she had just stepped out of the kitchen and was none too pleased about the interruption. Her straw-colored hair was pulled back brutally in a French roll behind her head as if she were punishing it. Tight-lipped, perpetually angry, her face creased and hardened with the markings of grief, she was still a beauty. A granite beauty. Like Bennie, hatred only solidified her features, erasing powdery soft prettiness and replacing it with a mean handsome. In Bennie I found this physically arousing. In Ruth Ann, downright frightening.

She studied us both in turn. First her brother. His face was bloodied, his knuckles raw and gnashed, pieces of straw stuck out of his baby fine hair. Then me. My eye was quickly swelling, my shirt was torn. I had horseshit up to my knees and a trickle of her brother's blood on my lower lip. Not a pretty sight.

"Bloody fools."

Couldn't help it, I had to smile. Bennie had called me that a few times. It was an expression she probably borrowed from Daniel. Words they had used to describe their fathers.

"I need to talk to you," I said.

Part of her was curious to know what I wanted, the other part wanted to finish me off with the shotgun. Lucky for me, curiosity won. Only slightly hesitating, she nodded towards the house. "There's coffee on the stove."

I brushed the dirt off my clothes. Then I pulled Zeth to his feet, and brushed him off, too. Puzzled, he docilely watched me, hurt feelings making him look all lost and sad. There wasn't much to explain. Except while we were messing around in the sand, Ryder burned me and Bennie's frame down. Zeth was an accomplice. He was lucky all he was getting out of it was a bruised lip and hurt feelings.

Ryder I would deal with later ... cautiously. You could not just jump on Ryder's back and give him a good beating like this knucklehead kid. Ryder kept an eight-inch Yankee-sticker in his boot: a wickedly thin double-edged knife. And he could wield it more gracefully than an Apache. I discovered it there by accident. One night in Santa Fe, I came up behind him in the dark and slipped my arms around his waist, surprising him. The silver-handled sticker was pressed against my throat before I even had a chance to whisper something nice in his ear. Course he apologized right nicely that evening. Ryder fought with guns and knives, never with fists. He was too conceited to bloody his face.

I followed Ruth Ann to the back of the house into the kitchen. Compared to the dining room the kitchen was small and humble. It had one of them fancy enamel stoves with a bread warmer on top. A huge black kettle of coffee bubbled away on the back burner.

The little cowboy sat at the table propped up on a pillow. He was eating a jam sandwich, making a mess of himself and everything within his reach. I pulled out a chair next to him. Ruth Ann busied herself at the stove.

"Why were you fighting with my brother?" She placed a cup of brew in front of me.

The coffee, like everything else, was too hot. I poured cream into it to cool it down. "Guess I'm just in a rotten mood today." That was true enough.

"Why are you in a rotten mood?" It was pretty plain she was not interested in my moods, good or bad, she was being sarcastic, sticking needles in me.

"I'm getting impatient with people who play with matches."

Not bothering to disguise the worry in her voice, she quickly turned from the stove. "Bennie? Was he hurt?"

"It was just a warning. This time."

Steadily, I helped the baby lift a milk glass that was too big for him.

"Don't touch him," she snapped.

I did not pull my hand away. "He looks like his uncle."

"He looks like his father."

"Then they sure looked alike."

"I wouldn't know. I've seen Bennie maybe once or twice. Usually from a distance, and briefly. Daniel pointed him out to me once when he was boarding a train to Boston."

"He didn't know nothing about the baby."

"No one knew anything about the baby. Except my family, of course."

"Ben Colsen didn't know?"

She shook her head, wiped a stray damp strand of hair off her forehead and sighed softly, either from the heat or the memories.

"Maybe it would have changed things if he had."

"No, it would not have." Her voice was cold and confident, but this time the anger was not directed at me. "It did not change anything on this side of the mountain, and it would not have changed things on that side of the mountain."

I stayed quiet and fiddled with the baby. I did not know enough about the circumstances to presume to advise her. In dealing with Bennie I learned it was smarter to let him wrestle with his rage alone. Interfering, advising, or just flat saying something usually made him aim that rage right at me.

"Did you tell him?"

"Bennie? Sure. Why not?"

No longer able to provide a good reason, she shrugged. "I suppose it isn't a secret anymore. Everyone knows. Babies do not sprout from cabbage heads. I'm a scarlet woman, Mr. Taylor. My child is a bastard child."

"I'm a scarlet man, Miz Anderson. I've been called a bastard fairly often, too."

The slightest spark of humor flashed in her eyes. "I imagine you have."

"It's the only kin Bennie has left. This baby."

She wanted to stay angry with me, stay angry with the world, and tell me to mind my own business, but she was softening. I could see it in the way she let her shoulders droop, her face relax, the way she no longer minded if I touched her child. Slowly, piece by piece, she unlatched her armor and let it fall to the floor.

"Does it really matter?" she asked, quietly.

"It would to me. Kinfolk are important."

She smiled, ironically. "You sound like my father."

"Guess I do. Maybe they're important because I don't have any of my own. None to speak of."

"No mother or father?"

"It's been a long time since I've seen them. I've been on my own since I was twelve. We don't see eye to eye on a lot things."

"Neither did the Colsens, Mr. Taylor. Or the Andersons."

"You can call me Dakota, ma'am." We stayed quiet as she considered whether she was ready for first-name familiarity. "My folks have their reasons, me being a gunfighter and all."

"And your father being a preacher. He must be disappointed with the profession you chose." I glanced up at her, surprised that she knew. "Zeth told me," she explained.

"Oh."

"He talks about you constantly. He's probably upset that he has angered you in some way. He's quite taken with you. You and Ryder. He gets that way with..." Suddenly embarrassed that she had said too much, she fidgeted with her apron, untying, then retying the bow. "Men. It's sort of idol worship. He's young and silly."

Avoiding her eyes, I nodded and pretended like I did not know what she was talking about even though I sure enough did. "I suppose I shouldn't have been so hard on him. But I think he may have had something to do with burning Bennie out."

"Not Zeth. He's incapable of bad deeds. Is that what they did, burn him out? Again?"

"Yeah. Did you see anybody leave here last night? Early evening?"

"Ryder McCloud ... and Zeth."

"Together?"

"They spend most of their time together. Ryder McCloud is not a man I want my brother to admire. Nothing personal, but neither are you."

"It was Ryder who lit the match."

"Zeth is easily influenced, easily persuaded by men like Ryder, but he wouldn't hurt Bennie."

I nodded slowly and let her have her way. Hers was a tender defense armored by a headstrong refusal to lose her brother to the same craziness she had lost other loved ones to. I wasn't convinced Zeth was completely innocent, but it didn't matter. She was right: Zeth was young and silly. He was not on my hit list.

"All I'm trying to do is keep Bennie alive. And, if I get lucky, find the people who killed his folks."

"Are you?" Her face soured. "Then why did you take my father's money?"

"I figured you folks owed him something." Course that was not true, but it was the most decent explanation I could come up with at the moment.

"Us folks?"

"Your folks. Your father."

She wiped jam off the baby's face and murmured, "You're right about that."

Through the kitchen window, I watched as four horses galloped under the arch, kicking up a whirlwind of dust, in an all-fire hurry to get somewhere. The poker game was over.

"The men are back from town."

"Where's your pa?"

"Pender. They're holding a town meeting there to discuss the water shortage." She smiled, weakly. "The drought has reached that far north. He rode up with Joel Webb to see if there was anything they could do. I can't imagine what."

The men rode to the barn and dropped off their saddles one by one. Zeth, still red-eyed and confused, met Ryder outside the corral. Their conversation was loud and animated by Zeth waving his arms, shouting, spitting all his anger at me out on Ryder. Gently, Ryder lifted his chin, inspected the damage. Then Zeth pointed towards the kitchen.

Anxious to get going before Ryder reached the house, the words slipped quickly, almost thoughtlessly, out of my mouth. "I found the Eternal Spring."

Ruth Ann hesitated, then slowly slipped into the chair next to me. "No one has ever seen it."

"I've seen it."

"It's like a fairy tale. Papa used to tell us about the Eternal Spring as a bedtime story."

"I'm not the only one who has seen it. The water is disappearing because someone built a dam blocking the stream. It has nothing to do with a drought."

"Who? Why?"

"I was hoping you could tell me. Zeth said you and Daniel spent a lot of time in the canyon. Maybe you saw something, or Daniel may have said something."

Stumped, she held out her hands. "I don't think Daniel was aware of it, even as a myth. I told him the story once, but he just laughed. He thought it was a nice story."

That did not surprise me. "Yeah, I sort of figured that."

"Why would anyone stop the water? They must have been aware of the devastation it would cause."

"Apparently, it was someone who wanted to cause devastation, someone who had something to gain from it." I scanned her face, gauging her response. "Or someone who held a grudge against the people of Turnpike and wanted to punish them."

"Ben Colsen?"

"It could have been him. Or someone who wanted everyone to think it was Ben Colsen, and turn a town against him."

"My father."

"He's the first one I thought of."

"He had been demanding that Ben sell to him for years. Maybe it was his way of forcing him out. If people thought Ben was hoarding the water ... my God, they would kill him."

"The entrance of the cave is about so big." I spread my hands a foot apart. "Your father is too big to fit through the opening. So is Zeth."

"What about Ryder? He's your size."

"Ryder landed in town only a few days before me. The water has been dammed longer than that." I peered over Ruth Ann's head, keeping my eye on the action outside. Zeth was still giving Ryder a rundown of all the sorry things I had done to him. "I don't believe your father knows where the Eternal Spring is located. He talks about it like he's talking about heaven. Besides he wouldn't let his cattle die and take a chance on losing his entire herd just to stick a briar in Ben Colsen's saddle. And now that Colsen is dead, there's no reason for him not to go on up there and release the water."

"Except he still has Bennie to reckon with."

"Bennie's no threat to your pa. I think your pa knows that."

Ruth Ann got up and walked to the stove. Her mind preoccupied, she carried the kettle over, and wordlessly refilled our cups. I didn't want the coffee. Ryder was finally getting riled. Spooky-like, he stared towards the house, knowing I was sitting here drinking coffee. It usually took a lot of talking and pushing to get Ryder angry. Zeth had done the talking. That morning, I had done the pushing.

"You don't know my father. He's likely to do anything to get what he wants. I'm warning you, Dakota, he's dangerous. Sooner or later, one way or another, he gets what he wants. Unless you're willing to kill him he'll beat you."

Kindly, I smiled and stared into the coffee. I had no intention of killing James T., or losing to him. "You don't want me to kill your pa, that's mad talk. You blame him for what happened to Daniel."

"He could have stopped it," she said, coldly.

"Maybe he could have, but he didn't. Now he can't go back and change things, even though he's wishing he could. Carrying around that kind of anger weakens a person's thinking. Trust me, I know. I make my living depending on people's anger, and their unwillingness to forgive."

She lifted Danny out of the chair and quietly began to wash him up. "Maybe so."

"It's like Bennie. He's got a right proper reason to be angry, just like you do. His neck is lying in a guillotine, but he's too busy being mad and seeking justice to notice. He's likely to get his head chopped off."

Abruptly, she stopped washing the baby and eyeballed me hard. I almost squirmed under her gaze. "You really care about him, don't you?"

Embarrassed, I gulped the coffee, burned my tongue. "Pardon me? No ... I was hired to protect him, that's all. He ain't making it easy."

"One can hardly blame him." She combed Danny's hair back with her fingers. "I wish there was something I could do to help."

"There is. In fact, there's a couple of things I need to ask of you."

"What are they?"

"Tomorrow we're taking the sheep to Flagstaff. Your old man has his boys taking potshots at them, and they're overdue for shearing. They know we're going to move them. There'll be a welcoming committee waiting at the bottom of the mountain. The only other way out is through the canyon and across Anderson property. When everyone is at the bottom of the mountain I need you to signal me."

The thought excited her. Inactivity was a breeding ground for resentment. If she could move, become involved again, the pain of yesterday would become a long, ugly memory instead of part of everyday living. "That shouldn't be a problem."

"Also, there is a locked gate up on the east fork. I can break through it, that's easy enough, but it would save us some time if you could open it."

A worried frown dented her forehead. "Taking the sheep northeast will lead you straight into Devil's Canyon."

"Yep."

"The canyon is deadly this time of the year. No one goes into Devil's Canyon in the middle of summer. Not even the Indian."

"I know. But I would rather take my chances with the sun than with your old man and his army."

"You said you needed a couple of things. What else?"

"I have a friend coming in on the train from Flagstaff on Friday afternoon. I won't be here to pick him up at the depot. If you can pick him up and find him a place to stay I'd be grateful."

"He can stay here. But if you're going to Flagstaff, why don't you just meet him there?"

I smiled and pushed my empty cup away. Outside, Ryder handed the reins of his horse to Pat. He removed his riding gloves and approached the house at a quick, angry stride. No doubt about it, there was going to be trouble.

Quickly, I picked up my hat and dropped it on my head. "My intentions are to transport the sheep to Flagstaff, and that's what I'm going to try my best to do. But I got a hunch we won't be getting very far."

I got out of the kitchen, out the back door, on my horse, and halfway through the arch before Ryder made it to the porch. Grinning slightly, he stopped on the second step, and took a long, hard look at my back fading into the dry countryside.

# 13

Surefooted, somewhat graceful, the sheep flowed easily through the crevice between the boulders, spilled down the trail, and emptied onto Anderson's fields like waves crashing onto a forbidden shore. Every once in a while a fat one got stuck and I had to dismount and shove her ahead to keep from interrupting the flow. When one sheep got confused they all got confused. Other than that, and their constant noise making, they moved easily, much easier than stubborn steers, which was something I would never admit to Bennie. Or anyone else.

I rode at the head of the herd to make sure they did not drift off the path and head up the mountain where it would take days to gather them. In the open fields we were able to keep them in a controllable bunch. Bennie rode at the end, straight in the saddle. Chin up, eyes alert, he waved a branch over the sheep like a wand, looking like a pretty dang dignified sheepherder.

A portly ram with wool hanging down to its knees plugged the hole. I booted it through just as Bennie came up beside me.

"Geezus, they stink," I complained when he got within hearing distance.

"Stop kicking my sheep," he grumped, like I knew he would. "And sheep manure doesn't smell half as bad as cow manure."

"Well, ain't that something I'm glad to know. I wouldn't want to go to my grave not knowing that."

"This is going to be a long drive."

"Tell me about it, Junior."

His black eyes sparked with impatience. He swung the walker around and trotted back to his post, forgetting what it was he had come to tell me. I had that effect on Junior: frustrating him so bad he became absentminded in my company. I chuckled as I watched the walker disappear into a sea of gray wool.

Truth is, I was enjoying myself. It felt good to be back in the saddle, moving, going somewhere. I enjoyed riding with Bennie, like I enjoyed working side by side building the big house. We never said much, hardly spoke more than a handful of words, but we were acutely aware of the other's presence, of our natural ability to get things done. Silently we communicated what the other needed, getting along just fine until one of us opened our mouth and spoke. Usually me.

The morning's shooting lesson was a hopeless attempt to teach anyone anything. Bennie feared the gun and was too headstrong to admit it. The resounding explosion, the sudden jerk of the wrist as he pulled the trigger, startled him quicker than a gun-shy horse.

I placed empty whiskey bottles ten feet away, stood behind him, and maybe pulled him in a lot closer than necessary. I held his arms straight out, tight, to keep his hand from snapping back, and scoped in his aim. There was no way he could miss. Before he pulled the trigger, he closed his eyes. He missed.

Then I placed a rock the size of his head two feet away. He missed that, too. Impatiently, a little testily perhaps, I told him the bullet wasn't going to leap out and bite him on the nose. He said I was being facetious, whatever the hell that meant. To keep from punching each other we gave up.

We came up on the first gate by the lower east fork. Shimmering in a ripple of heat waves, Ruth Ann sat on a rotund bay. She wore leather chaps and a leather hat to protect herself against the dry heat. When she saw us coming she leaped off the horse, swung the gate open, and beckoned us through. We picked up the pace and pushed the herd into wide-open fields. They kicked up a suffocating tornado of dust and sand.

When the last straggler was guided in, and the gate was closed, I turned my mare to thank her.

"Zeth knows" were the first words out of her mouth.

I surveyed the horizon, half expecting the posse to be riding down on us. It looked peaceful and empty, a world of its own. "Think he'll say anything?"

"Not right away. I asked him to give us a head start, but he's a good son, and he'll do what he has to do to please Papa."

"How much time?"

"Not much. You have to hurry, Dakota. They're all worked up. There's twenty, maybe more of them, and they're riding hard. Ryder is riding at the head. They're not going to take a chance on the sheep reaching Flagstaff."

The animals gratefully milled in the fields. They were heavy with wool, and I did not want to drive them in the heat any harder than we were. But I wasn't real eager to confront Anderson's twenty guns. Or Ryder's two.

My gaze glued to the horizon, I nodded slowly. "Appreciate it."

She hung on the fence, longingly watching the sheep. Gold strands of hair fell from her hat and itched her eyelids. "I'm the one who appreciates it. Those sheep were Daniel's life. We spent many nights in the canyon watching them. Daniel was afraid a coyote or a wild dog would get a young one." She glanced at Bennie, maybe hoping he shared her memories. Bennie looked away. She smiled up at me instead. "Go. Hurry."

"Yes, ma'am."

We gathered the sheep in a light bundle, and pushed them ahead. Behind us, Ruth Ann wrapped strands of barbed wire around the gate latch in an attempt to slow down the riders.

Bennie had not said a word to her. Not one word. I looked over at him. Arched and starched in the saddle, deep in unpleasant thought, a slight frown disrupted his beauty. One of these days I was going to slap the snot right out of him.

As we moved farther north the air became lighter, clearer, less thick with dust and heat. On the horizon, directly in front of us, a pink-and-orange mountain mass rose out of the flatlands. It was spotted with some greenery. Stalwart little evergreens stayed hidden among the cool shadows of the boulders. Other than that, it had nothing to offer a man but solid rock and shifting sands. A few miles in was Devil's Canyon, heatstroke, and hard times. We would reach the base of the mountain by nightfall.

In the open fields we could see for miles. Riders, twenty strong, would come across the desert like a herd of bison, loud and visible. But slipping intricately through the narrow maze of buttes, with rocky cliffs on each side, an army could hide out. We had no choice but to walk right down the middle of them with a herd of sheep.

Quickly, Bennie trotted up beside me. Before I could reprimand him for leaving our rear unprotected, he pointed east across the desert.

"Someone's coming."

In the center of a small dust cloud were maybe half a dozen riders. They were coming towards us, fast.

"Is it Anderson?"

Squinting through blurry vision, I couldn't tell. Most likely Anderson would not ride in from the east. He would either attempt to sneak up behind us, which would be impossible, or meet us face on in Devil's Canyon, which I was betting on.

"Herd the sheep into a tight circle. There's no point in having them spooked and scattering across the plains."

Deftly, Bennie moved the sheep into a protected position, if it were possible for two men to protect several hundred sheep. They made whole lot of noise protesting, but like good sheep they finally did what they were supposed to. They were like me: impatient for the cool running waters of Flagstaff, where a man or a sheep could nap leisurely against the trunks of ponderosa pines swaying soothingly in a light wind. No troubles.

The riders finally moved into my line of vision, which was too dang close for comfort. Indians. Worse. They were Indians riding war ponies and wearing ornate war dress. These boys were on a hunt, and it wasn't four-legged critters they were hunting.

In Hudson I heard tell of a renegade band of Indians burning out some settlers east of Turnpike. Cochise's men. They had a bounty on their heads, something like twenty dollars a scalp. I was lazily looking into that bounty before Junior came along and disturbed me. The way things looked now, they were going to get our scalps for free.

Last I heard the renegades were moving west, leaving smoldering cabins and looted shantytowns along the way. No doubt they were what had brought the soldier into the saloon to wet his throat. If I hadn't been watching Ryder's trigger finger I would have paid more attention to the moccasins the soldier wore. He was a scout, tracking Indians. White scouts wore moccasins in case they accidently left prints behind. Of course every Indian west of the Mississippi already had that figured out and it was getting to be something of a barroom and tepee joke.

Bennie was back beside me. He looked as if he had never seen an Indian before in his life. Maybe he hadn't.

"Are they hostile?"

"War paint. War ponies. War spears. Sort of."

"What are we going to do?"

"Seeing as how you couldn't shoot a mountain if I placed one in front of you, and it's just me against them, I suppose we're going to sit here and smile and be real nice and see what they want."

"I imagine they want to kill us."

"Then it's been a pleasure knowing you, Junior. Sometimes."

Bennie's groan showed serious disappointment in me. What he did not know was that I had already calculated a mode of defense. The trick was to get the rifle, good for long distances, steadied between the horse's ears, and a pistol firing at the same time. That way I could take three or four of them down before they knew what hit them. The others would be thrown off guard.

"I read an article about you in the *Bostonian Gazette*. It said you held off sixteen sheriff's deputies with a single rifle."

My eyes never wavered from the approaching warriors. I snorted a little. That was a story I never heard before.

"It said the posse limped back to town with every man wounded. They couldn't find any more townsmen brave enough to go up against you."

Although I was as proud as I could be, some of the things posted about me were truly amazing. The *Arizona Mill Press* said I was a lecherous womanizer. It warned husbands to keep an eye on their wives whenever I was in town. I got a good laugh out of that one. They should have warned the women to watch out for their men.

"That's why I placed an advertisement in the *Gazette*. They often print articles about gunfighters and their extraordinary feats. I assumed, since gunfighters are an egotistical bunch reading about their own heroics, one would find my advertisement."

"You advertised? For a gunfighter?"

"Well, yes..."

"Geezus..."

"That's how I met Ryder."

"Ryder answered your ad?"

"Well, yes..."

"Geezus..."

"He went over to Anderson's side when he discovered I didn't have the money to pay him. And when I refused to get ... amorous."

"Ryder always was smarter than me."

"It's rather difficult getting amorous when you've just buried your entire family." Bennie frowned. "He's a bit of a cad."

"Jackal."

"Whatever. Anyway, he rode onto the Double A and offered his services. That's when I began searching for you. After reading the article about the dishonored deputies. An article of half-truths it appears."

"I'll leave any time, Junior. Hell, I'll leave right now. Gladly."

"Don't be silly." Bennie fidgeted nervously in the saddle. "Are we really just going to sit here and do nothing?"

Not wanting to dismantle his image of me completely, I said, "This ain't a posse, these are Indian warriors. It takes one of them to five sheriff's deputies. They're spirits, Junior. They don't die easy."

Like a wild, unexpected tornado whirling across the desert, they rode down on us, then split in the middle just as they were about to trample our horses. Whooping and hollering, they circled the sheep. Quick count. There were ten of them. Hopi. If they had been Apache we would be sitting dead on our horses. Cochise was still rattling around out there somewhere.

"Hold still," I muttered under my breath.

Intrigued that we neither ran nor fought them, the apparent leader recircled and stopped in front of us. Our horses were nose to nose.

The leader, a young warrior destined to be chief, studied us with the ancient eyes of a sage. He was a beauty, with muscles as sleek and graceful as a panther's. Unbraided, his hair fell across his shoulders and halfway to his waist, like ebony cornsilk. Red clay was streaked wildly across his cheekbones, giving him a reckless look. His chest was covered by a breastplate made of bone and crudely hammered silver and turquoise.

No sir, there was no man on earth more beautiful than a painted Indian warrior.

My heart thumped wildly from an odd but exhilarating combination of fear and physical appreciation of his beauty. We locked eyes, probing deeply, staring each other down. All the while his pony drifted off to the side.

When there is a gulf between language and culture, all we have left to communicate with are the eyes. To break his stare meant I was a coward, that I feared him. To show the smallest glimmer of anger would show disrespect. But to hold his gaze meant not only did I not fear him, I also respected him. We were equals. We were both warriors.

Nodding silent recognition of this, he looked away and studied Bennie. Fascinated by Bennie's dark hair and eyes, he wetted his forefinger, leaned over, and rubbed Bennie's bicep roughly. Captivated in more ways than one, Bennie held dutifully still.

The leader said something to his friends and they laughed. They thought Bennie was Indian. With the Arizona sun toasting his skin, he looked Indian.

I could speak Cherokee, Sioux, and the language of most of the northern California tribes. As luck would have it, I could speak enough Shoshone, a language similar to the Hopi's, to understand him. A little.

"You are trespassing on Hopi land."

"For that I apologize. But I have a great need to take these sheep through."

"These are your animals?"

No need to quibble over what was Bennie's and what was mine. The only thing of value we possessed at the moment were our lives. "They're mine."

He looked them over.

"I'll give you ten," I offered. "In return for your hospitality and safe passage through Hopi land."

He could have taken them all. But that's not how men of respect earn respect. If he took the sheep by force, the great warrior would be reduced to a thief. A rustler, like the white men who stripped what they wanted from the Hopi, and left them with barely enough to feed their families.

On the other hand, he wasn't stupid. And he wasn't going to settle for ten.

"Fifty," he said.

"Nah," I shook my head, grinning. That was too much. He knew it. "Twenty."

"Forty."

Now we treaded lightly on a shaky ledge. To keep face with his braves he could not assent too much. Nor could I appear cowardly and submit too quickly. I met him in the middle, on safe ground. There, I could keep my life, he could keep his pride.

"Thirty," I said.

Scanning the herd, a petulant look swept across his bronzed features. "Our families are big."

"Thirty," I repeated with a definite air of authority.

"This I agree to. Thirty. Of the fattest."

One quick flip of his hand and the braves started to weed out fat, healthy sheep, poking them lightly with their spears.

The warrior held out his hand. A white man's gesture. I took it, squeezed firmly.

"I am Swift Running Deer."

"I am Dakota."

"You have the name of the land of the Sioux."

I nodded. "Land I'm familiar with. My birthplace."

"My grandfather talks of a giant man who has the name of the land of the Sioux."

"Living Cloud?"

"It is you he speaks of."

I had saved Living Cloud's life. Ten years ago when I was a hotshot kid with a new Spencer rifle and a reputation as wild as the buffalo I hunted on that day. I joined up with some drunken hunters and rode with them for a while, sharing their whiskey and their grub. When a herd rumbled across the plains, we dropped off our horses and hid in the underbrush, lining up like Mexican soldiers at the Alamo.

The buffalo weren't wild. They were slow-moving, gentle beasts. Cumbersome prehistoric animals, their heads were massive like the heads of lions. I had never seen a buffalo before, and they were something to behold, that's for sure. Quietly, I lowered my Spencer to watch them, to appreciate their calm.

The hunters opened fire. They fired on everything. Nursing mothers and their calves, half-grown bulls, dropped by the dozens. It was only a few men with a few guns, but by nightfall there would be no buffalo left.

My stomach had started turning, getting queasy, and I turned around and let loose my breakfast on the ground. One of the old boys said, "That's Garth's cookin' fer ya." And another said, "He's too much of a tenderfoot to be drinking rye whiskey." And they just kept firing, dropping them massive beasts in the dirt.

Out of the center of the herd rode an Indian, shrieking like a woman in birth pain. His silver hair streamed loose in the wind. His coats fluttered off the back of his paint. A warrior's spear was raised defiantly above his head. A ghost rider riding to defend the buffalo.

They fired on him, too. Wounded, he fell from the horse and ran into a ravine. Like a pack of bloodhounds they tracked him and cornered him with no trouble. He bled profusely from a gaping wound in his side. The hunters kidded him a little, called him Pocahontas. I remember them laughing. I stood at the top of the ravine, looking down on them. Then I lifted my new Spencer that had never been fired before and pumped the chamber empty on them buffalo hunters.

What I remember most, what comes along and pokes at me once in a while, forcing me to stop and ponder my ways, was that it did not bother me to watch them men drop. Not half as much as watching them buffalo. Pa always said, "You got a real bad spirit dwelling inside you, Dakota." Reckon he could be right.

The old Indian's eyes had clouded and he'd stumbled forward. I packed the wound with a root-and-mud concoction. The herbs stopped the bleeding, and I built a travois out of alder wood. Days later, when he was strong enough, I carried him back to his people.

Now I looked into the eyes of the ghost rider's grandson. His granddaddy had probably told and retold him the story a hundred times or so. Maybe there were parts of it he did not believe, that had become an old man's fable, but it wasn't necessary for me to retell the story. He knew. Knew a half-crazy kid, not old enough for marrying let alone killing, had saved his grandfather's life.

Again the warrior looked at Bennie, circled him, and examined his black hair. "This one," he said, "has the eyes and hair of the Navaho."

"Heck, no." That shook me. There was only one group of people the Hopi resented more than the white man and that was the Navaho. "He's English. His family traveled all the way from a European continent. I know he doesn't look it, but he is."

"What's he saying?" Bennie asked.

"English?" The word rolled off Swift Running Deer's tongue eloquently. Still he doubted me. "Navaho."

"He thinks you're Navaho."

"Navaho?"

"Hold still."

"How can I hold still when he keeps prodding me?"

"Listen to the way he speaks," I told the warrior.

"Speak," he demanded.

Patience not one of his better habits, Bennie lifted an eyebrow, getting ready to argue with the man with a spear. Already he had given them a chunk of his herd, now he was to become a puppet-doll, a source of their amusement, their curiosity.

"Speak," Swift Running Deer insisted more loudly.

"Good Lord."

Suppressing an outright chuckle, I looked towards the looming mountain, inwardly smiling at Bennie's discomfort.

"My name is Benjamin Colsen, Jr. I am from London, England, therefore, I am English, not Navaho. And those are my sheep you are stealing."

Playfully, they laughed. They did not understand a single word, they simply enjoyed the rhythm of his dialect.

Satisfied, Swift Running Deer concluded, "He is English, not Navaho." He motioned for the braves to move the sheep out. "You come to my grandfather's village sometime. Bring the English."

As swiftly as they had come, they departed. Their waning war cries mingled with the consistent baaing of the sheep. Thoughtfully, I watched them until they were no more than a blur against the horizon, reflecting on my time with Living Cloud, chieftain and great shaman.

Bennie reeled the walker around and rode to the back. "Those sheep are coming out of your wages," he said, testily.

I started to holler, "What wages?" but thought better of it. It was still a long way across the desert. And there was the slightest possibility, the smallest chance, the nights might grow cold.

# 14

Nightfall shrouded us like a cool blanket of arms. Darkness provided a welcome relief from the blinding aqua blue sky. The mountain mass was still a good two hours away. I did not want to stumble through it in the dark, and we both needed a good night's sleep before tackling the cliffs. We bunked down where we dropped our saddles. Wide open in a still lake of sand, we were fat plum pickings. But that couldn't be helped, there wasn't any cover. A three-quarter moon would alert me to anyone coming across the desert.

There was only one bedroll. Mine. Bennie had lost everything, except the walker and his riding gear, in the fire. I threw him the blanket and he made up his bed. It wasn't easy, but I got a fire going long enough to warm something to eat.

There was nothingness around us. Two tiny humans crouched over a tiny campfire while a great big mountain glowered down on them. A coyote yelled in the mountain. It was probably starving. I was going to have to sleep with both eyes open tonight. One on Anderson's men, one on roving coyotes.

Bennie's face was caked with dust, his delicate student hands cracked and broken. He took his canteen from his saddle, splashed cold water on his face, then vigorously rubbed off the dirt.

"You shouldn't use too much water."

"I know. Sorry."

"There's a standing well about twenty miles out of Devil's Canyon, and that's it until we get to Flagstaff. I can hardly wait, Junior. I'm going to find me a cool bed, warm bath, and a hot steak two inches thick."

Bennie smiled. The idea appealed to him. "How long will it take us?"

"A week, if luck's on our side."

"Really?" That surprised him. "I didn't realize it would take that long."

"If we had come straight down off the mountain, we would have made it in a couple of days. Through Devil's Canyon is the long way, the crazy man's way." I caught his eyes in the glow of the campfire. "Do you want to turn back?"

"No. We haven't much choice."

"That a boy." I burrowed into the sand, it was still warm, and rested my head against my saddle. "Was your father a big man?"

"Not really. Why do you ask?"

"Smaller than me?"

"You're not very small."

"Come on, Junior, it's been a long day. Just answer my questions without argumentative comments."

He laughed quietly. "If that's possible."

I smiled in the dark. "Was he?"

"Much smaller."

"What about Daniel?"

"He was about my size. Maybe bigger."

Bennie was a couple of inches shorter than me, maybe five-ten, but with broader shoulders and a thicker chest. I was six feet of nothing but legs. Still, one ounce more and I would not have fit through that hole. That ruled out Daniel. But not the old man.

"Have you heard of the Eternal Spring?"

Bennie smiled, indulgently. "It's an Indian myth. Is it water flowing from a rock? Of course I've heard of it. People in Turnpike are almost religious about it."

"What did your old man think about it?"

"My father?" Bennie shrugged. "Not much I'm afraid. It's a silly Indian myth. He was an educated man, he didn't believe in ghost stories."

"I found it."

"Really..." He was still smiling. Junior did not believe me.

"The reason folks in Turnpike are religious about it is because it's their water supply."

"According to the myth."

"It's a fact, Junior. And it's sitting right at the top of one of your mountains. The highest one. Trouble is someone found it before I did and built a wall twenty feet high damming it. That's why the water is disappearing. I think that's what got your folks killed."

Slowly, he turned to face me. "Do you think my father did it?"

"Would he?"

Frowning with uncertainty, he turned away, and stared at the stars. He stayed quiet for so long I thought he was counting the damn things. "I don't know."

I did not to push him for a clearer answer. The possibility that his father was responsible disturbed him. I would have liked to explain to him that we were not accountable for the actions of our elders, even if they were kin. If Ben Colsen hoarded the water to punish his tormentors in Turnpike and got his family killed for doing so, it was not Bennie's fault, not Bennie's sin. I wanted to explain that to him and ease some guilt.

But I didn't. Instead, I pulled my hat over my eyes. "Well, Dakota Taylor better get some sleep or he ain't going to be no good for nothing come morning."

It was the right thing to say. Bennie responded, almost cheerfully. "That is not your real name."

"Sure it is," I mumbled from beneath my hat.

"No, that's a gunfighter's name."

"I am a gunfighter."

"You weren't born a gunfighter."

"Sure I was. I came out of the womb packing two Colts with filed-down triggers, spring loaded, and ready for trouble." Showing off a little, I snatched the pistols out of my holsters and fired off fake shots, pretending to shoot stars out of the sky.

Bennie chuckled. "You're such a child sometimes."

"When my mama saw these two guns she gave me a name as big as an Indian nation."

He refused to believe my story and continued to challenge me. "Don't be a coward. Don't be a yellow-bellied..." He started laughing. "What is it?"

"Sapsucker."

"Yes. Don't be a sapsucker. What is your real name?"

Stubbornly silent, I watched the stars, way up in the sky, flickering, winking, dancing. I wouldn't have enjoyed Bennie more if I'd fed him a couple of bottles of cheap liquor and cornered him in a dark, private room. "Truth is, Dakota *is* my real name. I was born bouncing and wobbling in the back of a buckboard in the Black Hills while being chased by a band of Sioux warriors who called themselves the Dakota. They caught up with us, ready to have a skinning party. But when they saw that Ma was giving birth they backed off, real respectful-like, and escorted us through. She gave me their name. It means 'allies.'"

"Allies?"

"Yep."

Bennie considered the significance of the meaning for a few moments. Then, he mentally debated whether or not he was going to believe me. It was one of my better stories, to be sure.

"Got off to a good start, didn't I?"

"Off to a questionable one, that's for certain. Your true name is probably Bob or Garfield..."

I chuckled. "Garfield?"

"You're too much of a coward to admit it." He rolled over under the blanket, trying to wring comfort out of a hard saddle and a harder ground.

I ignored his fighting words. My eyes and ears were alert to every sound, every movement. I was waiting for Anderson and his boys to come thudding across the desert, waiting for some scrawny old coyote to come and start feeding on tender lamb.

How could Ben Colsen, old as he was, small as he was, move them boulders? Some piled twenty feet high? And for what purpose beyond irritating a lot of folks into wanting to kill him? Spite could make a person do some pretty stupid things. But would he cut off an entire town's water supply? If he ever hoped to become a part of the community, that sure wasn't the way to do it.

Suddenly Bennie turned back over. "I want a name. Something big and fearsome, like Texas or California. Think of me a name."

"Nothing wrong with the name you got. Benjamin Colsen, Jr. That's a fine name for a lawyer."

He placed his arms under his head, and said with a sigh of resignation, "Benjamin Colsen, Jr., Esquire. I'm not so sure."

"Don't you want to be a lawyer?"

"My father wanted me to be a lawyer."

"So?"

"So my father is dead."

"Well, what do you want to be? A sheep farmer?"

"A cowboy," he said, sarcastically. Trouble glinted in his bright eyes.

"Forget it. I'm still smarting over this morning's shooting lessons. You'll never be a cowboy, Junior."

"I don't suppose." He rolled back over and huddled deep into the blanket. "If you get cold I don't mind sharing."

Before I could leap to my feet and crawl under the blanket, he repeated like a dang schoolteacher or something, "*If* you get cold."

It wasn't cold. In fact, it was still warmer than a baker's kitchen. I prayed for snow.

It was early. A morning haze softly veiled the mountain like a fine misty cobweb. I studied the complex beehive of cliffs and valleys that lay ahead of us. We would have to take the sheep straight through. If Anderson and his men were hidden in the cliffs we would be trapped tighter than bugs in a brat's jar. And I had me a hunch, a deadly hunch, they were going to be there to greet us.

We had not seen hide nor hair of them on the miles that stretched across the horizon, which pretty much meant they were not coming. That way. All Anderson had to do was take the train to Pender and double back. That would have put them in Devil's Canyon sometime in the cool of last night.

Extinguishing the campfire by kicking sand on it, I leaned over and gently shook Bennie. He awoke in a panic, ready to fight, like a two-year-old coming out of a nightmare. Disoriented, he quickly searched his surroundings before getting his bearings.

"Time to go, Junior. We don't want to be in those cliffs when the afternoon sun hits."

Dead tired, he yawned and rubbed his eyes with the back of his hand. Then he jumped to his feet, picked up the blanket, snapped it briskly to get the sand out, grabbed his saddle, and plopped it on the horse. Sleepwalking. If there had been a wall nearby he would have walked right into it.

Apprehensively, with an eerie hesitation, we rounded the sheep into a tight herd and took them in.

Ahead of us was the only trail in and out. It was narrow. The sheep filed through, four to five wide. Sharp rock formations with jagged peaks, some small, some large, reached for the sky around us. Nature's statues. The cliffs rose dramatically on each side like massive praying hands. If Mother Nature elected to applaud we would be squashed between her stone palms like a couple of gnats.

Bennie sensed the urgency of our situation and stayed quiet, eyes swinging from canyon wall to canyon wall, from rugged cliff to rugged cliff. We rode slowly to keep our body temperature down, and to keep the animals from overheating. If luck were on our side, we would be out of the cliffs before the noon sun sat high in the sky. If not, we would join the rest of the skeletal remains cast off to the side, bleached white by the sun.

We rode in four miles. So far, so good. Bennie loosened in the saddle, relaxing a bit. I didn't. I kept my eyes on the rocks, my nose sniffing the air.

I stopped the buckskin twenty feet in front of what the Navaho called the Sandpit. It was a drop-off filled with drifting sand more treacherous than swamp water. It continuously sloped downward, traveling on for two hot miles. We were sure to lose some sheep in the sand. Not losing a horse depended on God.

The sun was already a blur, melted across the sky by the intensity of its own heat. A purple ring circled it as if it were hopelessly trying to contain the lethal rays. Bennie silently moved up behind me with the sheep.

Up in the rocks, light reflected and flashed off cold, blue steel. It was just a spark, barely enough to warn me. Paralyzed by my own premonitions, I reined the buckskin around wildly.

"Get down!" I shouted.

A thunderstorm of rifles opened fire like a violent cloud breaking overhead. Bullets shattered against the canyon walls and ricocheted back on us. A snippet of shrapnel bit my shoulder, a fiery hot bee sting. Unsteadily, I pulled both handguns and fired off round after round.

Invisible men were concealed behind the rocks. Their heads bobbed up and down like ducks on water. I blasted both barrels in their direction. I heard a holler. A man tumbled down the cliff, clutching his chest. Before I emptied both chambers, I wounded a couple more.

The sheep stampeded into the Sandpit. The buckskin whirled out of control. I struggled to rein her in and head the sheep back out, but the bullets kept her squirming.

Bennie's walker reared on him, then turned circles like a dancing bear. I plunged through the sheep to reach him. The dust was choking, blinding, and I kept losing sight of him. Finally, his horse threw him. He landed in the middle of the stampeding sheep. They were thick as black molasses as I waded through and pulled him to his feet.

"Take cover behind those rocks!"

We ran towards the safety of the rocks, outstepping a trail of bullets following close behind, and somersaulted behind a boulder. A barrage of bullets chipped away at it. Lead splintered around us. I pushed Bennie farther ahead, out of the range of fire.

The gunfire stopped as quickly as it had started. We climbed to an opening. It was protected by a small fortress of boulders, and I had a clear view of the canyon floor. We were safe here. Safe from Anderson's bullets, but not from the sun creeping over the eastern wall.

"Dakota!"

It was Anderson. I scrambled to a rock and peered down on him. Brazenly, he stood at the bottom of the canyon out in the open. Zeth and Ryder stood on each side of him, like two stone lions guarding the king's throne. It was kind of stupid of them. I could have picked them off with one bullet each.

"Don't want to hurt you, boy!"

That was obvious. And it was the only thing that kept me from dropping him where he stood. If Old Man Anderson wanted us dead we would be lying on the canyon floor looking worse than prickly cactus.

"That's mighty good of you, sir. I'd appreciate it if you would just let us through."

"You know what my situation is. I can't let them sheep go to market. Not without some legal guarantee the boy will turn the deed over to me."

"That's blackmail," Bennie grumbled.

I waited a few seconds. "Well?"

"Well what?"

"You gonna deal?"

"Of course I'm not going to deal. Tell him to kiss my arse."

"You sure? You sure that's what you want me to tell him? Him and his twenty guns compared to our..." I counted. Two six-shooters and one rifle. "...Three?"

"I don't care what you tell him." Bennie scuttled to another rock, keeping his head down.

I paused, scratched my head. We were jammed tight up here. There was no way out. None. Still, as if I really meant it, I shouted, "No deal, James T."

"That's okay. I can wait. We have plenty of time, plenty of food, plenty of water."

Geezus ... water.

We had two full canteens. They were on the horses along with our food and ammunition. I scrambled from boulder to boulder scanning the sides for our horses. Both of them were huddled on a flat plateau halfway down the mountain. They had found a clump of acacia to chew on. In a partial clearing, they were not only visible to me and Bennie, they were in full view of Anderson and his men.

"Can we get to them?" Bennie asked.

I judged the distance between the horses and Anderson. Regardless of thirst or hunger the mare would stay where she was, patiently waiting for my return. The walker had befriended her and stayed close to her side. To go for them now would be suicidal. Under the shadows of dark I would stand a better chance.

But the way the sun beat down on us, we would not be alive by nightfall.

My voice fierce with seriousness, I growled at Bennie, "You stay here."

Silent as a rattlesnake, I snuck down the embankment, slithered between boulders, and in and out of crevices. Only spitting distance away, I came up behind the horses and took cover behind a sandstone. The walker tensed, raised its head, swung it back and forth. I stopped, frozen in stance, careful not to spook them.

Tentatively, as if I were testing the water for leeches, I stuck out a boot. A bullet whizzed by me, striking the dirt with a mean hiss. Shit.

"Don't try it, Dakota. I got you covered."

Ryder.

Nothing would stop Ryder from killing Bennie. That is where his paycheck lay. The question was, would he kill me? Over a lousy canteen of water?

From past experience, I knew better than to play cards with Ryder. It was impossible to tell when he was bluffing. We were both childishly stubborn, and we were both sore losers. But I had no choice. We had maybe six hours before heatstroke melted our brains and turned us into lunatics. Six hours before dehydration squeezed the fluid out of our pores and left nothing but our skin and bones resting on the side of the mountain. It was a gamble I was going to have to take.

Bolting from the rock, I ran swift and alert as a white-tail. And as hunted. Ryder opened fire, purposely missing me, but not by much. The closer I got to the horses the closer the bullets got to me. I dived behind another stone.

"Geezus..." I muttered under my breath.

"Don't try it again."

I stood and started to run again. A wall of bullets blocked my path, pinning me down. There was only one gun. His gun.

"Dammit, Dakota..."

I could hear, almost feel, the frustration in Ryder's voice. The fear that Anderson's men, that Bennie Colsen, might witness something he could not do, tightened his grip on the trigger. But it was nothing compared to the frustration in my gut, a frustration that drove me on against reason.

For a crazy moment I was going to force Ryder to kill me. Just to annoy him. Just to see if he would. I started to stand and try again.

Bennie was beside me, tugging on my arm, pulling me out of the line of fire.

"What the hell are you doing?" I shouted. I had no idea where he came from or how he got there. Either he was a quieter rattlesnake than me, or Ryder let him through knowing he could talk some sense into me.

"Come back up."

"I told you to stay where you were." I was shouting so loud my voice rattled the canyon walls.

"Come back up."

"I'm only ten feet away."

"It's useless. He'll kill you. Come back up ... please." His eyes were bright with concern. Guess I had him pretty spooked. I know I had Ryder spooked, otherwise Bennie Colsen would be dead.

That Bennie had taken a chance with Ryder's careless mercy made me double mad. Still, the rage and frustration swimming around in my gut softened a little. Dying was not what held me back. Getting what I wanted, beating Ryder at this card game, was sure enough worth dying for. But that would leave Bennie wide open to Ryder's aim. Without me, there would be no mercy.

I wiped the sweat from my eyes, my nose on my sleeve, and took a deep breath. Then I shouted through the canyon. "Ryder! You can't see in the dark, you sonofabitch."

Relieved that I had not called his bluff, that I had thrown my cards on the table, and still liked him enough to speak with him, Ryder chuckled from behind his boulder. Then he lifted his arm in a playful salute. But he knew, knew the game was not over, knew I would be back. And I knew he would be waiting for me.

# 15

Noon. High noon. I never thought a man could sweat like that. We had been trapped for four hours. No shelter. No shade. No water. A hundred and twenty degrees. Even the air relinquished its oxygen to the sun, the soil its nutrients, the plant and animal life their bloodlines. The sun, pulsating, blinding, intensified as each second clocked on. The sun, now more our enemy than Ryder McCloud and James T. Anderson.

Deep in the Nevada desert I had once lost my mount and was forced to suffer the heat out. I learned how to work with it, how to shut my body down to preserve energy and fluid; how to shut my mind down to keep from going mad. Bennie was not so lucky. His body was regulated for the damp fogs of England, the harsh winters of Boston. His face was burning red, his lips were chapped and blistered. He had difficulty breathing, taking quick short gasps to prevent his lungs from scalding. There wasn't any way to comfort him. The only thing I could do was keep his mind occupied and off the heat. And the best way to do that was to keep him fighting. Against me.

"Sell it," I said. "Just sell the damn thing, collect your money, go back to school, be a lawyer, be comfortable. It ain't worth dying for, Junior."

He looked at me with such contempt, I had to admit, I was sorry for saying it. Not for meaning it, just saying it. After everything we had been through, I did not want Bennie looking at me with contempt.

To avoid his eyes, I took a bullet count. Ten, eleven left. I dropped one. It fell between two rocks into a deep crevice, jamming tight without any help from anyone.

"They killed my family," he said, wearily.

"Not them." I dug for the bullet.

With long, slim fingers, Bennie leaned over and plucked the shell from the rocks. He dropped it into the palm of my hand. "Why don't you believe it was Anderson?"

"They're Christians."

I thought that might make him laugh, but all he could manage was a slight smile through parched lips. "Dakota ... really."

"I'm serious. They're decent Christian folks. Decent Christian folks don't shoot children. They might be stout and greedy, like Old Man Anderson, and he'd probably even hang your daddy if he felt justified, but he wouldn't kill them kids. That's where he'd draw the line. He ain't a killer."

"He's trying to kill us right now."

"Self-defense. You ain't giving him much choice. You hired a gunfighter, and backed him into a corner. Christian folks need to morally justify the bad things they do. If they can't find a good reason in the Bible then they'll create their own and say it's in the Bible." I was comfortably into my sermon now. When you are hungry, talk, it will keep your mind off your stomach. When you are scared, talk, it will keep your mind off the bogeyman outside your door. And when you are dying, talk, it will delay the inevitable. "Because the rest of us poor slobs don't read the Bible it's easy to pull the wool over our eyes and believe whatever they say, okay everything they do."

Bennie studied me for a minute, trying to decide if I was joking. I wasn't. Men don't joke when they are a couple of hours away from death, or when their throats are so dry it could be used for a camel run, or when they get beaten before they have a chance to throw a punch. Instead, they become pitifully philosophical.

"I read the Bible," he said.

"I don't." I dropped a handgun in his lap as if that were going to keep him from frying.

"Then how do you know so much about decent Christian folks?"

"My old man was one. He was the most religious man you'll ever meet, scared to death of Jesus. He was greedy and he was a liar and he was a thief, but he would never do anyone bodily harm without some sort of justification."

"What happened to you? What made you different from him?" He fingered the gun lightly.

"I'm not that much different from him, Junior, which is probably why I don't like him. The only difference is I don't draw no lines. I don't need no pious reasoning behind my actions. I don't need to justify anything. Maybe I'm a little meaner."

"Would you murder my family if someone hired you to do it?"

"Junior, I'm willing to kill anyone you point out."

"This is not cold-blooded murder, Dakota. This is retaliation for what they did. I can't just let them slaughter my family and get away with it."

"Right. Justification."

"Don't tell me you can't see the difference."

"Dead is dead. I ain't asking no questions. This isn't my battle, it's yours. I'm just waiting for payday like Ryder. If it were my battle, I would sell that pile of rock and go back to school. Dying on this mountain isn't going to bring your folks back."

If Bennie's contempt bothered me then I sure didn't know how to keep my mouth shut. He looked at me with pure hatred now. He started to stand, but I pulled him back down, out of the line of fire.

Instead, he crawled away on all fours to the next boulder. As far away from me as our hideout would allow. "You're really vile," he said from his rock.

"You've noticed that."

Geezus, it was hot. And the sun hadn't finished climbing to the top yet. I once again judged the distance between us and the canteens. Vaguely I wondered if Ryder might have dozed off, or left his post for a cup of coffee. I wondered if I had the gumption to try it again.

"Junior, we're going to fry like two lizards in a skillet if we don't get that water."

He closed his eyes, rested his head against the rock, and lightly tapped it against the stone. My handgun rested loosely between his legs. Sweat dotted his forehead and upper lip. His blue cotton shirt was stained in a triangle down his chest and back. His skin changed from red to bronze before me. Even under these conditions, Bennie Colsen was the finest-looking man I had ever seen in my life. A perfumed showgirl would not look that good. All stubble and rawhide, I was sure I didn't look good.

"You shouldn't have taken the gold," he mumbled without enough energy to really scold me.

"Probably not. Guess I just got him all riled up."

"Dakota! Colsen!"

I waved my hat above the boulder. "We're still here!"

"The afternoon sun is going to kill you both. You'll never make it through the night. There's food and water down here. I just want to talk, make an honest deal."

Bennie snorted. "An honest deal."

"What sort of deal?"

"I'm not making any deals," Bennie hissed at me, coming alive all of the sudden.

"Shut up, Junior."

"I'll give him a fair price for the land. More than what it's worth to him."

A prime target, Bennie leaped up and waved the pistol. "You don't know what it's worth to me."

Scrambling across the hot sand, I tackled him. "Get down. What's the matter with you?"

He kicked and slapped at me, jabbing me hard with his knees and elbows. "I thought you said he wasn't a killer."

"I said he didn't kill your family. I didn't say he wouldn't shoot someone waving a gun at him."

"You're trying to sell me out." He punched me in the stomach, flailing blindly as if he had finally lost his mind.

I grabbed both wrists, pinned his arms above his head, and placed a knee firmly on his chest. "I'm not selling you out. I'm trying to keep us from drying up like two pieces of jerky. With you dead anyone can walk in and claim your land. Just keep your mouth shut, Junior, and trust me."

All the fight went out of him and he lay still, breathing hard. The sun had gotten to him. Minutes away from heatstroke his dark eyes clouded over with a murky film. He needed water. Fast.

"Anderson! I got me a maniac kid here on my hands. I can't make no proper deals under these conditions. Call your men off and we'll talk about it real peaceable-like."

"I'm not making any deals," Bennie whispered to the air.

Roughly, I placed my hand over his mouth to silence him. Rocks broke loose, crumbled lightly, and fell down the bluff. I grabbed the Winchester and placed a precious shell in the chamber.

Bennie sat up. "What?"

"They're circling us."

"The horses."

The buckskin snorted, irritated, disturbed. Sure enough, they were going for the horses.

Careful not to lose my balance, I moved across the sharp rocks like a mountain cat. Behind a miniature rock fort, I crouched down and raised the rifle steadily. The horses scuttled and whinnied a little then held still. Someone was hidden in the rocks. He was out of sight, but I could hear, sense, his movements. It was Ryder. Positive I would succeed the second time, he wasn't waiting for me to come back after the water.

To reach the horses he would have to come into the clearing. If he did I would have a clear shot at him. But he was a jackal, much smarter than that. He stayed in the shadows, waved his arms, and started hollering, attempting to scare off the horses.

"Move! Move!" he shouted. Uncertain, unsure, the buckskin stayed put. Then he started pelting them with rocks. "Get on ... get out of here!"

In a few more seconds they would have bolted. The walker pinned its ears back, snorted, and backed up, alarming the buckskin. Both were ready to flee. If they did, the water would go with them.

Ryder was out of my scope. Even if I was able to get a good bead on him, I only would have nicked an arm. And the gunfire would scare the horses into a dead run. I had no ammunition to waste. I could not lose the canteens.

Purely desperate, I aimed at the walker and fired. Quickly swinging the rifle, I aimed at the buckskin, took a deep breath, and fired. Almost simultaneously they fell. My blood pounded wildly in my ears. I waited a few seconds, ready to pump another bullet into them if they kicked. My aim had been merciful, hitting its mark exactly. Neither horse moved.

Bennie scrambled over the stone and fell in beside me. "What did you do that for?"

"Couldn't afford to lose the water," I grumbled. Killing horses did not amuse me, especially killing my horse. Now I was determined to make it worth something.

"Give me the pistol."

He hesitated.

"Give me the gawdamn pistol!" Savagely, I yanked it out of his hand, then shoved the rifle towards him. I was mad, all right. Mad and thirsty. Quietly, agilely, I snuck down the cliff. If Ryder could get that close to me, I could get that close to him.

Within seconds, I came up behind him. He stood on a wide, flat rock. His hat off, he wiped sweat from his brow with a kerchief, and stared at the bodies of the horses.

"Ryder!" I shouted.

Spinning quickly on his heels he started to go for his gun. Then he realized it was me, slowly smiled, and nodded towards the horses. "I can't believe you did that."

"Move out of my way."

"Only a crazy sonofabitch would kill his own horse."

"That's what I am, Ryder, a crazy sonofabitch. Now you get out of my way and let me have that water."

He considered it for maybe one second before his voice grew cool and his eyes narrowed. "You know I can't do that, Dakota. I got a job to do here."

"You talk about this job as if you have no control over it."

"In this profession what we want or feel or think don't count. We can't afford to let it, you know that. You're the one who has lost control."

"Maybe I have. Sometimes it reaches a point where what we're doing doesn't make sense anymore. And we have to stop and ask ourselves what's right and what's wrong. What's happening here is wrong. I can't ignore that. I need to do what's right this time."

"You'd be a fool to."

"Maybe I don't mind being a fool."

"Then go. I'll let you do that. I'll let you ride out of here."

"With Bennie."

"Alone."

"Give me the water, Ryder."

He zeroed in on a spot somewhere above my head. "I can't."

That was the final word. There was no point in talking. Professional gunmen did not solve differences with words. We relied solely on the sword. One of us would have to back down. It couldn't be me. My life depended on one canteen of water. And Bennie's life depended on me. Because of pride, God in heaven and old Satan himself knew it would not be Ryder McCloud that would back down off this mountain. Pride was as critical as water.

If my lips had not been blistered and chapped, my mouth dry, I would have shouted, "Don't do it, Ryder." But I could only shake my head slowly, begging him off with my eyes. Then he twitched. Just a slight muscle twitch in the right shoulder. Just enough to warn me.

"Don't do it, Ryder!"

Our hands dropped and both Colts were up. Two explosions rocked the natural calm of the mountains, explosions that guaranteed one man was going to die. I had heard the roar of that death call hundreds of times, and it always belonged to me. The sound of my gun.

Ryder's right-hand pistol suddenly leaped in the air like a silver frog. It clattered against a boulder before skidding to a stop. The left-hand pistol was only halfway out of its holster. Stunned, he dropped it back in.

Wordlessly, I stared at him, ready to fire again, if need be. That time I had shown him the mercy he had shown me. But now my Colts were pointed at his chest.

A wide grin swept across his rugged face. His eyes shone bright with dangerous excitement. "You win."

"I always do."

Calmly, valiantly, he accepted defeat. He pulled his black stallion out of the shaded area of the boulders and lifted himself into the saddle. "One of these nights I'm going to catch you in the right mood again."

I found his gun lying among the rocks, picked it up, and rubbed the dust and scratches off. Silently, I slipped it back in his holster. I attempted to smile through cracked lips, but all I could do was squeeze his knee. "I'm counting on it."

A red stain, moving fast, covered his waist just above his belt. He leaned into it, attempting to hide it from me. A smooth trickle of blood crept down his hand. He was wounded. I started to pull him off the horse and holler for one of Anderson's men to ride back for a doctor. But Ryder reined the stallion back and whirled around.

"Adios, amigo," he said.

Recklessly, still clutching his side, he ran the stallion down the cliffs. A flint black Pegasus without wings and a wild wounded renegade upon its back. They rode north, away from Anderson. Away from Zeth. Away from me.

Once again, I did not have time to say good-bye, to blow kisses, to do the things I wanted to do whenever Ryder hit the saddle. But some hot, muggy night, when I was in the right mood, I would encounter Ryder McCloud again. I'd bet my last Union penny on it.

Guns popped off from every direction. Bullets whistled past my head. I could smell the gunpowder, feel the shells tug at me. The canteens were still on the other side of the world.

When in doubt, attack like the Indians do. Whooping my fool head off with a steady stream of obscenities, I sprinted towards the horses. Anderson's men knew what I was after, and they were aiming to kill. But, this time, they had to do it on their own. They did not have a cool, steady hand like Ryder's to do their fighting for them.

I hopped over the body of the buckskin, which provided minimal coverage, grappled over its fat belly, and blindly fumbled for the canteen. Bullets riddled the body. Lead seared my flesh as it pierced my hand and shattered bones.

There was no point going for the ammunition belt. The buckskin had fallen on top of the saddlebag that held my ammunition. It would be pure luck if I retrieved the canteen. Ignoring the pain in my hand, I grabbed it up. I got it ... now I had to get back.

The crack of the Winchester alerted me. Bennie was shooting pretty good. Not great, but good. My chances for survival were maybe half a dozen bullets away. If I was going to make a run for it, I had to do it while Bennie and the Winchester were able to cover me. I ran like a crazy man.

Once I was out of the clearing, I had the giant boulders to hide behind. Within minutes I snuck up on Bennie.

"Good job, Junior."

Falling next to him, I uncapped the canteen and poured the cool liquid down my throat, letting it splash over my chin and down my chest. Sweet apricot brandy never tasted so good. Bennie stared at my hand as if a giant desert tarantula was sitting on it. I handed him the canteen with my good hand.

"We're out of ammunition," he said.

I did not bleed to death. It hurt like hell, but the bullet passed clear through the fleshy part of my hand. The blood clotted and dried. Ma always told people that we weren't bleeders. I thought it was an odd thing to be telling people, but now I knew what she meant. Anyone else would have bled all over the mountainside and died.

Nor was I especially bothered by the fact that my right hand had been damaged. I twiddled my fingers. They all worked, but the pain was severe enough to keep me from using it right away. Course it didn't matter. I was just as fast with my left hand.

So as the bitch of a sun lowered behind the western mountain, and an unnoticeable moon lit up our hideout like a torch, and I fingered a rifle that was as useless as a broomstick, I pacified myself with the knowledge that I was not a bleeder. And even with my right hand out of commission, I was still the fastest gun in the West. Ryder would vouch for that.

Bennie doctored me a little. When he realized the wound was as serious as shoving a stick through my hand, he backed off and hid in the shadows of his rock, getting ornery again.

At least the moon cooled us both off.

"Now what?"

"Don't know, Junior. You don't like any of my suggestions. You had better come up with a couple of your own."

"You're going to have to kill Anderson. That's what I hired you to do in the first place. Before you started playing diplomat."

"Wrong. You hired me to kill the men who massacred your family."

"Same thing."

I chewed on a dry twig. Breakfast was only a long, pleasant memory. Worse, my tobacco pouch was tied snugly to my saddle halfway down the mountain. "Like I said, just point them out. But you're going to have to live with the knowledge of having an innocent man killed. It ain't going to be my responsibility."

"He's not innocent."

Another argument brewed in Junior's chest. I was tired and my hand hurt and I wasn't in the mood. Pulling my Stetson over my eyes to get some sleep, I mumbled, "I'll kill him in the morning. Just walk on down there and hit him over the head with this here rifle."

I didn't see it, but Junior smiled. Then he picked up a rock and threw it at me.

Funny thing about God and prayers. If you pray for something on Tuesday when you need it, most likely you'll be getting it on Friday when you don't, like He was just getting your message or something. It did not snow, but an icy cold wind, hinting at an early snow, whistled through the canyon and across the small plateau where we were bunked down. At first it started with a gentle flutter, tapping tumbleweed lightly against stones, and snapping brittle branches off dry brush. Hours later it was howling, meaner than a pack of coyotes.

Hot or cold. The mountains are never still, never trustworthy. The numbing wind penetrated my flimsy flannel shirt. I rubbed my arms to keep the circulation flowing. Bennie's clothes were thinner than mine. I could hear his teeth chattering. Moving like an Apache in the dark, he stretched out beside me. Then he pressed hard against my side and tucked his ice cold hands inside my shirt, making me shiver. But not from the cold. I gritted my teeth and tried to sleep.

I couldn't sleep. It was not the nippy night air, or the fear of Anderson's men sneaking up on us in the dark, or Bennie's heart thumping mildly against my arm that kept me awake. When I closed my eyes I saw the buckskin drop, the red stain spread across Ryder's shirt. Violent images that jolted me awake.

Miz Mary Turner, a lover of women, once asked me how I, as a lover of men, could bear to kill other men. "I don't understand," she scolded me, as we sat around her potbellied stove in her cottage behind the Cactus Saloon. "One minute you boys are wrestling and playing with each other. The next you're pulling guns and killing each other. A woman would never do that to another woman." Her great bosom quaked like tapioca pudding when she shook her head. "I will never understand you boys. Never."

Mirrored by her wisdom my answer was feeble and sense-less. I said something like, not all men deserved love, certainly not my love. That men have been competing and warring with one another since the beginning of time. We were warriors. Tribesmen. Conquerors. It could not be helped. It was a man's nature.

She roared. Then she almost spit in my face and threatened to throw me out of her warm bungalow, so I shrugged and said, "Don't know, Miz Mary. I truly don't." And I truly didn't.

Ryder deserved love, certainly deserved my love. But during our gunplay I wounded him. It was a pure and simple accident, I never meant to draw blood. My eyesight was getting worse. My aim was a little crooked.

At the Santa Fe Hotel, with a bottle of whiskey on the night table, and one in our guts, Ryder had turned on his pillow. Quickly, almost in jest, he said, "I love ya, Dakota."

"No shit." I laughed like an idiot until I noticed he wasn't laughing. He lay there, eyes half lidded, half smiling. Nervously, I said: "Love among gunfighters. Ain't that something for the history books."

He rode out the next morning while I was still asleep. I never saw him again. Until Turnpike.

Bennie stirred in his sleep and snuggled against my chest, seeking nothing more than warmth. Dropping my arm across him, I pulled him closer and rested my chin on his forehead. His skin still burned hot against the cool air.

"'For the one I love most lay sleeping by me under the same cover in the cool night. In the stillness of the autumn moonbeams his face was inclined toward me, And his arm lay lightly around my breast, and that night I was happy.'"

Sorry, Ryder, old friend. But protecting Bennie Colsen was no longer a requirement or a responsibility. Protecting Bennie Colsen had become an obsession.

# 16

Perched atop a boulder, I looked directly down into their camp. A small fire flickered, a pot of coffee rested in the coals. I could almost taste the bacon sizzling. Men casually sauntered around the campfire, eating, talking, laughing. Not too scared, not too worried, they were having a gawdamn party. If I had had a bullet I would have shot someone.

"Anderson!" I called. "We're ready to deal."

Bennie did not argue. He did not want to spend another night in these cliffs any more than I did. And, as each hour passed, more sheep would find certain death in the Sandpit. Educated and practical, he finally summed up our situation: no food, no ammo, no way out. Time to surrender. I could have told him that a whole twenty-four hours ago.

James T. lifted his bulk, dumped his coffee on the ground, and peered up at my shadowy figure. As far as I could tell he was unarmed. "Come on down and we'll talk it over."

Chuckling to myself, I spurred him one last time before raising the white flag. "Tell you what, you and your boys ride back to town and we'll meet you there."

It brought a wry smile to his face. "I'm afraid you can't be trusted. You stole two thousand dollars from me."

That got my back up. I didn't like being called a thief. "I didn't steal it, you gave it to me."

His curly blond hair turning whiter in the sun, his face redder than a face should be, Zeth approached his father and said something. Impatiently, his father waved him off. An argument ensued. They were shouting but not loud enough for their words to drift up the mountain. I pricked my ears, straining to hear, and leaned over too far, almost losing my balance. Finally, bright-faced and angry, Zeth stomped away. Maury moved up alongside James T. and took Zeth's place. He spit tobacco out of the corner of his mouth and squinted up at me. The man who was missing, the man who no longer stood by Anderson's side, was halfway to Flagstaff by now.

Bennie rested against the rock I was sitting atop of. Exhaustion faded his smooth face and voice. "Give him back the gold."

"Heck, no, Junior. We got to get something out of this deal."

"If I'm willing to give him my mountain the least you can do is give him back the gold."

"It ain't the mountain he wants." In my pocket I had something more precious than land and gold. Water. "James T.!" There was no need to holler, I already had his full attention. "I found the Eternal Spring."

Maury glanced back at Pat squatting in front of the fire and laughed. Pat laughed. Then everyone laughed. Anderson kicked some sand with the toe of his boot, suppressing a grin.

"They don't believe you," Junior mumbled.

"I'll be damned."

He smiled up at me, benignly, like he felt sorry for me or something. "They don't believe you because there isn't an Eternal Spring. Everybody knows that. People talk about it but they don't really believe it. The Eternal Spring is a cozy myth handed down from generation to generation. Anderson knows it doesn't exist. He's not an imbecile."

"It exists."

"Come on down, Dakota, and tell us about it," said Anderson, patronizing as all hell.

"If you want the water I'm warning you to put away your guns, saddle up, and ride out of here. I'll go to my grave with the knowledge."

As if he were in a trance, Bennie rose from the dust and dropped my handgun in my holster. He started down the mountain, heading straight into Anderson's camp. I leaped off the rock and followed him.

"What are you doing?"

"This is no way for civilized men to behave."

"Are you crazy? These aren't civilized men. This isn't even civilization."

"This is no way for civilized men to behave," he repeated.

The sun had gotten to him. He was almost catatonic, mumbling to himself and shaking his head like a loony old man. If Anderson's men fired on him it would have been an easy kill. Completely unarmed, I could not defend him, except maybe step in front and take the bullet.

The men parted when Bennie walked through them. They watched him carefully, politely, as if he were a conquered princess or something. Strangely enough, all their guns were pointed at me. I dropped my Winchester. They lowered their rifles.

Bennie approached Anderson without faltering, coming face-to-face with the man who had made his life miserable. For the longest time they studied one another without words. It was the first time either of them had actually seen the other up close. Anderson cleared his throat, shifted on his feet uncomfortably, seeing as how he was the one burdened with guilt. But it was Bennie who spoke first.

"I want the sheep, the profits I get for them, and the wool. I also want safe passage to Flagstaff, and fair market value for the land."

There wasn't much Anderson could debate. He had won. But the win was bittersweet. A dirty battle had been fought to obtain what wasn't rightfully his. Compassion was carved on his rough features. Not pity, but compassion.

"Fair enough," he said, simply. Then he turned to the cook, a full-bearded man with bright red whiskers. "Fix them some breakfast, Whiskey."

Although I was sure enough hungry, I hesitated. "I need to bring the sheep out of the Sandpit before we lose the entire herd."

"Don't worry about the sheep. My boys will round them up." Anderson motioned to Maury.

"Boss..." Maury started to protest.

"Round them up," Anderson commanded, "and take them back to the Double A for food and water. We'll take them to Flagstaff by way of Pender." He looked at Bennie as if he had overstepped his authority and added, in way of explanation, "It's cooler and safer." He headed towards the chuck wagon to oversee our breakfast.

I stood there grinning. Cowpokes herding sheep. What a sight. "They stink something awful," I told them.

Bennie brushed by me. "Stay with them, Dakota. They'll probably leave half the herd scattered."

Shit.

Now it was Maury grinning. "I'll let you know when we're ready to ride." Then he added, sardonically, "...boss."

Anderson hollered at me from the chuck wagon. "Sit down and have breakfast first."

Ol' Whiskey slapped together biscuits and gravy in a matter of minutes. Over the campfire, he warmed up thick black coffee that had been allowed to cool. It could have been a right proper meal at the Cactus Saloon for all I cared.

I'd been trying to avoid Zeth since I came down off the mountain. And he was trying to avoid me. Avoid me, but not ignore me. If you could voodoo someone with looks of anger, with thoughts of malice, I would be living a cursed life. He stood off to himself, leaning against a salmon pink, jagged peak of broken rock. Arms folded across his chest, his eyes rested heavily on me as he worked himself into a sweat. I had seen that look many times: an unspoken challenge across a barroom floor, a silent threat from across a street.

Well, Zeth Anderson was not going to get a fight from me. Today I was retired from fighting. Today my Colts honored the Sabbath. Tomorrow might be another story.

Purposely ignoring his unspoken challenge, I drank the mud coffee and watched the cowhands ready the horses. Anderson handed Bennie a document that had been signed.

"I had my lawyer, Stephen James, write this up. He's right reputable. I think you'll find everything's in order, and my offer's a good one."

Bennie set his plate on the ground, took the paper, and slowly read it over. I leaned over his shoulder to read the pages. I didn't understand too much of what it said, but the dollar signs seemed fitting enough. Bennie scribbled a few notes on the paper. Then he started to put down his name.

"You don't have to sign that," I said.

As if I might have one final magic trick in my pocket to prevent it from happening, Bennie searched my face hopefully. I did have magic. I had the Eternal Spring. But nobody believed me.

Anderson looked at me, too, as if I were crazy. "Stay out of this, son..." he warned.

Quickly Bennie scribbled his name on the line, then handed the paper back to Anderson. He picked up his plate and continued eating. Brooding silence.

"I want you to understand something," Anderson said, pocketing the document. "Your father and I never caused each other undue harm. He had something I needed, and he was as stubborn as an old mule about sharing it with me and my family. Still, whatever happened between us was fair and square."

"Like what just transpired?"

"Son, I'm a desperate man. Rules change when you become desperate. Water is a precious thing, something you'll kill and die for if it comes to that. Without that water everything I own will be gone."

"Like everything I owned?"

The old man studied him hard. His own needs outweighed any sympathy he might have for Bennie. "You're young, you can start over. I'm giving you a fair price for the land. You can finish up your schooling, buy some acreage back east where it's more suitable. I think your pa would have wanted that."

I thought for a second, when his mouth twisted and his eyes turned sharp, Bennie was going to spit at him. Instead he nodded his head passively. Had to admit, the kid knew when he was whipped.

Too bad I could not say the same about the other kid. Uneasily, I shifted under Zeth's glare. Finally I cast my plate aside and walked over to the rock where he stood.

"What's this all about? You still sore at me for taking a swing at you in the barn?"

"Is Ryder dead?"

Is Ryder dead? Geezus. My eyes followed the outlines of the cliffs, resting somewhere in the vicinity of where the gunfight took place. "No. He rode out."

"Liar."

I felt like popping him a good one in the mouth. But I had made up my mind: no fighting today. "I ain't lying to you, kid."

"Why would he?"

I shrugged. I wasn't going to tell him that I stripped Ryder down and disarmed him. Ryder had pride, and would tell the story his way. I turned to walk away. Roughly, Zeth grabbed me by the shoulder and pulled me around.

"I asked you a question."

Three men rose from the campfire, fingering their gunbelts. Anderson's men. Zeth's men. It didn't matter. I could take all three of them down before this clumsy, foolish boy could even palm the butt of his handgun.

Killing foolish, clumsy kids was my life's work. But, today in particular, dog-tired, my hand thumping painfully with infection, defeat grinding in my gut like pebbles of glass, and a quiet, private promise fresh in my mind, I refused to confront another.

"And I done gave you my answer. Now you let go of my arm."

Again I tried to walk away, but he held fast. Taking a deep breath, I slowly started counting to myself. Now, I'm not willing to crawl off and lick my wounds very often. Today I was willing. Today, because of Bennie, I was willing to accept my failings as long as I could muster a certain amount of dignity to go with it. But Zeth had to release my arm. Despite newborn resolutions, I was not going to be a standing coward in front of Anderson's men.

James T. got to his feet. "Zeth," he shouted. "What the hell are you doing, boy?"

"Stay out of this, Pa."

The old man started forward. Alarm registered on his face when he realized what was taking place. Pat Jordan followed close on his heels. Pat was a squirrelly one. He was hankering for an opportunity to take me on. But he was not going to get a fight out of me today.

"Zeth Anderson, you get your butt over here, right now." His father practically pointed at the spot where he wanted Zeth to stand.

Good. I hoped he would pull the stupid kid by the ear, send him to his room. Seeing him scolded was all I needed to feel vindicated.

"This ain't your fight, Pa. This is between me and him."

Geezus ... Anderson suddenly backed off. Then he motioned for his men to do the same. He was not going to intercede. This was the way of the West. A father's way of teaching his young son a lesson, seeing what he was made of, an initiation into manhood. Fine and well. All he was going to end up with was a dead kid.

"Don't be stupid..." I growled at Zeth.

"Ryder taught me a few things." He tried to sound and look as tough as Ryder would. Yet his actions betrayed his youth. His voice strained and he visibly fought back tears.

"He didn't teach you enough."

Zeth took two steps backwards. His arms dangled at his sides, he shook his wrists to loosen them up. His face turned hard as he eyeballed me for the last time with a challenge he was forcing me to take.

Briefly, I glanced at Anderson. Come on, James T., put a stop to this. Pride ain't worth burying your only son over. Afraid he would show weakness if he met my eyes, the old man looked away.

Hard and mean, I looked at Zeth. Not hesitating another second, I took two quick steps forward and slugged him. It was a sucker punch, one he didn't expect, one that was going to give him a headache for a couple of days. He landed with a dry thud on the ground, shook his head, tried to stand, but fell back down.

James T. was on him. He pulled him to his feet, dragged him to a private rock, and hollered some long, hard sense into him.

Good common sense like never ever back yourself and your people into a corner and challenge a professional gunfighter.

Smarting a whole lot, my face flushed, my jaw rigid, I plopped next to Bennie, maybe looking for some comfort there. It scared me how sitting next to Junior was enough to calm my worries, and how I was beginning to seek him out for that purpose.

"What was that all about?"

"Guess he's a little annoyed with me."

"Was he going to draw on you?"

My mind raced. I didn't answer.

"How silly," Bennie concluded with a whisper. "He would have killed you."

I grinned slightly at the irony of it. My guns were empty. Cold and useless. During the craziest moments with Zeth, I had forgotten that. No ammo. I was not in the habit of walking with two empty barrels, and I had just dumb-ass forgot I wasn't loaded. I had not drawn on Zeth because today I wanted to be a better man, a thinker, not a fighter. Someone like Bennie Colsen, civilized, cool, self-contained, not some Wild West crackerjack with a penchant to pop off whenever someone looked at me wrong. It had saved my life.

Impulsively, I lifted my hand to touch Bennie's cheek. There was something I needed to tell him with that gesture. Something I'd never have the guts to say with words.

"The men are ready to ride." Maury watched me oddly.

Not really giving a shit what Maury thought, I nodded, got up, stretched the aches and pains out of my legs. Bennie did the same.

"Where do you think you're going?"

"With you."

"The hell you are. You ride back with Anderson, get a bath, some sleep, and a proper meal. Let him take care of you. I'll bring the sheep back safely."

"I don't think so."

"Then you're going to have to walk. There ain't enough horses..."

With a flash of enthusiasm, Junior babbled right over me. "I'll find one." Then he dashed away before I had a chance to stop him.

He wasn't staying. Period.

Oddly at peace with myself, I lit a cigarette, and carefully studied the patterns of a rock formation. If you looked long and hard enough you could make out faces in the patterns, usually ugly creature-looking things. Bennie was back beside me in less than a minute.

"I'm ready."

"You're not staying, Junior."

"They're my sheep." He bumped past me, then turned around, abruptly. "I really wish you would stop treating me as if I were incompetent."

I suppose I should have answered back, but this time Junior wasn't smarting off. What was said was said in a mature voice. A valid request.

"Did you find a horse?"

"Yes."

"Then come on, let's go get the sheep."

Picking up my Winchester, I walked to where the men had readied the horses, hoping they would give me some ammo. I felt naked as newborn without a bullet or two in my pocket.

# 17

It took two days to round the sheep up and herd them out of the Sandpit back to the Double A Ranch. I was glad, we were all glad, that Bennie had stayed. He was familiar with sheep, and the nature of sheep. The cowhands acted as if they were afraid to touch them. Like kids riding their first ponies, they did not want to appear scared or ignorant and risk being laughed at by the other kids.

"Can't we just rope 'em?" Pat asked, completely at a loss.

Nope. Sheep had to be led or tackled or lifted. You couldn't just throw a rope around them and drag them home. They were slippery, their heads were smaller than their necks. Maury gracefully swung his lariat and caught a critter around the neck, nice and pretty. The critter slipped out of the noose, slicker than a New Orleans magician. Then Pat double lassoed, front and back. Stubborn as a mule, the old ram laid down the ground. I stayed on my horse and laughed.

"Bennie uses a stick," I told Pat, trying to be helpful.

Pat nodded, looked around for a stick. Serious as all hell.

In the end they were grateful for Bennie's expertise and gentle guidance. More for his ability to wrestle a lamb to the ground without minding the stink.

I was grateful for his company.

At night, me and the boys played some cards. Bennie attempted to teach us a card game called bridge or something, but halfway through the game we figured we were too dense to learn and threw the cards down in disgust. He vowed to never teach us anything again. We were thankful and went back to playing poker.

Whiskey produced a harmonica, and blew a soft whining tune, "My Ol' Kentucky Home." Passive as babies, grown men stared into the campfire, silenced by a distant homesickness. Would there come a day when we'd stop being saddle tramps, stake out a plot of land, build a modest cabin we could call home, and settle down? One by one, I studied the grizzled, hard faces circling the campfire, softening with respect for the melody, and seriously doubted it. For better or worse, this was the only life we knew.

Then Whiskey launched into "Buffalo Gals," and faces brightened. Now that was more our style. Comically and fun-spirited, Maury and Pat danced the do-si-do, kicking their legs, entwining arms to circle, and clapping time. We busted bellies laughing, even Junior, who had been stiff with mistrust since we had walked down the mountain and surrendered.

The harmonica and the fiddle ... they either made a person feel like crying or dancing, no in-between.

Modest as all hell, Bennie walked halfway across the desert to tend to nature's business in private. Whiskey tapped the harmonica on his knee and wiped some spittle from his beard. "Too bad about that young 'un's folks."

That was all that was said about the killings or the mountain or the water. These were not the men who rode onto the Colsen property that night.

Sometimes I would catch one of them watching Bennie, wondering what it was like to carry that much tragedy around on your shoulders, and still keep your knees from being bent; what it was like to be a foreigner in a foreign country, to be that hated, that persecuted. That important.

Midday on the third day we moved across the flats of the Double A Ranch. The golden adobe sandcastle beckoned us like a lightkeeper's beacon. Without any prompting from us, the sheep quickened their pace as if they sensed that the corrals up ahead provided rest, food, and water. For us it was a shave, cool bath, and soft bed. Instinctively, we quickened our pace, too.

Out on the front porch stood our welcoming committee. James T. held the dog by the collar to keep it from running at the sheep. Rusty Cunningham stood next to him. The familiar glint of his red hair shimmered in the sun like a new copper penny.

Feeling heroic, maybe showing off some for Rusty's sake, I galloped into the yard at full speed, swinging off the horse before it came to a complete stop. Two quick strides up the steps, and I had his hand in mine. I shook it vigorously, shamelessly. Rusty in the untamed territories without his mother, now that would be interesting.

"Boy, am I glad to see you."

"Utterly amazed to see you," he smiled, wickedly or wisely, hard to tell which.

Rusty stood six feet four, thin as a rail. He never wore a hat. Gloves always, but never a hat. He seldom ventured outdoors and never needed one. His skin was clear and translucent. Emerald eyes and copper hair were the only colors on his entire body, except for when he got excited. Then the blood rushed to his cheeks, turning him bright red. It was the only tattletale sign of his excitement. Nothing else gave it away.

He was excited now. Although he stayed calm in front of our host, his face reddened deeply at the sight of me. I hadn't seen him in over a year. My fault.

Anderson brushed past me and stepped down off the porch. His eyes and mind were pinned on Bennie. "Get them sheep in," he hollered, taking up his command post once again, maybe showing off some for Bennie's sake.

A dozen ranch hands tended to the sheep. They did not need me. Bennie stood on a rail and leaned over the fence where he could keep a keen eye on his assets. He did not need me, either. I turned my attention back to Rusty.

"When did you get in?"

"Yesterday. A very charming woman picked me up at the depot, brought me here, and made me feel as if I were a long-lost cousin. Wonderful family. I can't say much for the people in town, though." Rusty grimaced. "They certainly aren't very friendly."

"Didn't you meet Lester?"

He looked at me quizzically. "Who?"

"Never mind." I grinned.

"Naturally I was surprised to hear from you. I had no idea you were in Arizona. Of course, I never have any idea where you might be. The last time I heard you were in, let me see..." He paused, did some exaggerated figuring in his head. "New Mexico. When you were in trouble there. You and Ryder McCloud. Apparently you're in trouble here, too."

Shrugging, I smiled sheepishly. "Not my trouble this time. Did you bring what I needed?"

He arched an eyebrow, a slender orange moth fluttering on his forehead. "What do you need with that?"

Now was not the time to discuss it. I had given Rusty a brief rundown of what I needed over the telegraph wires, but offered no explanations. He had simply come when I called. As always. "I'll tell you later. Where did you..."

"In the barn. Well hidden."

"Did anyone see you bring it in?"

"Of course not. I wouldn't want my hosts to think I'm a lunatic."

"Even though you are." Playfully, I rubbed the crown of his head. "Losing your hair, buddy."

He slapped my hand away. "Stop that."

"Where's the witch?"

"Who?" He scolded me with his eyes, but a slight smile twitched at the corner of his mouth. "She's inside with Grace."

"Your mother?" I almost spit the word out on the ground as if it were castor oil. It was worse than castor oil. "She's inside the house?"

"Of course she's in the house. I wouldn't leave her out in the sun."

"I would."

"I couldn't leave her home alone. Who would give her her medicine?"

"Geezus..."

"Don't mope." He looped a thin arm through my mine and led me towards the house, away from the ranchers who were still bedding down the sheep. "I have something to show you. And some rather interesting news, you may or may not be pleased to hear."

The information was mumbled secretly in my ear, information that I had been waiting and needing to hear, information that confirmed my suspicions. Once again my sixth sense had been right. Like a tenacious bloodhound, I was getting closer. In fact, I was only sniffing distance away from the man who had killed Bennie's family. And that one man would help me gather up the rest of the men. One by one, I would bring them to justice. My kind of my justice. If there had not had been an audience I would have kissed my redheaded friend, but I saved all displays of gratitude for later.

Rusty led me into the foyer, still whispering shrewdly. Abruptly, I stopped. There she was: meanest woman this side of the Mississippi. Probably on the other side, too.

To escape the heat, they sat in the foyer. The sun hadn't come around the front of the house yet and the foyer was still pleasant and cool. Chair next to chair they sat, Grace and witch. They sipped tea, nibbled cookies, relishing the coolness of the foyer. Raising a petal cup to her lips, she twittered at Mrs. Anderson's jokes and lightly touched her knee with a scented kerchief that I could smell all the way over to the door. In public she was almost human, proper and well mannered. For a while. Until something or someone annoyed her. Then she was as salty as a drunken sailor.

She wore a long black dress. She always wore a long black dress, and it was the same black dress. The woman had money. She owned the Cactus Saloon. When she grew tired of Mr. Cunningham she slipped cyanide in his brandy and took over his financial dealings. Course Rusty says she didn't. I swear she did. Murderer or not, she could afford another dress. But she just kept patching that one together.

A lace shawl was draped chastely around sharply protruding shoulder blades. Tiny, frail, and brittle, she looked like a spider. A spider with a long nose and bulbous eyes. Her gray hair, as tough as barbed wire, was pulled back in a tight bun, causing her eyebrows to shoot straight up as if she were constantly alarmed.

"I smell sheep!" she suddenly snapped, then searched the room for the sheep-smelling culprit. Me.

She almost spotted me. Quickly, I ducked behind Rusty's back and gave his hips a quick squeeze. "I'd better go find Junior."

"Who's Junior...?"

But I was already gone. I escaped into the kitchen and bumped into Bennie coming into the foyer. Dusty face; dirty, rumpled clothes, Benjamin was beginning to look like a cowboy. Smell like one, too. The pretty polished student was hidden somewhere under the grime. It was going to take a good, long soaking to find him.

"Help," I said.

"What?"

"Oh, I don't know what the hell I'm doing here," the witch cackled from the other room.

I whisked Bennie out of the kitchen, through the dining room, down a narrow hall, and into the study. Then I slammed the door shut and locked it. "We're safe in here," I said.

Looking over my shoulder, Bennie's face slackened. "I don't think so."

Ruth Ann sat in the straight-backed chair by the fireplace reading an expensive leatherbound book. On a blanket spread out at her feet, Danny played with a cornhusk doll. They both looked up at our abrupt entrance with wide-eyed surprise.

"I'm sorry, ma'am," I mumbled, quickly removing my hat. "I didn't know anyone..."

"No, please," she said, rising from the chair, "come in. I made fresh lemonade. You must be tired and thirsty."

Bennie turned to leave. If I hadn't locked the door he would have been out of there in a second.

"Bennie," Ruth Ann said, firmly, "I would like you to stay."

"Then I'd better be going."

"Don't leave," Bennie said quickly. He grabbed my sleeve and held me there. It was more than just bullets Junior thought I could protect him from.

Uncomfortable, awkward as all hell, I found a chair in a far corner and attempted to blend into the backdrop. But Bennie sat right next to me.

"Did you bring the sheep back safely?" She poured lemonade.

"Yes, ma'am. Your pa did." I didn't confess that we had lost the mountain to her pa like she predicted we would. "Thank you for picking Rusty up at the depot and putting him up here. That was mighty kind of you. "

"It was no problem. Mr. Cunningham's a delight." She handed me a glass of lemonade and made a sour face. "His mother's a bit ... odd."

"Odd." I repeated. That was one way of putting it.

Danny toddled over to me as if he recognized me or something, all smiles and glad-to-see-yous. He got ahold of my thumb and squeezed it like a baby python. "I told you he kind of looks like you."

Bennie stared at him for a full minute without saying anything. Finally he acknowledged the miniature Colsen. "He looks like Daniel."

"He takes after the Colsens," Ruth Ann agreed. "He certainly doesn't have our fair hair and skin."

"My mother was Spanish." It slipped out of his mouth without any thought. Faintly. Not knowing what else to say, the poor kid said the first thing that came to mind. It was pretty irrelevant but what the heck.

"No shit?" I attempted to help him out. "That explains the dark coloring."

Bennie smiled, weakly. "Daniel and I resembled Mother. Marcie and Sammy looked like Father."

Taking a seat close to him, Ruth Ann said with a quiet urgency, "Tell me about them."

"I didn't know them. I only knew their history. My mother was a Spanish princess who was forced to leave Spain when she was quite young. She migrated to England where she met my father and they came here. They were persecuted in England. Dark-skinned people, people of different nationalities, cultures, and backgrounds, aren't expected to interbreed. They came to America thinking it would be better here. It wasn't." Bennie shrugged. "That's all I know. I'm sorry."

"Because you've been away at school?"

"Yes."

"Daniel bragged on you all the time. He was quite proud of having a brother at Harvard."

That seemed to surprise Bennie. "Daniel did?"

Ruth Ann smiled, contentedly. "He talked about you constantly. About how intelligent you are, how you were going to be a lawyer, how his father was so proud of you."

"My father?"

A silence hung in the air. Again, I shuffled uncomfortably and carefully studied the scuffed toe of my boot. These memories belonged to them, I was eavesdropping. But I could not leave the room without drawing attention to myself.

Memories rolled over her like fresh breezes coming through an open window. "Daniel told me stories of all the silly things you did together as children, in England, and here in Turnpike. He had many stories to tell, Bennie. He missed having you at the ranch."

"Just having temporary visits into their lives is what I regret most. Like the baby. I didn't know anything about the baby. I wish Daniel had been able to trust me enough to confide something as important as that."

"No one knew about the baby except my father."

"Mother didn't?"

She shook her head. "I'm sorry, no. For obvious reasons we had to keep quiet. If they had let us marry it would have been different. We were planning to run away together. We were going to go to the Nevada territories and marry there. But Ben ran into financial trouble."

"You knew about that?" I asked.

"Daniel told me. He decided to wait until his father got back on his feet. He didn't want to leave him on his own." Now that the memories turned cruel, her smile grew dim. "He said there would be plenty of time."

"Did your father know anything about Ben's financial situation?"

"My father knows everything. I have no idea how he came about the information. Lord knows, I didn't tell him. He told Zeth they would wait him out. That Ol' Ben – that's what he called him – would be begging to sell sooner or later. Then the water started to disappear and no one was willing to wait for anything."

The baby had somehow successfully maneuvered up my leg. He held still in my lap for a flat second before spying Bennie and precariously began to crawl across the chairs to reach him.

Ruth Ann moved towards the fireplace and silently stared into the dark hole. When she spoke again the generosity was gone, and her voice reverberated with anger. "None of this had to happen. Daniel would still be alive, my child would have a father, you would have your family, if only they would have spoken with each other, if they had worked together. We could have been a family. They were very much alike." She twirled around to face Bennie, her eyes brimming. "You know what's really senseless about the whole thing? Deep down they admired and respected each other."

They. Meaning pa and pa. Father and father. Patriarch and patriarch. The stubbornest of human beings. The most dangerous. The most destructive.

"My father did not hate your father," Ruth Ann said, in a soft tone of amazement. "But one of them had to die before that became clear to the survivor."

"It's all over now," Bennie said, gently. "The battle is finished. I think the Andersons won."

Relaxed now, he fiddled with the baby. He did not need me any more. Ruth Ann's move to the mantel gave me the exit I needed. I stood and put on my hat.

"I'm going to check on the sheep before it gets dark."

His mind on something else for a change, maybe something pleasant, Bennie only glanced at me. I left them with their lemonade to get to know each other.

James T. was at the barn, personally seeing to the grooming of the horses. We had ridden them fast and hard. Zeth stood on the other side of Anderson's thoroughbred stallion, combing it down. When he saw me, he threw the currycomb to the floor, and bumped past me. He hit my shoulder hard enough to push me back against the stall. His anger was understandable and I let him go.

"Don't know what's gotten into that boy." Anderson shook his head, bent over, picked up the comb, and resumed brushing the horse.

"He'll get over it. Whatever it is." I knew what it was. "That's a fine-looking horse," I said of the stallion.

"Part Morgan. Part thoroughbred. Makes a fast but sturdy companion."

"You know your horses."

"That I do. I know everything there is to know about horses and cattle. I can tell you the biological difference between a longhorn and a shorthorn besides just the size of the horn." He looked up from the horse's underbelly. "But women and children," he shook his head, laughing. "Now they're a real mystery."

"You done pretty good."

The old man paused, nodded his head. "That I have, son, that I have."

Standing back, he inspected the stallion. He dang near sparkled, he was that slick. "He's good stock. A good breeder."

I nodded slowly. "Yes, sir."

"You want him?"

The offer was a generous one, but stallions were too much horse for me. In constant need of loving, they were pesky and irritable, like some men I knew. "I'm in need of a horse. But I don't need one that fine."

It did not seem to surprise him that I would reject it. He shrugged and said, "There's more," then ushered me to the back of the barn.

Outside, two dozen horses lounged easily in the shaded part of the corrals. Although they had once been beautiful, healthy stock, they, too, were feeling the effects of the water shortage. It suddenly became clear to me that I had to move fast. Bennie was out of danger, but the ranchers in Turnpike were going under.

Come morning, Anderson was prepared to send every man up the mountain in search of the spring. I would have led them to it, even though they still figured I was full of stuffing, but I was not going to be there come morning.

"Pick one out."

I hesitated. James T. was determined to overcompensate for his bad deeds. Repentance is what my old man called it. I knew a lot about repentance. Pa had always tried to get me to repent for one sin or another. But I had me a list of sins deeper and longer than the notches on my gunbelt. To cover them all, I would have had to start repenting before I was born.

"Go ahead," he urged. "The least I can do is replace your horse."

That was true. A man without a horse was a man without legs.

A dapper palomino gelding danced in the far corner of the corral, sort of enjoying its own company. If there had been a mirror hanging in the barn he would have been staring at his own reflection. He had long legs, a cascading white mane that almost blinded him, and a matching tail. Probably faster than all get-out.

Normally I prefer the slow, stout horses, a mountain horse like the buckskin, a work mule. This horse was a show pony, a pretty prancer full of conceit. Something Ryder McCloud would ride.

He shook his mane off his forehead and swung his head towards me. He had dark yellow eyes, scary eyes that contrasted nicely with his pale yellow hair.

"That one," I made up my mind. "But I'm going to pay for it."

Anderson shrugged. "Do what you got to do. I'll let you have him for two dollars."

Reaching deep into my pocket, I pulled out a few coins and paid him with his own gold. Then we shook hands. Deal closed.

Well now, I thought, as I watched the palomino circle the corral, I got me a real prissy horse. To match the prissy man I was sure enough going to get.

The dinner bell split open the night air. I looked towards the porch where the Indian cook banged on the triangle as if it had done her wrong.

"Let's go eat," said Anderson.

"Dinner?" I paused. The thought scared me, all right. Scared me more than a band of Comanches and Apaches and Sioux chasing after my scalp. Scared me more than every sheriff, deputy, or United States marshall hot on my trail. Scared me more than any fresh-faced, fast-as-a-lizard kid with a brand-new gunfighter's special sitting in his holster, goading me on, making me mad. Dinner with the witch. Now that's what I considered downright frightening.

# 18

Zeth. Rusty. Bennie. Feast or famine.

Hidden in the shadows, I stood at the end of the hall on the second level of the adobe. I finished my smoke, then ground it into the hardwood floor. Here stood a man who had come to a triple fork in the road and could not decide which road to take. Beyond me lay three closed doors. Three potential bed partners. Tough decisions.

Dinner had gone well, considering. Considering I was placed right next to the witch. She was as much aware of me sitting next to her as I was of her sitting next to me. And neither of us liked it. But we were guests and we behaved like guests. Dutifully, we ignored each other. She was almost pleasant. Almost. Plus, I was hungry, starved-like hungry, and I kept my mouth shut and ate. She ate, but she didn't keep her mouth shut.

Her and James T. dominated the conversation. Luckily, they took a liking to one another, and did not mind rudely talking over each other. He was like a man who had stumbled on a gold vein, talkative, exuberant, making plans, drawing up maps and blueprints for tomorrow. Who could blame him? A week ago he was doomed. Today he was a winner.

Zeth was sullen and withdrawn. Ryder had been his first love, his first chance to express feelings that could drive a man crazy keeping secret. Hundreds of miles could be traveled before finding someone who shared the same inclinations as you. A hundred-mile ride through desolate, hostile territories; a hundred-mile trail, alone, with just yourself for company.

If you were wise and experienced like me, you knew where to look. I painted arrows, put up road signs, all leading to my rendezvous. At each stop, there was a man I could bed down with for the evening. A comrade. As long as Zeth stayed on the ranch, which he was likely to do regardless of his nature, a chance meeting with a man like Ryder would not happen twice in his lifetime. He was condemned to a life of lonely, and for that he blamed me. On payday, Ryder would have upped and left anyway. But to a youth with a star like Ryder McCloud in his eye, cold hard facts wouldn't be appreciated or believed.

Then there were Bennie and Ruth Ann, the two who had lost the most. Visibly, with some effort, they attempted to follow the conversation. But they were not there. Their minds were haunted, wandering, quietly assessing and accepting their losses.

Thank the Lord for Rusty and his tales of drunken lumberjacks and burlesque entertainers in Flagstaff. Even Rusty's mother, getting tired and turning into a curmudgeon, was a pleasant diversion from the heaviness of the thoughts and emotions of the folks around Anderson's table. They each looked mighty proper, but they all wished they were somewhere else. Including me.

We survived dinner, had the obligatory brandy in the study, and were informally directed to our rooms, which everyone happily disappeared into. Except me. Be danged if I was going to spend another night sleeping alone.

I had been up in the Montana territories two winters before. I had hired on with a big outfit driving a thousand head of cattle through an early snowstorm. Over fifty men had signed on, fifty men and not one to bunk down with. Isolated in a blizzard, feet so cold you had to check with your eyes to see if your shoes were still there, and not one of them cowhands touched each other, for warmth or otherwise.

Hushed talk around the chuck wagon was about a trial taking place, as we sat there, in the territorial tribunal. Some fellow had been caught fooling with a neighbor's eldest son. A crime against nature was the charge they brought him up on. A crime every man around the campfire had committed at one time or another in his life. We shook our heads and unanimously agreed what a disgusting act it was. Then we blew warmth on our hands to keep the little fingers from falling off, hunched our shoulders to keep the sleet out of our ears, and stayed touching distance away from each other. But most of us knew better.

I knew better. Because I knew nature. Growing up in the back of a traveling preacher's wagon with its snake oils and magic cures and hands-on healing, I became close kin to nature. In Wichita, Kansas, Pa stuck a pig's liver under my shirt and pulled it out in front of the townsfolk that had gathered around his wagon. He held it in the air, wiggled it, then declared how he had removed some disease from my belly. The women fainted. The men gathered around the wagon and waved their hard-earned dollars in the air to have their pig livers removed, too.

It became pretty embarrassing stuff. To keep from partaking in Pa's rituals and fleecing of hard-working folks, I snuck out of the tent before anyone got up. I hid in a lot of bushes, in a lot of forests, in a lot of livery stables, and behind a lot of barns. From there, I observed nature close up. And I ain't never seen a female cow that didn't show interest in another female cow. Or a male duck who didn't appreciate another male duck. Or a stallion that didn't mount another stallion. And that was nature. Pure and simple.

Course I was not real eager to be brought before a tribunal for bedding down with my host's son, and have to explain all this stuff about nature to people who would not listen if Ol' Mother Nature herself did the explaining, so I skipped Zeth's room. I knew he was sore with me, but I figured I could do some sincere apologizing and talk him out of it.

Reluctantly, I walked past Bennie's closed door. If it had been left partially open, the slightest crack, I would have snuck in, pretended I got lost in the dark, and maybe been invited to stay for a while. But it was shut tight. I would not be surprised if it were bolted from the inside. I never knew what Bennie wanted or needed from me, and he wasn't shy about hurting feelings and saying no. Tonight I did not want to hear any rejections.

So I went to where I knew I was always wanted.

I searched in the half-light for the doorknob and stepped into Rusty's room. Hell and almighty, he was a sight for mistreated eyes. He was sitting up in bed with his cotton nightclothes on and one of them stupid-looking nightcaps he always wore, even though I warned him I wouldn't bed down with him any more if he didn't get rid of it. He wore round reading spectacles that magnified his eyes and made him look like a hoot owl. Even after I stepped in, he feigned interest in a book. But really he had been waiting for me.

His mother was sleeping downstairs in Grace's room, so he didn't have to keep his voice low. He made a little noise because I had been neglecting my shaving, but I told him it was hard to shave when you've been stuck on a mountain with twenty guns pointed at you.

Then I told him about Bennie and the Colsens, purposely leaving out the part about how I felt when I was around Bennie, how I got deaf and dumb when I saw him watching me, how I was willing and eager to make a fool out of myself just to get a smile. How I was ruining my bad reputation. I didn't tell Rusty any of that. But Rusty was intuitive and sensed it anyway.

Finally I told him about Ryder. My voice grew small when I got to the part where I put a bullet in him. How I had accidently ripped open flesh on a smooth, perfect body I cherished more than my own. Rusty pulled me close, feeling sorry for me like he always did. It wasn't long before we weren't telling each other anything any more, and he didn't mind my scruffy face, after all.

Something wasn't right. It felt good to be in his arms again. Being away from Rusty for a year or two usually heightened subdued passions enough to put me to sleep afterwards. Making love to Rusty was the exact opposite of making love to Ryder. With Ryder we usually ransacked the room before it was over. With Rusty it was tranquil, peaceful. A tranquility I did not appreciate until I'd been shot at, beaten up, and lost every Union penny to my name. Lying next to Rusty I felt sane, protected, like coming home, like lying in a mother's arms. Maybe the way Bennie had felt lying in my arms on the mountain.

Bennie ... geezus.

As usual, he was the problem. As I ran my tongue down Rusty's milk white leg, I pictured Bennie's legs, bronze and muscular. Touching my lips to Rusty's thin mouth, I thought about Bennie's mouth, full, twisted a little with that sardonic scowl. When I pulled my fingers through Rusty's copper hair, tugging gently, I thought about Bennie's hair, raven and as straight as the warrior's. From head to toe, my mind, my body, was with Bennie.

"Uh ... Dakota."

"Huh?"

"You're not with me."

"Huh?"

Rusty smiled patiently at my stupidity. I think it was my stupidity that had kept him fascinated all these years. Unlike Bennie, who became irritable with my stupidity, Rusty thought it was charming.

"You're not with me," he repeated.

"What do you mean I'm not with you?"

Squeezing my forearm, he attempted to explain without causing an argument or stepping all over my pride. "It's okay, doll, you're probably tired."

I rolled off him, all set to make a big deal out of nothing. "What do you mean I'm tired?"

He propped up on one elbow, softly smiled down at me, and tapped my temple. "Preoccupied by thought. Too much has happened, with the sheep and all."

There was a lot of truth to that. But it wasn't the sheep I was preoccupied with. It was the sheep's owner. I felt like an adulterer, a wayward son.

Rusty bunked back down and kissed me on the cheek. "Sweet dreams," he whispered. Rusty Cunningham really had a way of making me feel young and dopey. The exact way I made everyone else feel.

Within minutes he was snoring, almost purring. Careful not to disturb him, I slid out of bed and walked to the window. It was dark, there wasn't much of a moon, just a thin sliver. Pointless but pretty. The days were growing shorter, darkening earlier. Soon it would be autumn, then winter. Another cycle passing.

By the end of the week the sheep would be in Flagstaff, sheared and sold. Then what would Bennie do? Back to Massachusetts. Back to school. On with his life. He would probably be a rich, fat lawyer someday. Married to a woman he didn't love, she would be intellectual as all hell, and she would know who Walter Whitman was. Befitting for the son of a Spanish princess.

What would I do? Stay on at Rusty's for a couple of days until his mother got tired of me and booted me out. Then what? Look for another bounty ... another card game ... another gunfight. Another night spent with a nameless stranger who felt good and smelled good, and may or may not have looked good, it was usually too dark to tell. I would probably end up facedown on Main Street with a bullet in my heart by the time I was thirty-five years old. Befitting for the son of a cheating preacher man.

I groaned, like I had an ache or something and felt bad for myself, felt pitiful. I was thinking too much and too hard and should go get drunk and stop looking at the moon and feeling sorry for myself.

But a moon like that could sure make a man feel melancholy.

I looked towards Bennie's mountain. Bennie's ex-mountain, now part of the Double A Ranch. It was nothing but a big, dark shadow like thunderheads on the horizon. The stream was up there. I had seen it. Bennie and Old Man Anderson and gullible Zeth and Pat and Maury could snicker all they wanted. I had seen it, swum it, touched it.

Lightly, I felt the cuts on my stomach. They were all but healed, the wounds scarred over.

When I returned from tomorrow's journey, I would haul my disbelieving comrades up that sheep trail, through the white thorn and prickly brush, and rub their noses in the water. Then I would just stand there and let them hem and haw and scratch their heads while they figured out who had built the dam. I did not take kindly to being laughed at. In my reckless days men died for lesser offenses.

With no intention of waking him, I snuck down the hall and slipped into Bennie's room. I stood at the foot of the bed and watched him sleep. He slept on his stomach, his arms enfolding his pillow like it was human or something.

The mattress squeaked as I sat on the edge of the bed. Afraid the noise might wake him, I held perfectly still. He was a sound sleeper. Truth was, I didn't know what I was doing there or what I wanted. My responsibilities to Bennie were coming to an end. And maybe I wasn't looking forward to that happening.

Placing my hand on the back of his neck, I squeezed gently. He opened his eyes, two pinpoints of light, two windows opening. Intuitively, he knew it was me. He didn't move or make a noise. Cocooned in sleep, he just lay there. Then he stretched his arms like lazy butterfly wings.

"Dakota?"

"Yeah."

He waited for an explanation. Somewhere in the room, hidden in the dark, a pendulum clock chimed three times.

I rubbed between his shoulder blades, smooth and warm.

"I know who killed your family," I said.

Sort of. I didn't really know, not right offhand, who killed his family. I could not give him a name even though he bolted upright in bed, shook my hand off, and demanded one immediately. But I knew the answer was as close as the barn.

Shoeless, with our boots in hand, we tiptoed downstairs to keep from waking everyone and walked out to the barn. There wasn't much light shining from the pointless moon. The horses snorted and grumbled a little when they could not easily identify the two intruders waking them. Clumsily, I stumbled in the dark until I found a lantern and lit it.

"Over here," I said.

"Why the big mystery? Why don't you just tell me? This is not a game, you know..." Bennie followed the light as we walked to the end of the barn, annoying me all the way.

"I know more than anyone that this isn't a game. The fact is, I don't know exactly who did it. Not yet. Soon enough we'll both know."

Rusty, clever and discreet, had buried the crate in the hayloft under a pile of loose straw. We climbed the short ladder to the loft. Once there, I pushed aside mounds of straw, exposing a new, sealed wooden crate. On the side, stamped in bold black letters, read: DANGER. Beneath it was stamped: U.S. ARMY. Rusty knew a soldier who knew a soldier who stole the dang thing. Friends. Life wasn't much fun without them.

I found a long-handled branding iron hanging on the wall and pried the lock open. Bennie took a step back. "Good Lord..."

Ignoring him, I pushed aside sawdust shavings and took out a brown envelope fat with documents gathered by trusty Rusty. They were banking documents from the Bank of Flagstaff.

"Junior, I got a good hunch that the name of the person signed to these here documents is the same man who dammed the water." I paused, before adding softly, "And the man who killed your folks."

He slowly slipped the envelope out of my hand. Shoulder to shoulder, we sat on the crate as he unfolded the documents. Bennie read faster than me and turned the pages before I was finished reading. It didn't matter. It was the last page that interested me. The one with the signature scribbled in indigo ink at the bottom. Silently we sat there and stared at the name.

Relief swept over me like a cool ripple of water. Relief, not anger. I had found the man who killed the Colsen family. It was written down in black and white.

The reality of finally knowing overwhelmed Bennie, and he bit down hard on his lower lip. Visibly, he struggled to rein in a rage that had been bubbling inside him like a volcano threatening to erupt since the day I met him. He gave into it. Tears pricked his eyes and smoothly spilled down his cheeks. A silent crier. I didn't look at him. A man should be allowed to cry in private, without an audience, even if there was someone else in the building. I pretended to study the design on a European saddle that hung from a rafter. Loosely, I counted the bales of hay piled in the loft. Then I tugged at my tobacco pouch and rolled a strong smoke.

Angrily smearing tears away with the back of his hand, Junior finally whispered, all hot and mad, "Kill him."

Now, I would have obliged him, loaded up every empty chamber in the Colts, called the killer out, and taken him down unmercifully in the dark, the way he had taken down them kids.

But killing a man was not that simple. Especially now that I had sprouted some morals.

"There's still a few things I need to find out."

"Such as?"

"Why."

He rustled the papers. "This explains why. He was after the ranch."

"It's pretty plain he was after your ranch. Him and a couple of dozen more. This document doesn't explain all of it."

"I don't care about the rest."

"You don't want to know who dammed the spring? If it was the same man? And if it had anything to with your folks' death?"

"No."

"Even if it was your father who stopped the water?"

His patience was all tattered and torn. He had made too many concessions, had given up too much. Now he smelled blood and wanted a taste of it. It was all he could do to keep from hollering at me. "What difference does it make? Are you suggesting that if my father did dam the water this man was justified in killing..."

"I'm not suggesting any such thing, Junior," I said calmly, but firmly. We stayed absolutely quiet and still for a minute before I added, "I need to know for sure."

Plumb exhausted, Bennie rubbed his temples. I should have let him sleep, should not have burdened him until I had gathered all the facts. Maybe not even until I had presented him with a bullet-ridden body. But there was something else I needed to do. Something that would take me away from him longer than I wanted.

"I'm going to be gone for a couple of days."

As expected, the thought disturbed him. "Why?"

"There's someone I need to see. Someone who can help clear up a few things."

"All we need to know is right here on this paper."

I clamped my hand around his wrist and squeezed just hard enough to stress my point. "I can't kill a man, then find out later it was the wrong man. I don't want to live with that. Do you?"

Speechless, he stared into the shadows. The light from the lantern flickered on his face. A bat flitted by, its shadow magnified a hundred times in the lamplight, making it look huge and dangerous.

"All this paper does is point me in the right direction. If I go in that direction I'll have your killer, and I'll bring him in. I'll do your family justice, Junior, I promise you that."

Without pulling his hand away, I felt his entire body slacken, conceding once again. "Can I go with you?"

He already knew what my answer would be. "The Andersons will take good care of you. Rusty will keep you company."

Junior smiled, limply. A ring of dampness circled his eyes. "Where did you meet him?"

"Rusty? Oh, hell, that was so long ago I don't hardly remember. I think it was at the Barbary Coast Saloon in San Francisco. He was singing there, he sings like a canary. A redheaded canary." That drew another weak smile. "We got to be pretty good friends. Rusty's the only person on earth I'd trust with my life. Him and Miz Mary Turner."

"Are you friend-friends, or just friends?"

"What's the difference?"

"A friend-friend is when you have stronger feelings than you normally would for someone. More intimate feelings."

"Really?" Junior sure knew a lot about love between men. "A friend-friend, I guess."

"Oh." He studied my face as if he found it difficult to believe I was capable of friend-friend feelings, that gunfighters were not intimate types. There was some truth to that. "Then he's lucky, your friend."

That made me flush redder and hotter than a chili pepper, and I leaned back against the wall, out of the light so Junior couldn't see. "Did you ever have a friend-friend?"

He shrugged and turned bashful all of the sudden. "No. I've been mostly studious. I thought if I kept my mind on books I wouldn't have to deal with those feelings."

"Don't you get lonely?"

"Oh, sure. Sometimes I get terribly lonely. Once I almost took a train to upstate New York to see Mr. Whitman. Fortunately, I came to my senses before I got there."

"Fortunately?"

"I might have made an arse out of myself."

Smiling slightly, I tapped the cigarette on my knee before lighting it. "Nothing wrong with that."

His face brightened a little as he said, "You should know," while I nodded my head, knowing dang well that was what he was going to say.

"Maybe, Junior, when this is all over, we'll get ourselves a couple of fresh horses and ride across the Americas to visit your Mr. Whitman. I'll make sure you don't act like an ass."

"That would be an adventure." There was another long, uncomfortable silence. "When are you leaving?"

I looked out the window. It would be light soon. "I'm going to saddle up now."

Suddenly he stood up and dusted off the back of his jeans. "Well, I'll say good night then. Do be careful."

A little confused by his sudden departure, I watched as he climbed down the ladder. His head disappeared beneath the loft. Then he came into view again at the bottom of the ladder. He walked down the long aisle of the barn, and outside into the soft dusk. He didn't turn around, didn't look back, trying to be as cavalier about my going as all hell.

I stubbed my cigarette out in the straw. Junior was getting sweet on me. I wondered if he would ever admit it.

# 19

It would have been easier if I knew where I was going. Easier, still, if I had been riding a horse that did not mind being ridden. The palomino was corral broke, and that was about it. In open spaces he strained at the bit and fought to bolt ahead, or he tried to turn and head back to the barn for supper. It took a few hours of riding before I got him calmed down and rode smoothly.

A day's journey took me into the table flats northeast of Turnpike. The ride was pleasant, cool. As I left behind the land of cacti and soil erosion, and moved north, the desert gave way to rose-colored mountain masses. The land was aglow with an early burnt orange sunset. Wisps of maroon clouds sparsely painted the sky. Castles of small buttes cast long shadows across the level floor. When I crossed under them I rode into night, then back into day.

Scattered vegetation relieved my starved eyesight. Mesquite branches rose from the dunes like the arms of a man buried alive. Short deep green carpets of juniper and cedar lay low against the rocks. After the brief winter rains, the land would be spectacular with beauty. The cacti and vegetation would blossom and spread across the sand, a sea of whites and yellows and purples. I had seen it that way before. Years ago when I'd carried a wounded Indian back to his people.

The Hopi built their adobe fortresses where even the slyest and bravest of Grant's soldiers would not dare to tread. On the flat ledges and small plateaus of the larger mesas, up against the wall, almost camouflaged against the mountain. There, the smallest braves could see foot or horse soldiers approaching, signal, and the people would scatter into the crevices of the plateaus like sand fleas, concealing themselves behind boulders and stones. There, the men and women could hold off a cavalcade of soldiers or marauding Indians with spears, arrows, and stones. There, where the table flat of the mountain was shrouded by a billowing cloud mass was where I would find Living Cloud, the great Hopi shaman.

I climbed unaggressively, as if I were out for a Sunday picnic or a quiet stroll in the majestic mountains. At the bottom of the mesa I left my rifle and handguns. The eyes of these children were like the eyes of young hawks. If they saw the guns, they would signal their people that an armed white man approached, and I would be ambushed before I reached the first plateau. Weapons were not needed here. Even if they were, I would not use them. I came uninvited. Until they knew my name, the name of the Sioux, I would be only one more suspicious white man, potentially dangerous, potentially destructive.

Hidden behind the rocks, the children saw me coming. Their eyes followed me, watching for signs of hostility. I was a lone rider, unarmed, and they let me ride through.

They allowed me to ride into the compound, right up to the two armed sentries guarding the village. Wordlessly the guards stepped in front of my horse and brought him to a stop. Their expressions were vague, but not unfriendly. A white man riding into their compound did not appear to bother them.

"Living Cloud," I said.

Not allowing me to dismount, they took the reins of my horse and led me into the village. Women looked up from their pottery tables with curiosity. Mistrust showed slightly on their weathered faces. Small children, barely visible except for round chocolate eyes, peered out from behind their skirts.

The village consisted mainly of old men, women, and children. There were very few young men. Because of Cochise's rampages all young Indian men were suspect, and brutally put to death. In the white man's world, an Indian was an Indian. Small details like a man's innocence were not worth an argument if that man had red skin. The bounty had asked for scalps. Whether those scalps belonged to a Hopi farmer or an avenging Apache, it made no difference. An Indian was an Indian.

We stopped in front of a three-terraced adobe built alongside the entire length of the mountainside. Directly outside the adobe, an elderly man huddled in front of a large loom meticulously weaving a purple robe. His back was bent at the shoulders and he appeared hunchbacked. What had once been long silver hair was now snow white, and cropped close to his head. A red rag was tied around his forehead to keep the hair from straying into his eyes as he worked. A face that had once been wrinkled was now mapped and cut deep with gullies and valleys. The years had been dragging on him.

"Great Shaman," one of the sentries said, "a white man has come."

Surprised at the deep pleasure I felt at seeing the old man again, I leaped off my horse and stepped into the weaving circle. Living Cloud's bones snapped audibly when he got to his feet. His eyes were dim, blinded, covered by a gray film. He lifted a gnarled hand to my face and slowly traced the outline of my brows and nose, then down to my mouth. He touched my mustache, a mustache that could not be grown on this baby face ten years ago.

"Ah..." he said. "The buffalo hunter."

Almost spryly, he wrapped thin arms around me and patted me heartily on the back before releasing me. "Sit," he told me. Then he shouted through a cutout window of the pueblo to a soft round woman grinding maize. "Bring food and drink. The Dakota is here."

At the sound of his voice, or at the sound of my name, the villagers relaxed and continued with their work. Only occasionally did they discreetly glance in my direction. The Hopi were a friendly and polite tribe, unless they had reason to be otherwise.

We sat cross-legged on the ground. Living Cloud patted me on the back, my arms, my legs, as if to reassure himself I was really there in the flesh. The plump woman, a wife of many, many years, placed a meal of ground corn and an odd berry drink I had never tasted before in front of us. I ate like a hungry man, a grateful man, and that pleased Living Cloud, pleased the woman. The drink was thick and bitter, almost like a soup .

"Tell me, buffalo hunter," Living Cloud said. "What brought you up the mountain this time? Another crazy Hopi to rescue?"

I grinned and shook my head. Then, soberly, I considered my words carefully. For a white man, even a white man who had done great things in the eyes of the Indian, to ask an Indian for his help, his wisdom, his magic, seemed shameless and presumptuous.

"There's something I need to ask of you. It's important. If it weren't, I wouldn't be bothering you with a white man's problem."

Blind as he was, he still examined me with the clear eyes of a visionary. Declarations or solemn promises were not needed. I knew, without words, there was nothing the shaman would not do to repay the life I had given.

"Speak freely," he said.

"I need to know of the Eternal Spring."

He was not surprised, only slightly moved. "You have been there. You have touched the magic spring."

"Not out of disrespect. For the preservation of my people." If that sounded absurd to him, he did not show it.

"The water god is angry. The water is drying. Perhaps it is your people he is angry with, and they have earned his punishment."

How did he know? The water tables of Turnpike did not reach this far north. And Living Cloud, in the aged condition he was in, could not have been down off the mountain in years.

"I'm sure he's angry with them. I doubt if there's a Hopi god that isn't punishing my people."

First he grinned. Toothless, purple gums were exposed through gray lips. Then he broke into loud, choking laughter. Quickly, he took a swallow of the berry drink to clear his throat. "You always speak the truth, buffalo hunter."

"When is the last time you have been to the spring?"

Sighing deeply, he silently cursed his age. "Many, many moons. I am an old man."

"Who brings gifts to the water god now? To appease his anger?"

I needed to know if anyone else had access to the spring. It never occurred to me until now that an Indian may have dammed the spring to force the white man out of their valley. Even Living Cloud, a peaceful man, might do so.

"Only a magic man can go into the cave. Anyone else the water will consume. It will steal the breath from their lungs."

"Then no one else knows of the spring but you?"

"And now you." Living Cloud's gaze drifted away from me. He overlooked the mountain range and the deep floor of clouds obscuring the valley below. "And my grandson, Swift Running Deer. He comes now."

A thunderous call started up and the village came alive with excited activity. Ten warriors whirled into the middle of the compound with a small herd of sheep. Packs of dogs barked and chased after them. The villagers ran behind the horses. It was Swift Running Deer and his braves.

Living Cloud grinned a gaping grin. "They think they are Apache. I tell them, You are farmers. Put down your spears and pick up the plough. Live in peaceful coexistence with the white man. But they have dreams of joining Cochise's army and winning. That one," he pointed to where he felt Swift Running Deer was, and he was right. Striding proudly through the crowd with his winnings, the young warrior was exactly where the old shaman predicted. "He is like his grandfather, trying to save the buffalo."

A trail of dusty children, barefooted and scantily clothed in loincloths, followed Swift Running Deer to the crudely built pens, chattering among themselves. Beautiful doe-eyed women, with thick hair tied like a ram's horns to the sides of their head, flocked around him, offering him drink. Young bucks watched him in awe, imitating his gestures, his moves.

Swift Running Deer was a hero to his people. Perhaps more of a hero than the medicine man who taught passive resistance. The Hopi were torn between preserving their culture and identities, and living peacefully among the white man, whose impending encroachment would destroy their way of life. There was nothing passive about Swift Running Deer. He knew where he stood among the white man. And he would keep his people from their bondage.

Another cocky young hero had walked through this village ten years ago. In his arms, he had carried a broken old man, a beloved shaman. Two dusty, scantily clad children had followed after him, emulating his gestures, running to bring water. One of them was Swift Running Deer. The other was a sister. A twin.

"What about the other child? A granddaughter. White Doe."

Living Cloud's face darkened, turned somber. "She is dead. Come. The Snake Dance begins."

Letting me guide him, Living Cloud took hold of my arm and directed me to a ceremonial clearing outside the pueblo. During winter the dances and ceremonies took place inside the kiva, a ceremonial chamber on the bottom floor of the adobe. Today the sun was hot, and the gods could observe the dance more clearly outside.

Dressed in colorful fabrics of orange and black, twenty men danced in double file, side by side, before splitting to form a neat circle. They lifted their faces to the sky and repeatedly sang a monotone chant. Their faces were painted white, their eyes black, as if they were masked bandits. Orange grass skirts made of yucca fiber hung past their knees. Under the skimpy grass skirts were shorter skirts dyed yellow and black. In contrast to their dress, their headdresses were modest: small hats of orange feathers placed near the forehead.

Two of the dancers once again moved side by side and hopped up to a circle containing two woven baskets. From the baskets they removed two rattlesnakes. Desert sidewinders. I sucked in my breath. I didn't like messing with them things.

The dancers gracefully lifted the snakes above their heads then lowered them to face level. They placed the sidewinders in their mouths and held them there. Then they stepped back into the circle and joined the other dancers. For some spooky reason the rattlers did not strike. Maybe the dancers handled them with fastidious care. Or maybe the snakes understood the significance of the ritual.

"Isn't it too early for the Snake Dance?"

"The water god is angry," Living Cloud repeated. "He is drying up the water, taking it back from us."

"It ain't the water god's idea, Living Cloud. It is man's. A man without magic did go to the Eternal Spring. He built a wall and stopped the water."

Engrossed by their movements and the chants, Living Cloud continued to watch the dancers as if he had not heard me. Quietly, he whispered, "This must be so."

Swift Running Deer suddenly squatted beside me. Everything he did, he did quickly, suddenly, with exuberance. I could see how he had earned his name.

"A white man is allowed to see our sacred dance?" he chided his grandfather.

"This is the great buffalo hunter. Nothing Hopi is secret to him."

"Dakota...," he smiled, once again taking my hand and shaking it. He looked over his shoulder. "Where's the English?"

"Stayed home."

He was still dressed in war gear, smelling of sweat and hard riding. My pulse quickened and I backed away from him, a little. He noticed and leaned back into me, a little.

"And how was your hunt?" Living Cloud asked with a smattering of sarcasm.

"Victorious. We brought back sheep." He swept his arms towards the makeshift corrals and grinned at me.

That pleased Living Cloud. He patted his grandson's knee. "This is good. Winter will not be as long with wool and meat."

"And we brought back the scalp of a blue soldier."

Blue soldier. Cavalry. The kid scout in Turnpike.

That did not please Living Cloud. "Warriors," he grunted. "Little wonder the water god is angry."

As if to appease the water god for his grandson's transgressions, Living Cloud picked up the chant, gliding smoothly into the rhythm of the dancers. Mutely, I watched the dancers handle the snakes, awed.

The warrior leaned closer and spoke quietly in my ear as if I were a co-conspirator. "My grandfather is too generous with the white man, ever since one saved his life. Before that he had no patience for them either."

"I have no patience with the deaths of my people," the old man snapped. His eyes might have failed him, but his ears were still as sharp as a coyote's. "The white man has many guns. We have only rocks, and children to throw them."

"But we have courage. And we have the Great Spirit on our side."

"Not all white men are your enemies," I muttered.

He rattled his spear. The scalp dangled grotesquely among pretty feathers and beads. "This one was our enemy."

"It wasn't you he was tracking. It was Cochise's men."

"We are all Cochise's men."

Again Living Cloud interrupted the chant, just long enough to scold him. "Marauders. Pretend Apaches."

And that finished the argument. With a slight smile of affection, mixed with patient and respectful tolerance, Swift Running Deer bowed to his grandfather by remaining silent. Using my shoulders to lift himself, he leaped to his feet and disappeared into the adobe to show off his scalp to the villagers.

Throughout the night, it would be that way. Swift Running Deer would come and go, be there, then gone. Like a bird, he would light beside me, say something quarrelsome, be scolded by his grandfather, then, good-natured and full of zest, he would fly away again. Up and down all night.

I stayed close to his grandfather's side and didn't wander throughout the village. To be allowed to participate in the Snake Dance was a great honor. Although my curiosity and my mission wanted to take me through the compound asking questions and gathering evidence that might link the Indians, Swift Running Deer in particular, to the Eternal Spring, I stayed where I was. Despite Living Cloud's affection towards me, I was still a stranger. A stranger with a white face.

Dusk came early, and the dancers continued to dance. Women brought out bushels of food and drink, and the ceremony turned into a ritualistic orgy of dance, food, and drink. A fat sheep was roasted on a spit. Many of the women and children picked up the dance on the side. The dancers, dripping with sweat, continued to beat their drums, praying for rain. The entire table flat was alive. It glowed with an energy the gods could not ignore if they wanted to. The dance would go on night and day for nine days, becoming more raucous, more demanding, until the gods grew weary and split open the sky with water.

Enchanted, I sat and drank the berry juice. It was laced with something catatonic, perhaps sap from the peyote plant. At first the bitterness was unappetizing, but the more Living Cloud poured into my cup, the more I drank, until I found the thick syrupy liquid agreeable. The chants, the juice, the blazing fire, lulled me to sleep. I felt drugged, but at peace. In fact, I felt so peaceful, I couldn't move my hands or legs.

The painted faces of the dancers loomed up on me, then quickly diminished. The light from the bonfire gave them a ghostly appearance. For a moment, I thought they were masked revelers at All Saints' Day in New Mexico. I thought I was with Ryder McCloud, drunk as a skunk, having fun, looking forward to the night. Then the stars reappeared. The Big Dipper was bigger than I had ever seen it before in my life. It appeared to be sitting on my head, and I almost swatted it with my hand.

Living Cloud placed a crippled hand on my arm, signaling that he was ready to rest. So was I.

"Dakota ... does the water being stopped bring harm to you?"

My mouth was numb, my head reeled from drunkenness. Without much clarity, I said, "It brings harm to someone I love."

Drunk talk. I'd swear by it when the berries wore off.

I stumbled to the pueblo. Dotted campfires lighted my way. Surprisingly, I climbed the ladder to the first terrace without falling on my face. I entered through a hole in the roof and climbed down a ladder to a medium-size room. My saddle and riding gear had been placed in a corner. A small fire flickered in the middle of the room in an adobe burner shaped like a small rounded hut. There were blankets spread out in front of it for my bed.

The room was about ten by ten. No windows, no doors, the only exit was up the ladder and through the hole. The design was very similar to the Eternal Spring. I did not like being trapped in this clay box without an easy exit. Fleetingly, I considered taking my saddle and finding a comfortable spot outside to bunk down in. But I reeled forward, asleep before my head hit the ground.

The sound of the ladder squeaking, the weight of a body wobbling it, awakened me. Someone moved silently through the dark. The fire was out and I could not see in the room. I cursed myself for not being outdoors where the moon served as my perpetual light. Pretending to sleep, to be unaware of the intruder, I slipped my hand under the blanket to where my bowie knife rested.

Silk hair tickled my back as Swift Running Deer leaned over me to see if I was awake. My hand clutched the knife, ready to spring, as I met his gaze.

"Grandfather will take the snakes to the Eternal Spring and release them. The water god will free the water then."

This was an unprecedented honor on my behalf, a demonstration of the respect I had unwittingly earned from the old man. It was also an undeserved generosity towards the white men in the valley.

"Can he make the trip?"

"He is old, but he is strong."

"Thanks," I said.

I expected him to move back out as quietly as he had slipped in, but Swift Running Deer stayed. He lay down beside me as if he planned on sleeping there. Outside, the chants grew louder. Through the hole, the orange glow of the bonfire lit up the night. I had been asleep for maybe four or five hours.

Coolly, the Indian laid the palm of his hand on my back and slowly, sensually, began to work the muscles with strong, callused hands. It felt good enough that I lay still for ten minutes as he kneaded up my back to my shoulders. Half dozing, half aroused, I could have lain there all night. I also could have used a little more berry juice.

"Maybe," the warrior said, quietly, "not all white men are our enemies."

I rolled over to meet him. "Maybe not."

This time Bennie never even entered my mind. The two men were completely different from each other. Like sampling two different foreign dishes, there was no comparison. The English was cool, civilized, withdrawn. The Indian was hot, wild, immodest as all hell.

Hemmed in by the adobe walls the night air grew cool. Rising from the tangled blankets, Swift Running Deer went about the task of relighting the stove. He piled pieces of stick in the center and blew on it until it flickered brightly in the room, a miniature replica of the bonfire blazing outside.

Goosebumps trickled up his arms and along his spine. Once he got the fire going, the flames danced against his skin, highlighting his hair. I soaked up as much of his beauty as I could with two eyes.

He watched me absorbing him, appreciating him, and laughed. I lifted up the corner of the blanket and silently invited him back in. He crawled into the warmth, then buried his head in the hollow of my armpit.

"You probably don't recall, but I remember when you were about yea high." I attempted to move an arm and demonstrate how high, but I was pretty much pinned down by his weight.

"My memory is not so good, but that is a day I will always remember. Everyone in the village will remember that day. The day you brought Grandfather home."

Loosely, I rubbed his arm with the tips of my fingers. "I had to leave the travois at the bottom of the mountain. My horse couldn't pull it over the rocks. And I remember thinking, Geezus, how am I going to carry him up the mountain?"

"He had been gone for months. He said a spirit had come to him in the night and told him to go to the Great Plains of the Nebraskas and sit with the buffalo. For what purpose, or what difference this would make, he did not know.

"Grandfather is our magic, our medicine man. Without him, the village seemed distant. Sickness and despair came over us. When you came into the village, there was great celebration. As a child all I could see was this white cowboy, a *gaucho*," he used the Spanish word with a bit of flare, "with big guns and a frail old man."

"Didn't you have a sister? A twin?"

"You, too, have a good memory. For an old man."

Gently, I pinched his arm. "Living Cloud said she was dead."

"To Living Cloud she is dead."

"What happened to her?"

Swift Running Deer shifted uncomfortably under the blankets, either because I held him too tight or because he did not want to talk about his sister. For a second I thought he was going to bound away as quickly as the animal he was named after.

"She is a white woman now. Her name is no longer White Doe. Her name is Sarah."

There was a long pause. I felt like apologizing, but it was not my fault. Whatever unnatural ways befell the Indian were not my doing. I was on their side. I lived among them more easily than I did white men. If I had lived among them, I would not be a gunfighter. I would not carry guns. I would take up the plough.

Mutely, sleepy with thought, I entwined strands of his hair around my fingers. As usual, trusty Rusty, his eyes, ears, and nose sharp as a straight razor, was right.

"This is why we are Cochise's men. Warriors for the Apache, and not the farmers of our fathers. If we do not fight the white man and his ways we will all become like him. We will wear white man's trousers, read the white man's holy book, sanction the white man's money..."

"Develop the white man's greed."

Searching my face, the Indian chuckled slightly. "You are not only a warrior, you are a warrior against your own people. Maybe you should ride with the Apache."

"There's only one white man I'm warring against." Almost smothered in his hair, I breathed deeply and inhaled its fragrance. It smelled of willow, sand, river. Of the earth. "If I ask you something, will you answer me truthfully?"

He lifted his head, met my gaze. "Ask."

"Did you dam the Eternal Spring?"

"What would be my purpose for stopping the water?"

"To drive the white man out of the desert plains."

"I want the white man out of the plains and off Hopi land. But I will drive them off with the spear, face-to-face, man to man. Not as a coward who sneaks in the night and builds walls and steals water from the mouths of children. We, too, have been without water because the water god does not hear us."

"Okay."

"Is that the man you seek, buffalo hunter? The one who built the wall?"

I nodded. I was too warm, too comfortable to speak. The air was thin in the adobe. It became difficult to keep my eyes open. "That is the man I seek."

"Listen." Swift Running Deer lightly placed his fingers across my mouth even though I was as silent as a spider spinning its web in the dark.

The soft, quiet patter of raindrops tapped shyly on the roof of the adobe, whispering to us. Then it began to beat down loudly, louder than the tom-toms, shouting its arrival.

In unison we whooped loudly, scrambled out of the blanket, and up the ladder to greet it. We stepped out on the roof of the bottom terrace and lifted dry faces to the heavens.

# 20

On foot they moved slowly up the trail as if they were four sluggish snails dragging millstones in the heat. A pack mule loaded down with picks and shovels labored over the sharp rocks. They looked like a mining outfit climbing untamed territory to stake a claim. Bennie led the way. Although he had never been up this side of the mountain he was familiar with the terrain and walked against it. Anderson and Zeth trudged behind him, panting heavily. Their pale faces thumped red from the heat. It did not surprise me to see Ruth Ann close behind. She moved easily, the only one who knew where she was going. These were the mountains she and Daniel had played in.

The sun was hot, brutal, unaware that only fifty miles north of us cool gentle rains bathed and massaged the earth. Not so in Turnpike. Living Cloud was right. The water god was madder than I had ever known a god to be, and he showed little mercy on Turnpike's inhabitants. Maybe the snakes would appease him.

At the top of the plateau, I waited patiently for them to arrive. I studied the crowns of their heads while I casually smoked my smoke and ignored the fact that I was pleased to see them. All of them. Like they were family or something. Behind me, Living Cloud and Swift Running Deer sat astride their pintos. When the climbers reached the top, they were not surprised to find me, but regarded the Indians suspiciously.

Swift Running Deer smiled when he saw Bennie. "Hello, English," he said in passable English. From there on, I would translate any conversations between the white men and the red men.

In his traditional Hopi garments, without his Apache war gear or saber to rattle, he did not look as intimidating. Bennie politely nodded recognition, then turned demanding eyes on me.

Whether one night had passed, or three days and three nights, I got this reckless urge whenever I saw Junior. An adrenaline pumping. Sometimes it made me feel peaceable and calm, a mature man always under control. Other times it made me feel restless and itchy, like a corralled stallion. Today it made me restless. I scratched my neck, kicked the dirt with my boot, avoided his eyes.

I figured those urges were of an earthy nature, maybe sexual. But I had been bedding down with Swift Running Deer for two nights, taking care of them urges, and my skin still itched under Bennie's gaze.

"What's this all about?" Anderson said, gruffly.

He was none too happy about climbing halfway to heaven to indulge my whims. It was only at Bennie's insistence, whom he had sort of adopted as a second son, that he had agreed. At this point, there was little James T. would not do to pacify Bennie. His debt was huge, unpayable. Atonement.

I didn't say anything, only studied the faces of my doubters for the last time. Swift Running Deer dismounted and squeezed through the two protective boulders. I followed him. Effortlessly, we slid the flat, gray stone away from the hole.

With a just a bit of the dramatics of my preacher father, I removed my hat and said, "Gentlemen ... and ma'am, the Eternal Spring."

Convinced I was playing a joke on him, Anderson hesitated before he moved towards the hole. He peered into the cave, then dropped to both knees. "My God ... it is."

Zeth hurried by me, flashing me a quick irritable look, and squatted next to his father. "Can we get down there?" Zeth said it. James T. was mute with shock.

"This is the only entrance," said Living Cloud.

Removing the picks from the pack mule, Swift Running Deer and I bashed at the opening. We peeled back the top layer of earth, careful not to drop sediment into the water and muddy the stream. When we had expanded the hole enough for James T. to squeeze through, we dropped a rope ladder and each of us climbed into the hole, splashing into the water. At the end, I carefully lowered the wiry old Indian down.

"It has been years." His vacant eyes misted over. "I can see the glow."

"What does he have in the basket?" Bennie whispered. The shaman clutched a basket tight to his chest.

I grinned at him. "You'll see."

Slowly, we waded through the water. It was deeper than when I had been there before. Living Cloud momentarily stopped us with a word of warning.

"Evil spirits are not permitted in the Eternal Spring. They cannot survive. The water will consume them, swallow them up."

That made each of us stop, gauge our evil barometer, quickly scan one another's faces, gauge their evil barometers, then wade on. Far as I could tell, I was the baddest member of the group, and I had played and swum safely here.

When we reached the bank where the ceremonial campfire had taken place many years ago, the water was up to our chests. We passed by the ring silently. The entire walk was made in silence. It was the quietest group of people I had ever waded in water with. You would have thought we were in a church or something. Our faces practically glowed with reverence, and it was not from the strange light.

When we rounded the bend, the dam, large and flat, and grotesquely out of place, sprang up in front of us.

"There it is," Ruth Ann said.

"What the hell is it?" Anderson demanded.

"Well, James T.," I answered, "it appears someone has been holding your water hostage. As long as the wall stays, the wells will continue to dry up in the valley."

"Who? The Indians?"

"This is sacred ground," I said. "The Indians would not desecrate it. It takes the selfishness of a white man to interfere with something this perfect."

"What is he doing?" Bennie was purely intrigued by the old shaman and carefully watched his every move.

The chieftain mumbled something in Hopi then crawled up on the bank. Sitting cross-legged, he placed the basket between his thighs and lifted the lid. Carefully, he pulled a sidewinder out of the basket.

"Good Lord..." Bennie whispered.

Fascinated as all hell, James T. watched silently, pleased.

"The snakes will carry our message to the water god. The water god will then release the water."

I translated his words to the best of my ability.

"We don't need snakes," Zeth growled. "Just fell the damn thing." Having Ryder skip out on him had taken the glow of youth from his face and the tone of kindness from his voice.

James T. nudged him with his elbow. "Quiet."

Living Cloud sang an incantation as he raised the rattler above his head. His voice echoed through the cave. Then slowly he lowered the snake, dipped it in the water, and released it.

Everyone froze. The sidewinder darted straight towards me and wiggled around my waist. I hate snakes. And I hate them twice as much when we're sharing the same pool of water. On land, you can outrun them. In the water, they're faster than you. It was only the sanctity of the moment, and my respect for Living Cloud, that kept me from bounding out of the water like a man on fire. Besides, I did not want to look like a yellow-bellied sapsucker in front of Junior and the warrior.

After the rattler sniffed me out it circled Junior. He didn't look too thrilled either. It dived and disappeared as if it had a mission to accomplish and was in a hurry to get it done.

Living Cloud finished his song when the snake could no longer be seen. Then he offered Hopi gifts of corn, wool, and flint. Finally, we were permitted to wade ashore. All of us scrambled up the embankment, grateful to be out of the water.

Anderson laid his palm against the sandstone wall. "Your father hated us so much he would do this," he said to Bennie.

"Ben did not build the wall," Ruth Ann said, not Bennie. Bennie still was not sure of what his father was capable of doing.

"How do you know?"

"Daniel would never have allowed it."

"What if he didn't know, Sis?" asked Zeth.

"Daniel knew this land. He walked it constantly, looking for strays or hunting wild dogs. He told me there was water here, but he didn't know where it came from, or that it was part of a legend. They were practical people, they didn't believe in legends."

Anderson studied the heavy-bouldered dam. "It would take machinery to move these rocks. Or dozens of men. Colsen could have hired it done."

"No," I interjected, "Ruth Ann is right. Ben Colsen didn't do it. He didn't know any more about the spring or the water than you. While folks were threatening him and his family over the water, he didn't even know what they were angry about. Ben Colsen died an innocent man."

"My father didn't believe the spring existed. He thought it was a myth."

Living Cloud grunted, understanding the English word *myth*. "You can't touch or see something you don't believe."

"Then who?" Anderson demanded, growing impatient with the guessing game. "Who else?"

"The same man who led the riders up the mountain the night the Colsens were murdered."

"Do you know who it was?" Anderson asked, gruffly.

"I know."

"Tell me and I'll see that the bastard hangs from the highest gallows. There will be no need for a gunfighter's brand of justice here."

I shook my head as I attempted to light a damp cigarette. "Sorry, James T. That's between me and him. I've been hired to do a job and I'll see that job through."

Swift Running Deer emptied the picks and shovels on the ground. Lifting a heavy-handled pick, he leveled a mighty blow, bashing it against the rock. Slowly, methodically, he took another swing. I dropped the cigarette, picked up a pick, and followed suit, hitting the stone with all my might. Sparks lit up beneath my pick.

The impact stung my palms. Then James T. lifted a pick. Then Zeth. Then Bennie. Then Ruth Ann. The only noise echoing through the hollow cave was the sound of steel picks clanging against sandstones.

It started with a small trickle, then gradually became an even flow. The water found an unstable duct and broke through. It crashed into the empty riverbed with a roar. The force washed most of the sandstone wall down with it. We stood back and watched it run farther into the cave, cascading down the mountain into the bottom wells of Turnpike.

Once again we were quiet with our individual thoughts as we waded back to the opening and climbed the ladder. One by one, we looked behind us for the last time. No one would come back to the mountaintop and touch the water again. That was a lonely thought.

Swift Running Deer was the last one out. He lifted the rope ladder and started to slide the rock over the opening. I stopped him. The old Indian was missing.

"Where's your grandfather?"

"He will stay."

Roughly, I grabbed the ladder and started to drop it to retrieve the old man. Then I remembered, I had no voice in Indian matters. I stared at Swift Running Deer for a moment, maybe trying to will him to reconsider and bring the old man up.

"It is his choice."

"Your village will be without a shaman."

"There are many villages without medicine men now. It has become a way. A new way. It is time for our village to fight with Cochise. Grandfather would never permit that."

I nodded slowly, handed him back the rope, and helped him slide the rock in place. It blocked out the gentle rays of water that reflected off Swift Running Deer's hair. He was right. Living Cloud would rather abide with the water god than live to witness the inevitable: his people at war.

Swift Running Deer leaped onto his pinto. He reached down and squeezed my hand. It was the last courtesy he would show to a white man. Turning his pony wildly, he let out an Apache war cry, and bolted down the mountain. A lone Apache warrior.

Our horses were waiting for us at the bottom of the mountain. When we rode into the canyon, I took the reins to Bennie's horse and led him away from the Andersons. No one noticed us leaving. Deep in thought, still silenced by the magic of the spring, no one said anything. Not even Bennie. Maybe he had come to trust me enough that he no longer protested or questioned my actions.

Steadily, we climbed the west side of the mountain, taking the trail the buckskin had engraved into the earth a few weeks earlier. When Bennie realized where I was leading him, he took back the reins of his horse and followed without giving me any trouble.

The sun lowered on the western horizon. It lit up the sky with orange and pink, and cooled us with its shadows. At the top of the mountain we rode up behind Big House Boulder. Our horses waded through ashes as we had waded through the water. I stopped the horse right where the big house used to stand.

Bennie finally piped up. "What are we doing?"

Afraid he might ask too many questions, not like my answers, and demand to ride back down the hill, I slid off the palomino and immediately loosened the girth. Then I took my saddle off real fast.

"Let's spend the night here."

"Why?"

Yep, he was rolling with the questions now. I wanted to say, "Because I missed you," but I didn't say anything. I just half lifted him off the horse and dropped his saddle on the ground next to mine.

"All right," he agreed. "But it's getting cold. We'll need a fire."

"I'll do that."

And I did it quickly. There was an urgency to my every move. Within minutes a cheerful fire burned on Bennie's mountain, taking the edge off the dark and the coolness, probably for the last time. Regardless of all my thinking and calculating, I did not know how to get his land back for him. That took brains. The dirty part I could do, the smart part seemed impossible.

Bennie stared into the fire, his hands tucked up his sleeves, a little chilled. "You told Anderson you know who killed them."

"Yep," I nodded. I squatted on my haunches and pushed the coals around with a stick.

"What did you find out about the name on the document?"

"He's our man, Junior."

"Are you sure?"

"Sure enough. Like I told you, I'll do your family justice."

Somber, thoughtful, Bennie took a deep breath, but he stayed silent.

"It'll be over soon enough," I assured him.

And no more would be said. Not before or after.

Bennie squatted next to me. "You should have seen James T.'s face when he saw the spring. He was like a child."

James T. ... Bennie had taken to calling him that. It was a term of affection, of familiarity.

"Yep," I nodded again, smiling into the fire.

"I think everything's going to be okay now. I really do."

"I hope so, Junior."

Already some of the pain had left his face, the burden lifted from his shoulders. He seemed brighter, quicker, less heavy with mourning.

"We should have brought food. I would have if I had known we were going to take this excursion into the mountains." He smiled out of the corner of his mouth.

"I'm not hungry. For food."

"I am."

"I could shoot you a mountain goat."

"No thanks."

"Make you a merry berry wine."

He looked at me oddly.

"It's a fact. I charmed the recipe right off an old Indian woman. It's a mixture of peyote, juice from the saguaro, and berries. It tastes like shit, but it'll keep you warm and happy. And make you crazier than hundred-proof whiskey from the still will. Guarantee it."

"No thank you again. You're already crazy enough."

Hypnotized by the fire, we stared into it, silenced. Bennie spoke first. "I think I know why we're here."

I nodded.

"I don't mind. I've grown quite fond of you, if I should be saying such a thing."

I nodded again. Yes, he should be saying such a thing. After all, come tomorrow morning, I would prepare to kill for him. Not for money, not for gold, but for him. And for this odd new ideal called justice. Ryder was probably snickering his fool head off somewhere.

"We could have accomplished the same thing at the Double A."

I shook my head no.

Lightly he placed his hand on the small of my back, right above my gunbelt. And that's all he needed to do. Slowly, wanting tonight to go on for a couple of years, I unbuttoned his shirt. He wore a flannel work shirt that was too big for him. It must have been Zeth's. The sleeves hung past his wrists. It made him look like a badly dressed puppet, not at all like the sharp young man I had encountered in the saloon at Hudson. But it didn't matter. Junior could be swathed in an old gunnysack and he would still be prettier than all the men and women of Paris or San Francisco.

As soon as I opened the last button, the shirt slipped off his right shoulder, exposing a brown sinewy arm that matched his chest. I kissed his shoulder, all gentle and nice-like. He tasted salty, and warm like the sun.

He held me there for a second while I breathed him in. Then he pushed me away and lay down on the ground. I unbuckled his belt. He spread his legs slightly as I lowered myself on top of him. I didn't say nothing. I'm a man of few words anyway, and I never thought much of people who try to talk and love at the same time. It's a purely physical thing.

I never thought to ask Junior if he had done this before. Or if he preferred a more sensitive, considerate approach. Desire overpowered politeness. When I slammed into him, his entire body stiffened in shock, and he threw his head back to let out an agonizing scream, but no sound escaped his throat.

Then the wildest, craziest smile swept across his face. He grasped the back of my neck, and rode harder than a Montana mustang. He was mumbling and breathing inaudible senseless words. I couldn't decipher them; his mouth was too full of my hot skin.

Surprising me somewhat, Junior was not shy when it came to lovemaking. He reminded me of Ryder, without the whiskey, looking for a little violence. His fingers dug into my back, his teeth nipped at my neck and shoulder, sometimes biting down hard, making me flinch, as I rocked against him. There was nothing civilized about him. He was meaner than any gold miner, gunfighter, gambler, or Indian that I had taken to bed. He arched, rubbing against my chest, and pushed me in deeper. Finally I exploded, and the whole mountain could have exploded with me for all I noticed.

Now that the first wave of gluttony had subsided, I went about the business of cherishing him, to show him how tender I could be. Very, very gently, I kissed his nose, his eyelids, the tips of his fingers, his belly. Each kiss was a kiss of gratitude. A profoundly sincere, straight-from-the-heart, thank-you-very-much, Junior.

Paralyzed by pleasure, I did not move for the longest time. I lay there holding him, smelling him, savoring him. The night had just begun. There was no need to hurry. I noticed that I still had my jeans and boots on, and I chuckled, a small laugh lost in the tangle of his hair.

"What's so funny?"

"Nothin'."

He leaned away from me, looked into my face, never satisfied with my answers.

"I'm still fully dressed," I explained.

"You are." He tugged at my shirt. It was ripped open but still in place. "I should do something about that."

"Don't move." I began to rock against him again. "Be nice this time."

His laugh was as jolly as a kid's on a tree swing. For a few seconds I enjoyed the privilege of watching him laugh. Then I silenced him by cupping my mouth over his. Second time around maybe I was a little gentler, a little less piggish, and took my time. He called my name, shouting it to no one except coyotes and lizards, because I sure wasn't listening.

The fire almost died. Reluctantly, I searched the dark for dry twigs and got it blazing. An autumn chill had come to the mountain. Bennie shivered slightly. I pulled him close, blanketing him with my heat. He started to settle against my chest, changed his mind, and quickly sat up, restless and energized. Sex did that to some folks, I guess. It woke them up, inflamed them. For me it was a tonic, making me lazy, putting me to sleep.

Bennie rummaged through my saddlebags, me too lazy to ask what he was searching for. He came upon the banking documents, looked at them briefly, then pushed them aside. "You have jerky."

Sex also did that to some people. Made them hungry.

"Venison."

He found the leather strip that held the jerky and wiped the mold away. "It'll do."

"Getting to be a real pioneer, Junior."

"Ah, this is what it takes."

We watched the fire. He sat on the opposite side and chewed the jerked venison. He was deep in thought, he had that quarrelsome look on his face. I almost dozed off.

"Does it bother you?" he finally asked, his mind too busy for its own good.

"What?"

"Liking men."

I glanced up from the fire. "I don't like men, Junior, I love men."

"That I can tell." He smiled across the fire.

"I love everything about them. The way they feel, the way they smell, the way they think. Their voices: high voices, low voices. I love young men and old men. Red or white. Thin or fat. Bald or with hair like Godiva's. I love the muscles in their backs and arms and legs and..." I reached across the fire and ran my hand down his neck, squeezing hard. "That muscle right there. There ain't nothing I don't love about a man."

"It's against the law," he said, dismally. "I'm afraid it always will be."

I chuckled. "There ain't no law west of the Mississippi."

"Isn't. You have terrible grammar." He smiled slightly, but he sure enough meant it. "Seriously, we could be arrested and prosecuted. It's happened already, even in America. There are cases in the law books in some eastern courts."

"Crime against nature."

"Yes." He acted surprised, pleased that I was smart enough to know that. "The men in the West aren't as discreet as you must

+214+

be in the East, and certainly in England. In England, although the death penalty has been abolished, they place offenders in carts and parade them through the streets. People are allowed, even encouraged to throw things at them. Stones, mud, animal manure. It's quite primitive. But it's a public spectacle people travel miles to attend, equivalent to a hanging."

"How come nobody does anything about it?"

"Such as? I think if anyone dared they would be considered guilty by association."

Picturing the brutal scenario that Junior painted with his words got me riled. I leaned forward and said roughly, "See this?" I held a Colt up to the flames. They flickered off the silver barrel and it immediately warmed in my hand. "This is my law. This is the only book I go by: law book or Good Book. The law hasn't been able to jail me for killing men with this gun, and it's this gun that's going to keep them from jailing me for loving men. This is what you do about it, Junior. You fight back. And you die fighting. You're going to learn how to use it before you go back east."

"I may not go back east."

Too mad and lazy to discuss it, I shrugged. "Whatever."

"I fully plan to marry some day..."

Laughing uproariously, my side almost aching from the humor of it, I punched my bedroll into shape and lay down. "You do that."

"Well, don't you?"

I peered out from under my hat. "I'll marry you."

I thought he was going to kick me or throw something for making fun of him. Instead, he moved across the sand and rested his face against my chest.

"I like your chest," he said. He trailed light, ticklish kisses down my ribs, pulled at my hair. Then he found a nipple and bit down hard, getting violent again.

"It's against the law."

"There ain't no law west of the Mississippi."

We'd hang in England for what we did next.

# 21

Colonel Samuel Colt invented the first repeating pistol thirty-five years ago. I don't know much about Colonel Colt, don't know if he was a tall man or a short man, if he was bearded or clean-shaven, if he was fair or partial, a saint or a sinner. But I am eternally grateful to Colonel Colt. His revolvers brought a certain democracy to the untamed territories.

My Colt .44s were ten years old. But like good whiskey they only improved with age. They were a matching pair. Only my keen eyes and sensitive touch could tell the difference between the two. I knew which gun went into the right-hand holster, and which one fitted the left. Wrong gun in the wrong holster could throw my timing off by a critical fraction of a second.

The guns were specially ordered for me by a gunsmith in Tombstone. They were long-barreled, silver, with scroll engraving on every crook and straight line of the gun except the handle. The handle was pure ivory. At the bottom corner of each handle, the initials D.T. were carved. The initials were not noticeable enough. So I had the gunsmith inlay them with gold.

I paid one hundred dollars for the pair. The gunsmith threw in the double holsters for free. One hundred dollars was a lot of money for a kid that hadn't done an honest day's work in his life.

But I found some luck at a card game, purchased them specially designed Colts, and had my picture taken with them right there in the shop to send to my ma. She did not appreciate it.

Ryder had told me the Colt Company was designing a short-barreled Peacemaker .45 and would be releasing it soon. They called the short-barrel the "gunfighter's special." Ryder waited on it with anticipation. They were supposed to be easier to handle, a quicker pull out of the holster, and more accurate. I waited on them Peacemakers, too, doubtful their aim could be any truer than the Colt .44s warming against my sides.

That morning I oiled the guns so slick it was a wonder the bullets didn't slip out of the barrels on their own. My right hand operated at ninety-nine percent, the soreness was gone, the muscles and tendons stretched and popped like new.

I stood at the top of Bennie's mountain, alone. That was the way I wanted it. I had sent Junior off the mountain early that morning. He protested, of course, and argued to stay. But I had some hard work to do. He would only distract me, make me want to play with him instead of tending to my guns, tending to my horse, and that could get me killed.

Snapping them beauties out of their holsters, I fired off round after round at bottles placed on a boulder one hundred feet in front of me. One by one the bottles exploded. Quicker than a camera could grab the illusion, slivers of glass flew into the air. I did not miss one. I rarely did.

Gracefully, I twirled and flipped the six-shooters in the palms of my hands. Then I dropped them back in their holsters, where they would stay. The next time they were removed it would not be bottles I was firing on. It would be something smarter, quicker, something that could fire back.

The leather straps were tightened around my thighs, the buckle fastened securely. I made sure every shell carried powder, and the ones that came from the barrels weren't duds. Finally, I swung into the saddle, talked quietly to the palomino, and climbed down the mountain to Turnpike.

At the depot, I nonchalantly chewed on a matchstick and read the train schedule. The trains were not coming as often. Turnpike was quickly turning into a ghost town. Without water there was no reason to come to this once-burgeoning cattle station. It would still be weeks before the bottom wells filled now that the spring was flowing again.

The flint was in my hand. Cool to the touch, it was flawless, the finest of flint. Twenty flared arrowheads could be made with that one chunk of flint. To an Indian it was a valuable piece of stone. To a shaman an appropriate gift to the water god. To a white man a paperweight.

Frank Rhinehart hurried in. Annoyed to find me still alive, he eyed me impatiently.

"Howdy, Frank," I said without turning around.

"I told you, Taylor, there isn't anything I can do for you here. I have no intention of transporting your..."

"Sheep."

"Sheep. Regardless of what James Anderson says."

"Good for you, Frank. You're not as spineless as I first figured. It takes a mighty, mighty man to stand up to James Anderson."

"I hear tell Anderson's men are herding the sheep to Flagstaff for the Colsen kid." The idea amused him and he chuckled slightly.

"As we speak."

"How did you manage that?" Rhinehart muttered. He moved behind the desk and started copying down notes.

"I'm not here to talk about sheep, Frank."

"No?"

Slowly, I turned away from the train schedule and smiled ugly. "Nah. I'm hear to talk about you." I flipped the flint in my hand.

Unperturbed, he reached out for it. It wasn't mine, I dropped it in his hand. "I'm sure you and I have nothing to discuss."

Smug little bastard. "Why did you dam the water?"

"I don't know what you're talking about."

"Six months ago Ben Colsen ran into some financial trouble, thanks to the friendly folks of Turnpike. Putting his land up for collateral, he borrowed a chunk of money from the Bank of Flagstaff. He figured he could pay it back after the shearing."

I paused, arched an eyebrow, and waited for a response. The clanging of pulleys lifting beef to the ceiling, smooth and efficient as a well-oiled machine, was the only sound in the warehouse.

"Should I care about any of this?"

"Sure should."

He got up from his desk and gathered armloads of paper as if he were going to take his business someplace else. Perhaps home, where there was no gunfighter to disturb him. "I'm a busy man, Taylor, I don't have time to..."

"Your brother, Paul Rhinehart, is a loan officer at the Bank of Flagstaff. Pure coincidence that Ben Colsen would end up doing business with him."

Scooting out from behind the desk, he moved towards the exit. The room was small. It took only one quick step to block the door. He sighed loudly, dropped the papers on the desk with a thud, and folded his arms. "Go ahead," he muttered.

"Thank you. A couple of weeks later, months before the shearing, poor old Ben, penniless and harassed, and at the end of his rope, if you'll pardon the expression, got a notice from the bank stating they wanted their money back. They wanted it paid in full, or they were going to seize the property. It was signed by your brother."

The notice was in my saddlebag on the prancer. But, at this point, notices and positive proof didn't mean much.

Still smug, Frank shrugged. "Maybe so. My brother signs a lot of documents."

"Funny thing is, and I've been asking myself this question, why would Paul Rhinehart want to seize that pile of rock? Why would the Bank of Flagstaff? The land is useless. It isn't good for anything except raising sheep. You can't make money off sheep. Not in cattle country, as Ben Colsen found out."

"This is a long, boring story."

"I had a friend of mine, Rusty Cunningham, talk to the bank president in Flagstaff to find out why they would want that mountain. The bank president said, not in these exact words, 'Hell, we don't want it.' Knowing the land had no value, they preferred the money and the interest they would make off Colsen and his unprofitable sheep."

Frank fiddled with the flint. "I really don't care."

"Course the bank president didn't know what you and your brother knew. There's an oasis at the top of the mountain, a magical spring of water."

"You're crazy."

"The Eternal Spring. Priceless."

Frank snorted. "Do you believe in ghosts too, Taylor?"

"Yeah."

Restlessly, Frank jumped to his feet and edged towards the door again. "You really are crazy."

"A lunatic. Your brother confiscated the property and arranged it so that you can put the first bid on it. The auction starts a week from tomorrow, but you've already sent in an anonymous bid. I hate to disappoint you, Frank, but the auction has been called off."

"What?"

"Bennie Colsen sold the mountain to James Anderson."

"When?" He suddenly panicked. Panic from greed, not fear.

"A while back. All your lying and cheating and sneaking, and all of your brother's lying and cheating and sneaking, is going to come to light. So you might as well admit what you've done and start looking for a good lawyer."

"I don't need a lawyer. What my brother did was perfectly legal, a loan official's prerogative. He did nothing illegal."

"Unethical and slimy, but not illegal. What about murder? Ain't that illegal?"

"I didn't murder anyone!"

My mouth was running at full speed like a getaway horse. I barely heard Rhinehart's protests of innocence. It didn't matter. I knew what I knew. Rhinehart could deny it until he shriveled up and fell over from old age. The man was guilty as hell, and had only a few minutes left to live. Adrenaline coursed through my veins. Numbness started in my toes and went straight to my emotions. That numbness always accompanied me before I reached for the Colts.

"Ben knew what was happening. He figured it out right away. If he was anything like his kid, he was stubborn and determined to stop you."

"Still that doesn't..."

"I got a few more coincidences, just be patient and hear me out."

"I'm not listening to any more of this."

Again he headed for the door. Again I put my arm across it and blocked it. "Course you are."

"I'll holler for my men. They'll be in here in ten seconds."

"Ten seconds is a long time. I'll have a bullet in you by then.

"Rusty Cunningham plays piano at the Cactus Saloon. He's got the voice of a canary and the nose of a ferret. Rusty knows everything about everybody. And he tells me that your brother, Paul, is married to an Indian woman. A Hopi."

"She's not Indian." It was spit out with more force than the rest of Frank's denials, even the one where I accused him of murder.

"Frank, dammit, don't lie. I swear, if you keep on lying I'm going to get mad. Now, it don't matter how many times your sister-in-law, Sarah, shades her hair a lighter color, or wears Parisian dresses and carries them frilly parasol things, or avoids the sun like I would avoid you if we lived in the same town, she's Indian. I know she's Indian. You know she's Indian. Everybody knows she's Indian. In fact, she's more than just Indian. She is White Doe, the granddaughter of the high priest shaman, Living Cloud."

"Gossip."

"Before he got all white-haired and full of rheumatism, Living Cloud went to the Eternal Spring every summer to give sacrifice to the water god." I held up the flint and twirled it in my hand. The light caught it. It flashed as if it were sending out sparks. "Sometimes he took his little granddaughter with him."

Fed up, he was shouting at me now. "What has this got to do with anything, Taylor?"

Real creepy-like, I gazed over the flint. "I'm going to kill the man who killed the Colsen family. Everybody in Turnpike knows that. That's why I'm here."

He grew silent. In the slaughterhouse I heard the grunts and shouts of the workers as they harnessed, then pulled the beef on the pulleys. The chains rattled against each other. I could almost smell the sweat, feel the heat in the slaughterhouse.

"Whoever built the dam killed the Colsens. That's my theory. You built the dam, Frank. You got together a couple of men, set up a pulley system similar to what you load the beef with, and you went to the Eternal Spring and built a wall in an attempt to dry out your neighbors."

"Why? Why should I?"

"To get rid of Ben Colsen. And to lay claim to the water."

"Look," Frank's voice was worried, but not sympathetic, "all I wanted was for Ben Colsen to sell to me. That's all. I'm a businessman. I own half this town. If I could control the water rights then I..."

"Could own and control the other half, including the ranchers, including James Anderson. They would have to come to you for water."

"What's wrong with that? If food and land can be marketed then why not water?" He waited for my reply as if I was going to bother to answer him. "The spring was what I was after, nothing more. I didn't want the mountain or the land. I drew up blueprints for a water company, and showed them to Ben Colsen. I gave him an opportunity to be partners."

"I call that optimistic. I also call it a pretty good motive for murder. When he refused, you killed him."

"I didn't need Ben Colsen dead. He was halfway to losing the mountain anyway. It was only a matter of time before he would have gone bankrupt. I only helped him along. It's James Anderson you should be talking to about killings."

"I've been talking to him."

"He had as much reason and more to lose. It's no secret he wanted the water just as badly as I did. His cattle are in a bad way. Now I'm willing to admit I had a part in Colsen forfeiting the ranch. I'm even willing to admit, I dammed the water. But that's all I needed to do. Why would I kill him?"

Leaning over, I placed both fists on the desk, one on each side of him, and pinned him there. We were eye to eye, nose to nose, mouth to mouth. If I wasn't careful I could taste his spittle. "Because, you weasely-eyed, sawed-off coward, Ben Colsen was more educated, a better businessman. You're just a tinhorn in comparison. He had a battalion of lawyers in Boston waiting to swoop down on you and the bank. You dammed the water to rile the townsfolk, which didn't take an awful lot of doing, then you got the old boys drunk and went for a ride. You didn't have the guts to kill Ben Colsen on your own, face-to-face, man to man. You're too small and scared.

"When everyone sobered up, they were ashamed of themselves, ashamed of what they had done. You would all like to bury it in the back of your heads and pretend it didn't happen. But Bennie Colsen came along, I came along, and we reminded everyone of what they did."

"You don't have any proof."

"I don't need no proof. I ain't no judge. I ain't no jury. I'm the executioner."

For the first time fear registered in his eyes. It finally occurred to him that he was dealing with a man whose moral fiber was lower than his, a man who didn't play by the rules.

"I am going to kill you," I guaranteed him. "As soon as I find an interesting way to do it."

"It wasn't me! I swear."

I removed a rolled cigarette from my hatband. Striking the match on his desktop, I lit it, inhaled deeply, and stared at him hard. "Bullshit."

"No, I swear."

"Who then?"

His hands fluttered nervously as he pointed at empty space. "I only rode along. I didn't kill anybody, I swear on the Bible, I didn't kill anybody. It was them."

My palms hit the desktop hard. My cigarette dangled from my lips. I leaned over and shouted in his face. "Them? Them? Give me some names."

Sweat popped out on his scalp. I could almost hear his brain whirling, his mind racing as he tried to think. "Uh ... Jacobs. Jacobs was there. Wilcox, Lanolin ... uh, Webb..."

The list went on.

Dusty Jacobs ... store proprietor. Bid Wilcox ... sheriff. Henry Lanolin ... blacksmith. Joel Webb ... rancher. Bobby Joe Watkins ... butcher. Charlie Eagleton ... saloonkeep. Joseph Ellis ... preacher. Yeah, preacher.

"Who was riding at the head?" I shouted. "Was it you? Did you take them in?"

"No!" Struggling with words, his voice finally broke and he became this tiny little man shouting in the dark, a wee little voice that could barely be heard. I thought for a second he was going to break down and cry, he was that scared. "I already told you who it was."

"Tell me again," I barked.

"It was James Anderson." Then he actually started to cry, afraid of me, afraid of Anderson. "The Lord is my witness, it was James Anderson."

I felt like crying, too.

# 22

F ear. The stifling, suffocating blanket of fear. Like slow tor-
ture, fear is something a man cannot live with for long.
Eventually it will drive him mad, or drive him to anger. It will
force him to do something foolish, something he wouldn't do if
his mind was free from fear. Fear, eating away at a man, was what
a gunfighter relied on. Another man's fear was my ally. My third
gun.

That is why I left Frank Rhinehart alive. Frank Rhinehart was
my plague of fear, my carrier. He would carry the disease from
one man to another. Each of them would look over his shoulder,
peer out his windows, stay awake at night, the bitter taste of fear
in his gut. The promise of my coming haunted them all like a
specter of death.

They armed themselves. Frightened, cornered men always
did. Rifles lay next to their beds. Loaded pistols were tucked under
their pillows and counters. Shotguns leaned against the door in
many kitchens, or were hidden under the straw in the barn.

By arming themselves they became my equal. I had never put
a bullet in an unarmed man. And I never would.

I stood on the outskirts of Turnpike. The palomino and I were
a blended shadow. It was hard to tell where the horse ended and

I began. How many days had passed since my conversation with Rhinehart was a blur. It could have been two, maybe three. I wanted to give them time. Time to gather their weapons, and time to let the disease of fear burn them like a fever.

My saddlebags were heavy with destruction. An eye for an eye ... tooth for a tooth ... there were no innocents here.

Slowly, silently, the palomino glided into town. I had removed its shoes that afternoon. No one would hear the clacking of steel hooves as we crossed the tracks and rode through Turnpike.

There was no moon, no stars. The night was overcast, remnants of the Hopi's rain dance. The streets were dark. The lanterns that had lit up windows a few hours ago, illuminating families sitting at kitchen tables, had all been extinguished. The player piano that had droned on in the saloon, barely audible over the constant hum of small talk and laughter, was silent. It was midnight. Befitting time for the avenging angel to come.

The only light came from my cigarette. Tense, I clenched it between my teeth. Its head brightened as I sucked in, then grew small as I exhaled.

I stopped in front of the church, ethereal with its virgin white hypocrisy. I could almost hear the congregation singing, hear the preacher preaching. Maybe he had preached about loving thy neighbor as the Colsen family's bodies stiffened under a pitiless Arizona sun. Maybe the congregation had sung a hymn, "Onward, Christian Soldiers," while a young boy dug five shallow graves.

Onward, Christian Soldiers ... indeed. I was the soldier now. In the dark of the night, I snuck in as quiet as Cochise's warriors. And as deadly.

From my saddlebag I removed a stick of dynamite. Steady-handed, I placed the tip of my cigarette to the fuse. It sputtered, sparkled, hissed, then swiftly started to burn. Allowing it one second to catch, I took perfect aim and threw it.

It rolled onto the porch and sat there, for a brief moment as harmless as a lightning bug. Instinctively, the palomino knew to back away. The dynamite exploded with a blinding flash of light. It was a masterpiece of accuracy.

The church remained standing, but the windows shattered and the doors blew off the hinges. A gradual licking of flames crawled up the doorjamb, threatening to eventually engulf the structure. Good. That's what I wanted. A slow burn.

As if the explosion had ripped open the night, the streets behind me filled with townsfolk running from their warm homes. Still in their nightclothes, still half asleep, they looked around in shock. They saw nothing but the eerie glow of red and orange burning their church down.

Within seconds, men started hollering and ran towards the church. The fire bell in the square rang out, calling for help, while the bucket brigade lined up in front of the water pump.

I was no longer a silent ghost in the night. I swung the gelding around and galloped into the center of Turnpike, unnoticed, unrestrained. While the palomino danced nervously beneath me, I stopped long enough to place the tip of my cigarette to another stick.

I threw it. It shattered the gold letters spelling out *General Mercantile* painted on the store window. In a few seconds, too long for me to wait, it blew apart. The walls collapsed like a house of cards, the store's contents scattered into the air in small bits and pieces.

The horse took two steps backwards, and I lit another stick, flinging it as far as my arm would take it. It landed on the walk outside the sheriff's office. Quiet little fella, it barely made as much noise as a steaming teapot.

Bid Wilcox bolted out the front door. He hopped on one foot, trying to get his boots on and pull his pants up at the same time. Then he noticed the black-powdered snake hissing at his feet and instantly dove for cover. The jailhouse, empty as usual, sent metal stakes spiraling through the air like Indian spears.

"What the hell's going on?" someone shouted, frantic, scared. It looked as if Armageddon itself had come.

"Get some water down here!" someone else shouted.

The destruction, the billowing fires were beyond the towns-folk now. There was nothing they could do to stop it. There was nothing they could do to stop me. I would not be stopped until every hinge on every door was removed, until every window in every building was broken, until nothing remained on the main street except railroad tracks and a pile of ashes. Like nothing remained on Bennie's mountain.

One by one, I rode to each building. Unseen, as if I were veiled by a protective sheet, I rode alone among hundreds of fleeing, fighting townspeople. I rode to the blacksmith's and left nothing behind. Rode to the saloon, it ignited within seconds. The butcher's, the livery stable, the cramped little telegraph office, all fell behind me.

Finally, I stopped in front of the Rhinehart Cattle Company and Depot. It stood empty and dark. My saddle groaned as I lowered myself to the ground. I wanted to stand and get a good long look at this one.

Not much was left of my cigarette, just a small tip squeezed between my fingers. I lit a stick and threw it. Lit another. Threw it. And another. Finally, I pulled the last stick of dynamite out of my saddlebag. Cautiously, almost ritualistically, I laid the tip of the cigarette to the fuse. Then I pitched it right into Frank Rhinehart's office. If he was in there, I did not know. I did not care.

With one mighty explosion, an explosion that would shake God right off His throne, the warehouse split in two. The tin roof streaked across the corrals and landed somewhere out of sight.

That's all. That's all I needed to do. The avenging angel was satisfied. Satiated. Proud and pleased.

Hysterically, the fire bell cried for more help. Men and women, boys and girls, gathered at the wells and the watering troughs. They brought with them pots, cups, anything, to douse an inferno that Satan himself would be right proud of.

My boots crunched through broken glass as I walked across the boardwalk and mounted the golden gelding. At the edge of town, I looked back one last time at the chaos and destruction I was leaving behind. The sign from the saloon fell to the walk. Ashes and cinders floated in the air to join and mingle with the other debris.

Someone in the water brigade, wearing suspenders thrown haphazardly over his long johns, spotted me. "Hey," he shouted, dropping the water bucket, "it's Dakota Taylor!"

The palomino reared up on his hind legs. Whirling recklessly, I galloped out of Turnpike, a ghost disappearing into the night.

I ran the horse at full speed until I reached the flats of the Double A Ranch. Once I was in the pastures, I followed the wagon trail, and slowed down to a trot. Under the arch, I reined in until I approached the sandcastle at a slow walk. The horse was almost dragging. Neither of us wanted to be here.

Wrong had never plagued me this bad in my life. My intuitions had never led me this far off the track. I could read tracks better than I could read books. But this time I had been mistaken. Like Ryder warned me, my feelings for Bennie, whatever they were and they were strong, had scrambled my keen sixth sense and interfered with my judgment. After this maybe I'd better start planting potatoes. Or get as far away from Junior and his black eyes as I could.

That wasn't going to be easy. Bennie waited for me at the top of the mountain. I had not explained anything. I just told him to be there with an outfitted horse. No questions.

I stood in front of the sandcastle for a long time. A part of me ached to turn the horse around and ride out, all the way out of Arizona. But I had a job to do. Finally I dismounted and took the four steps up the porch with a mean determination. With each step my spurs twirled, jingled. They were the only sound in the night. The dog lifted his old bones to halfheartedly greet me. I scratched behind his ear, stalling for time, before pushing the door open.

The foyer was dark. There wasn't any moon or stars to light my way. Not wanting to light a lamp and announce my arrival, I felt my way through the foyer, careful not to knock anything over.

On a hat rack just inside the foyer hung a leather holster with a six-shooter bulging from it. Anderson's .44 caliber. It was older than mine. Fumbling a little, I lifted it off the hook. It was heavy. It was loaded.

A lamp burned in the study, a thin sliver of light peeked out from under the closed door. I followed the light down the hall.

James T. sat in an overstuffed leather chair next to the fireplace. A single, dimly lit lantern sat on the table beside him. A small fire flickered in the black hole. The nights were getting cool.

He was reading the same leatherbound book Ruth Ann had been reading, not because it was interesting, but because it had been left open on the table. Literature and cognac acted as a sedative to help him sleep.

He peered over his round reading spectacles when I jingled in. Sitting there reading, cozy by the fire, with his eyeglasses, he looked like old Saint Nicholas, everybody's favorite uncle. He started to greet me, but held back when he saw the hard look on my face.

"I've been waiting for you," he said.

Gently, almost reverently, he closed the book in his lap. He took off his spectacles and placed them on the table. He studied me for a full minute, examining my face for the smallest sign of compassion or forgiveness. He must have found something there.

"We didn't mean for it to happen. We only went there to scare him, threaten him. It just all got out of hand, somehow."

I can't say how disappointed I was to hear them words come out of his mouth. A big chunk of me had hoped he would snort at the accusation, rage at Rhinehart for making it, and ride with me to Turnpike to string the weasel up. But this time, I guess, it was James T.'s turn to concede.

My face passive, my emotions made of steel, I remained silent and let him make his confessions.

"The water shortage had become intolerable. We were losing too many cattle. I called a town meeting at the saloon that evening. We went there to discuss the water, that's all. None of us had any intentions of discussing Ben Colsen.

"Saloons aren't the best places to hold your meetings. Charlie poured the drinks for free. Hours passed as we argued and wrangled about what we were going to do."

"And who was to blame," I said.

Anderson smiled weakly. "A man's gotta have someone to blame for his misfortune."

"Go on."

There was a long pause before Anderson painfully relived that night. "Ben Colsen's name came up. Someone, I think it was Joel Webb, stood and shouted, 'Colsen has water!' That's all that needed to be said. The saloon emptied and we were riding up the mountain.

"It was dark, a night like tonight, but not overcast. We stumbled around like drunken fools. None of us had been up the mountain before, we didn't know our way sober, let alone drunked up on liquor and hatred. We stopped outside the livery stable and got torches to light our way up the mountain." Miserable, James T. shook his head incredulously, and emphasized, "We brought the torches just to light our way. We had no notion of burning his home or bringing him harm."

Down the hall, a door creaked open. Bare feet padded quietly on the hardwood floor. The steps were heavy. They belonged to Zeth.

Brief panic flitted across Anderson's face. "My family doesn't know anything. I'd like to keep it that way."

"That hardly seems possible, at this point." My voice was flat. My eyes were cold. Successfully, I suppressed my own apprehension. If Zeth entered the study, he would automatically attempt to defend his father. And I would be forced to take them both down.

The footsteps went into the kitchen in search of a late-night snack. There had been fresh apple pie for dessert. Then Zeth returned to his bedroom and closed the door.

Anderson's entire body sagged with relief. Mine did, too. But I didn't show it.

"What happened next?" I prodded.

He leaned over and poured fresh cognac into his glass. "Our plan was to ride up to the house and call Ol' Ben out. We thought if we threatened him, we could scare him into sharing the water. What a man won't do for the good of others, maybe he'll do because he's been forced.

"I don't recollect what happened from there. He must have heard the horses coming, because he was waiting for us. I know he was scared, many people had been threatening his family for a long time, and he wasn't taking any chances. He fired on us. We started firing back, all of us, crazy, circling the house like a pack of wild dogs thirsty for sport and blood." There was a tired in his voice that had not been there one hour ago. "My gun was out. I was firing, too, son."

I did not respond. I was not the judge, not the jury. I had come here to do one thing, and one thing only. Anderson had a story to tell, to get off his chest. To die with a clear conscience was a priceless opportunity. Absolution.

"Next thing I know, the house was blazing..." James T. squinted against the memory of the fire.

"Who killed them kids?"

"I don't know. It could have been me. It could have been any one of us." Again he grew silent. Then he shook his head and became a strong-thinking and hard-voiced man again. "It don't matter who did it. We are all equally to blame, but I take full responsibility. One word from me and it would not have happened. I let it happen. Yes, sir, I was the man responsible."

That was all I needed to hear. James Anderson was a brave man taking rightful blame for a wrongdoing. I dropped his six-shooter on the table where he had dropped the bag of blood money. "Put it on."

He stared at the gun as if it were unrecognizable. "Only a fool would."

"Put it on," I repeated, mechanical, cool.

Evenly, without fear, he said, "I'm not going to draw on you, son."

I slipped a Colt out of my holster and leveled the barrel inches from his face. Slowly, I pulled back the hammer. "For the last time, put it on."

James T. looked down the barrel of the gun. His voice was calm, that of a proud man showing no fear. If he were to die, so be it, he had it coming. Remorse and regret were reserved for the Colsens, for Bennie, for Ruth Ann, for his fatherless grandson. His actions that night on the mountain were indefensible. Tonight he would not make a mockery out of the memory of the Colsen family and defend himself against me.

"If you really want justice then leave me alive. For as long as I live I will never forget the face of that little girl holding onto her mother. For as long as I live I will never sleep without that image in my mind."

Age nagged at him cruelly, in the stoop of his shoulders, in the slackened face. Carefully, he pushed the silver barrel aside. Grimacing a little, his knees aching with arthritis, he lifted his bulk out of the chair and hobbled to the door.

"Anderson!" I shouted. The force of my voice surprised even me.

He froze. His back was as wide open as the Great Plains. His shoulders slightly stiffened as he waited for the hot sting of a bullet to enter his flesh.

My arm was extended straight out. The Colt was clenched tight in the palm of my hand. My jaw was clamped shut firmly. The muscles in my shoulder and neck strained so hard that the barrel of the gun began to shake as I commanded myself to pull the trigger.

Too much had happened since the day I met Bennie Colsen in the saloon at Hudson. Physically my life remained the same. I rode just as hard, fought just as freely, considered myself part of the wind and part of the dust that came and went without settling too long. In that respect, nothing had changed. My face looked the same. My voice was the same. I walked the same and smelled the same and ate the same and I slept on my right side with my right hand under my pillow like I had done for years. But I did not feel the same. I did not think the same. I was not the same man.

The stranger holding his special, precious Colt could not pull the trigger. Not for money. Not to appease the ghosts of Ben Colsen and his wife and children. Not even for Junior could I shoot an old, unarmed man in the back.

I would let him live with his memories. Condemn him to dream his nightmare, night after night.

James T. took one more step and reached for the doorknob. He stepped into the hall before closing the door behind him.

I lowered the gun. The fire popped. A spark landed on the Navaho rug. Outside, the palomino whinnied impatiently. In the distance, a campfire flickered faintly at the top of the mountain. Bennie Colsen was waiting for me. No doubt a little annoyed that I had been gone too long.

# Other books of interest from
# ALYSON PUBLICATIONS

**THE GAY BOOK OF LISTS,** by Leigh Rutledge, $9.00. A fascinating and informative collection of lists, ranging from history (6 gay popes) to politics (9 perfectly disgusting reactions to AIDS) to useless (9 Victorian "cures" for masturbation).

**THE ALYSON ALMANAC,** by Alyson Publications, $9.00. Gay and lesbian history and biographies, scores of useful addresses and phone numbers, and much more are all gathered in this useful yet entertaining reference.

**COWBOY BLUES,** by Stephen Lewis, $7.00. Detective Jake Lieberman is called upon to investigate the disappearance of a young gay cowboy, and discovers that the case is only one part of a much wider scheme.

**THE ADVOCATE ADVISER,** by Pat Califia, $9.00. Whether she's discussing the etiquette of a holy union ceremony or the ethics of zoophilia, Califia's advice is always useful, often unorthodox, and sometimes quite funny.

**THE ALEXANDROS EXPEDITION,** by Patricia Sitkin, $6.00. When an old schoolmate is taken hostage by fanatics in the Middle East, Evan Talbot sets off on a rescue mission. What he doesn't know at the time is that the trip will also lead to his own coming out and to the realization of who it is that he really loves.

**EIGHT DAYS A WEEK,** by Larry Duplechan, $7.00. Can a black gay pop singer whose day starts at 11 p.m. find happiness with a white banker who's in bed by ten? This love story is one of the funniest you'll ever read.

**REFLECTIONS OF A ROCK LOBSTER,** by Aaron Fricke, $7.00. Aaron Fricke made national news when he sued his school for the right to take a male date to the prom. Here is his story of growing up gay in America.

**GOLDENBOY,** by Michael Nava, $9.00. Jim Pears is guilty; even his lawyer, Henry Rios, believes that. The evidence is overwhelming that Pears killed the co-worker who threatened to expose his homosexuality. But as Rios investigates the case, he finds that the pieces don't always fit together the way they should. Too many people *want* Jim Pears to be found guilty, regardless of the truth.

**THE LITTLE DEATH,** by Michael Nava, $8.00. When a friend dies under suspicious circumstances, gay lawyer Henry Rios is determined to find out why.

**VAMPIRES ANONYMOUS,** by Jeffrey McMahan, $9.00. Andrew, the wry vampire, was introduced in *Somewhere in the Night,* which won the author a Lambda Literary Award. Now Andrew is back, as he confronts an organization that has already lured many of his kin from their favorite recreation, and that is determined to deprive him of the nourishment he needs for survival.

**CODY,** by Keith Hale, $7.00. When Cody and Trotsky meet in high school, they feel as if they have always known each other. An intense bond of friendship develops even though one is gay, the other straight.

**BETTER ANGEL,** by Richard Meeker, $7.00. Fifty years ago, *Better Angel* provided one of the few positive images available of gay life. Today, it remains a touching story of a young man's discovery of his sexuality in the years between the World Wars.

**COMING OUT RIGHT,** by Wes Muchmore and William Hanson, $8.00. Coming out can be frightening and confusing, but with this recently updated book it's a little easier for you, your family member, or a friend who's taking that first step.

**FINALE,** edited by Michael Nava, $9.00. Murder and the macabre are explored in these carefully crafted stories by some of today's most gifted mystery and suspense writers. Michael Nava, author of the Henry Rios mysteries, has selected well-known authors like Samuel M. Steward and Katherine Forrest as well as newfound talent.

**THE GAY FIRESIDE COMPANION,** by Leigh Rutledge, $9.00. A rich compendium of unusual and interesting information by the master of gay trivia. Short articles cover a wide range of topics. A favorite gift item.

**LAVENDER LISTS,** by Lynne Y. Fletcher and Adrien Saks, $9.00. *Lavender Lists* starts where *The Gay Book of Lists* and *Lesbian Lists* left off! Dozens of clever and original lists give you interesting and entertaining snippets of gay and lesbian lore.

**THE MEN WITH THE PINK TRIANGLE,** by Heinz Heger, $8.00. Thousands of gay people suffered persecution at the hands of the Nazi regime. Of the few who survived the concentration camps, only one ever came forward to tell his story. This is his riveting account of those nightmarish years.

**THE TROUBLE WITH HARRY HAY,** by Stuart Timmons, cloth, $20.00. Harry Hay has led a colorful and original American life: a childhood of pampered wealth, a Hollywood acting career, a stint in the Communist Party, and the founding of the Mattachine Society – forerunner of today's gay movement.

**ONE TEENAGER IN TEN,** edited by Ann Heron, $5.00. One teenager in ten is gay. Here, twenty-six young people from around the country discuss their coming-out experiences. Their words will provide encouragement for other teenagers facing similar experiences.

**UNNATURAL QUOTATIONS,** by Leigh W. Rutledge, $9.00. Do you wonder what Frank Zappa thinks of lesbians and gay men? How about Anne Rice? This collection of quotations by or about gay men and lesbians reveals the positive and negative thoughts of hundreds of celebrities and historical personalities.

**WORLDS APART,** edited by Camilla Decarnin, Eric Garber, and Lyn Paleo, $8.00. The world of science fiction allows writers to freely explore alternative sexualities. These eleven stories take full advantage of that opportunity as they voyage into the futures that could await us. The authors of these stories explore issues of sexuality and gender relations in the context of futuristic societies. *Worlds Apart* challenges us by showing us our alternatives.

**GAY SEX,** by Jack Hart, $15.00. This lively, illustrated guide covers everything from the basics (Lubricants) to the lifesaving (Condom care) to the unexpected (Exhibitionism).

**BROTHER TO BROTHER,** edited by Essex Hemphill, $9.00. Black activist and poet Essex Hemphill has carried on in the footsteps of the late Joseph Beam (editor of *In the Life*) with this new anthology of fiction, essays, and poetry by black gay men.

**SOCIETY AND THE HEALTHY HOMOSEXUAL,** by George Weinberg, $8.00. The man who coined the term *homophobia* examines its causes, and its disastrous but often subtle effect on gay people. He cautions lesbians and gay men against assuming that universal problems such as loneliness stem from their sexual orientation.

**GAYS IN UNIFORM,** edited by Kate Dyer, $7.00. Why doesn't the Pentagon want you to read this book? When the Pentagon's own studies said gays should be allowed in the military the generals deep-sixed the reports.

**CHANGING PITCHES,** by Steve Kluger, $8.00. Pitcher Scotty Mackay gets teamed up with Jason Cornell, a catcher he hates. By August, Scotty's fallen in love with Jason, and he's got a major-league problem on his hands.

**THE BEST MAN,** by Paul Reidinger, $8.00. Best friends David and Katherine are both looking for the man of their dreams. Unfortunately, their individual searches lead them to the same man.

**CHINA HOUSE,** by Vincent Lardo, $7.00. A gay gothic novel with all the suspense, intrigue, and romance you'd expect from this accomplished author.

**I ONCE HAD A MASTER,** by John Preston, $9.00. In this collection of erotic stories, John Preston outlines the development of an S/M hero.

**THE LAVENDER COUCH,** by Marny Hall, $8.00. A lesbian psychotherapist gives valuable guidelines to gay men and lesbians interested in therapy.

**OUT OF ALL TIME,** by Terry Boughner, $7.00. In this entertaining survey of history's most interesting gay and lesbian figures, Terry Boughner tells the part of history that other books have left out.

**THE CARAVAGGIO SHAWL,** by Samuel M. Steward, $9.00. Gertrude Stein and Alice B. Toklas step out of the literary haut monde and into the Parisian underworld to track down a murderer and art thief. The two women, along with gay American writer Johnny McAndrews, rely on their wits to bring the murderer to justice.

---

## SUPPORT YOUR LOCAL BOOKSTORE

Most of the books described above are available at your nearest gay or feminist bookstore, and many of them will be available at other bookstores. If you can't get these books locally, order by mail using this form.

---

Enclosed is $_____ for the following books. (Add $1.00 postage when ordering just one book. If you order two or more, we'll pay the postage.)

1. _____

2. _____

3. _____

name: _____

address: _____

city: _____ state: _____ zip: _____

## ALYSON PUBLICATIONS
Dept. H-97, 40 Plympton St., Boston, MA 02118

*After December 31, 1993, please write for current catalog.*